The Knowing
To
Your Knowing

—A Journey of Self-Discovery—

Les Coombes

NATIONAL
LIBRARY
OF AUSTRALIA

A catalogue record for this book
Is available from the National
Library of Australia.
ISBN : 978-0-646-70753-2

Main text set in Garamond 12pt.
First Edition : November 2024

ꟅOREWORD

The Knowing to Your Knowing is not merely a story; it's an invitation to explore life's deeper questions and seek unexpected answers. At its core, it delves into the human quest for meaning, connection, and understanding.

We all grapple with existential uncertainty, wondering about our true selves beneath societal roles and daily distractions. We question our struggles' purpose and the path ahead. In Peter, Melissa, and Michael, you'll recognise aspects of yourself: those yearning for clarity, resisting change, and gradually embracing life's mysteries. This book examines the delicate balance between seeking and allowing, control and surrender. It addresses moments when life challenges us to relinquish certainty and trust in a greater unseen force. The Knowing isn't a destination but a process, a way of being which values the journey over answers.

As you read, reflect on your own journey. Consider the questions you've avoided or truths you've overlooked. The path to The Knowing isn't about finding concrete solutions; it's about embracing and living within the questions.

You'll encounter profound insights, doubts, and moments of stillness which resonate with different parts of you. Take your time with this story; it's meant to be felt as much as understood. Let the words guide you, but more importantly, let them create space for your reflections.

Thank you for joining me on this journey. May The Knowing awaken the quiet truths within you, waiting to be remembered, and may Your Knowing guide you toward deeper understanding and peace. As you progress through this story, I hope you'll discover the characters' truths and your own, those whispers of wisdom residing within each of us. Let Your Knowing mirror your inner journey, inspiring you to embrace life's mystery and beauty with an open heart.

Your Knowing is the inner voice which is often drowned out by life's distractions, fear, doubt, and the desire for certainty. It's the part of you which has always understood life's larger currents, even when the path seemed unclear. It's about reconnecting with your innate wisdom rather than seeking external answers.

As you progress through these pages, I hope you'll uncover not only the characters' truths but your own. Let The Knowing be a guide, but allow Your Knowing, your unique sense of what's right and true for you, to illuminate your journey. In moments of stillness, contemplation, and surrender, Your Knowing becomes clearest, reminding you of your connection to something greater and timeless.

This story serves as a mirror, reflecting the parts of you which are seeking, questioning, and growing. Trust Your Knowing will help you navigate these inner landscapes, leading you to embrace life's mystery with curiosity and openness. Trust in your inherent wisdom, for Your Knowing is your greatest guide.

As you read, you'll find many different levels of wisdom which will need to be read more than once. Allow the message's conveyed to penetrate to your very core, and enjoy, as I do, the freedom which Knowing brings. I believe The Knowing is humanity's hidden asset, and it's within every one of us, waiting to be discovered.

With gratitude
Les Coombes

ＮTRODUCTION

I've spent most of my life chasing after answers, believing if I could understand the world's logic, dissect life's mysteries, and put them into words, I might finally find peace. But after years of searching, writing, and questioning, I've realised something essential: peace isn't found in the answers, it's found in living with the questions, which is where The Knowing begins.

This isn't a book which promises revelations tied up in neat conclusions, nor is it about discovering one ultimate truth. Life doesn't offer those kinds of answers. I've learned, and you'll find in the pages ahead, the most profound truths aren't found by dissecting life but by experiencing it fully.

The Knowing is about a different kind of awareness, one which goes beyond the surface, beyond the need to make sense of everything. It's not about finding an ultimate truth which will tie everything neatly together, and neither does it require understanding. What you hold in your hands reflects my search, the search for meaning, for connection, for something beyond the surface of things. It's the journey of a man, myself, who has come to see truth isn't something to be solved but something to be experienced.

There's something I've come to understand as I've walked this path, the difference between knowing with your mind and knowing with your heart. We're taught to value logic and to reason our way through life. But the truth is, there's a different kind of knowing, a deeper kind. It doesn't fit into words or theories. It's something you feel, something which rises from the quiet space inside you. And it's called, The Knowing.

There are moments in life when the boundaries between what we think we know and what we actually feel blur. The Knowing is the space between those moments, the silence between the noise, the clarity which comes when you stop trying so hard to make sense of everything. It's not something which can be explained fully and if I'm honest, I still struggle with it. I've spent years writing, trying to grasp at meanings, to put life's complexities into something tangible. But now, I see the most important part of the journey isn't the words, it's the awareness which rises when the words fall away.

As you, the reader, move through this story, you'll follow characters, people like Melissa, Michael, and me, each on our journey, each of us confronting our fears and personal questions. And also, the same things many seek: meaning, purpose, love, and a sense of belonging. But there's more, you'll also find an invitation. An invitation to reflect on your life and to ask yourself:

'What if I allowed myself to live in a way which reflected The Knowing?'

The Knowing is not about figuring everything out. It's about recognising there is more in-depth wisdom within each of us, one which doesn't rely on logic or reason but on a quiet, unshakeable awareness life is unfolding exactly as it should. When you begin to live with this understanding, everything changes. You stop fighting against the current and instead, you allow yourself to be carried by it. You trust, even in moments of doubt, confusion, or pain, there is something larger at work, a deeper truth guiding you.

If you adapt your life to reflect The Knowing, you may find the battles you've been fighting no longer hold the same weight. The constant need to control, to understand, to be certain begins to fade, replaced by a quiet trust in the unfolding of life. Peace becomes less about avoiding struggle and more about embracing the present moment, knowing everything is part of a greater whole. This shift, this way of living, brings a kind of peace which is not fleeting but enduring. It allows you to meet life with openness, curiosity, and a deep sense of inner calm, even amid uncertainty.

The Knowing isn't about answers. It's about presence. It's about surrendering to the unfolding mystery of your life, trusting even when the road ahead is unclear, you're being guided by something deeper. I've learned the most profound truths aren't the ones you can explain, they're the ones you live.

As you begin this journey with me, I invite you to let go of the need to understand everything right away. Let yourself be curious, open, and even uncomfortable at times. Trust what you're seeking isn't far, it's already within you. And as you begin to live The Knowing it becomes Your Knowing.

I sincerely hope you'll find not just my story, but your own, and I trust you'll find Your Knowing reflected in your life, and in your struggles and joys. Most of all, I hope you'll come to trust the peace you seek isn't something distant or unattainable, it's already within you, waiting to be discovered.

Thank you for walking this journey with me. May Your Knowing guide you to the quiet truths which have always been there, waiting to be remembered. May you find in Your Knowing the peace, clarity, and connection which comes when we stop searching outside ourselves and begin to trust what's inside.

This is my story and, in some ways, it's yours too.

Welcome to The Knowing and to Your Knowing.

Peter

The Knowing to Your Knowing

—A Journey of Self Discovery—

Book 1 in The Knowing to Your Knowing Series

For all who know there's a better way

CHAPTERS

Chapter 1	The Joy of Discovery	1
Chapter 2	Michael's Place	7
Chapter 3	My Journey Begins	19
Chapter 4	Back to Michael's Place	28
Chapter 5	The Veil is Lifting	39
Chapter 6	Feeling the Pain	48
Chapter 7	Revelations	66
Chapter 8	The Rock	76
Chapter 9	The Heart Tree	81
Chapter 10	Peter Talks About Himself	88
Chapter 11	Michael and Melissa	92
Chapter 12	More About Melissa	97
Chapter 13	Michaels Advice to Melissa	100
Chapter 14	The Knowing	105
Chapter 15	Michael and Peter Talk	112
Chapter 16	Michael, The Healer	123
Chapter 17	Peter's Understanding of The Knowing	129
Chapter 18	Melissa's Embracing of The Knowing	135
Chapter 19	Finding The Knowing	142
Chapter 20	Accessing The Knowing	150
Chapter 21	A Personal Journey to The Knowing	159
Chapter 22	The Knowing to Your Knowing	167
Chapter 23	Michael's Journey to The Knowing in His Own Words	171
Chapter 24	Michael, Peter, and Melissa Share Experiences	177
Chapter 25	The Impact of The Knowing on Peter and Melissa	183
Chapter 26	Leonard and Michael	188
Chapter 27	The Knowing and Christianity	200
Chapter 28	The Knowing and Buddhism	206
Chapter 29	The Knowing and Hinduism	212
Chapter 30	A Lecture Given by Michael	218

CHAPTER 1

THE JOY OF DISCOVERY

'Our life is shaped by our mind; we become what we think.' — *Gautama Buddha*

It has been about five years since I first met Michael. It was early autumn, and Melissa and I had joined friends for a weekend at a mountain retreat. We met him the morning he arrived and invited him to join our group. As the weekend unfolded, we were glad we did. His wit and charm were refreshing, and his relaxed demeanour put everyone at ease. What struck me most was his sense of calm. Michael was different, his peacefulness set him apart from anyone I'd ever known. He never seemed ruffled, no task too daunting. I wanted to get to know him better, as his understanding of life's subtleties far surpassed my own.

The weather was perfect. Each day, the sky appeared bluer, more reminiscent of spring than autumn. If not for the trees shedding leaves and the chilly nights, one might have believed the seasons had shifted. The guest house was warm and inviting, and we gathered in the lounge each evening, where a fire crackled in the open hearth. The scent of wood smoke filled the air, and the soft glow of the flames wrapped the room in gentle warmth, creating a cosy atmosphere which relaxed us all.

Michael never seemed intentional in anything he did, yet he found himself at the centre of our group. This man and his words captivated most of us, and we naturally directed many questions towards him. He answered each one in a firm, quiet manner as if such conversations were second nature to him.

I've always lived my life intending to wring every drop of pleasure from each experience. I never considered my actions could ripple into the future or shape events yet to unfold. Yet, I was to learn, every action has a consequence, in the present, and in the unseen future as well. Realisation, however, was still ahead of me.

In another era, society might have condemned my hedonistic approach but today's values aren't the same. My philosophy was simple, live each moment as it comes, and leave providence to handle the details.

Melissa enjoyed life as much as I did, and while our friendship was warm and fulfilling, we had no plans to become seriously involved. She had a care-free spirit, a 'free soul,' as she often called herself. A true career woman, her greatest pleasure came from acquiring property and material possessions. She moved at such a pace it left many breathless, as she knew how to make money and wasn't afraid to spend it on whatever she wanted.

I've never been one to hold onto money; I spend it as quickly as I earn it. As long as I have money in the bank, a roof over my head and the freedom to live as I please, I'm content. An old saying says opposites attract, which described us. Melissa and I had been drifting in and out of each other's life for some time, and we envisioned no reason to change. We enjoyed each other's company, without strings attached, and the arrangement suited us perfectly.

Had it not been for Melissa, I never would have met Michael; quiet weekends in the country weren't my style. But she thought it would be fun, especially since our companions were old friends we hadn't seen in a while. Even though our lifestyles differed, she reasoned a break from our hectic schedules wouldn't hurt, and she was right. The weekend turned out to be fantastic, and for me it set in motion a series of events which eventually led to me writing this book.

Unfortunately, the weekend ended all too quickly, and as often happens when old friends come together, we promised to do it again sometime. I was particularly eager to get Michael's contact information, and he obliged, telling me with a smile our paths would cross sooner than I might expect. Maybe we would, I thought and pocketed his card.

Melissa and I said our goodbyes and began the drive back to the city. We discussed many things as we made our way through the night, but our conversation kept circling back to Michael and the lasting impression he had made.

Weeks slipped by, autumn gradually gave way to winter, and Melissa and I carried on with our lives, focusing on our separate pursuits. There's a quiet reassurance in knowing someone is always there when needed, and for years, we had been a constant for each other. Marriage was never something we entertained; it wasn't part of our reality. Why risk disrupting what we already cherish? We accepted each other as we were, flaws and all, with no desire to change or compromise who we were.

Lost in thought, I wandered into the kitchen to make coffee. It was late morning, and I often struggled to get started on days like this. The book I was working on wasn't progressing as I had hoped and I found myself doing everything to avoid thinking about it.

Outside, rain poured down in sheets, and icy winds battered the trees in the park. In winter, the city seemed to take on a dull, oppressive greyness which always left me feeling low. Even when the sun peeked through, it was weak, unable to chase away the shadows in the corners where winter's icy grip lingered. Those forgotten parts of the city always seemed to attract the lonely and desperate.

I stared out the kitchen window, watching raindrops dance on the glass. A shiver ran through me as I wished I was somewhere else. Normally, at this time of year, I would have been, but I had a deadline to meet, and its weight deepened the gloom which seemed to surround me.

'Rain, rain, go away' we used to sing as children, a faint echo from my childhood stirring in my mind. Go away indeed, I thought, pushing memories of my past aside. Those memories had long been consigned to the rubbish bin of history. Why dwell on them now? Haven't I come a long way since then?

My thoughts drifted to Melissa, and I wondered if she might be free to meet. It had been a while since we had spent a night together, and the thought of being with her stirred a familiar longing. It had always been this way between us. Neither of us wanted to commit, but we never missed an opportunity to be together. We had often cancelled other plans whenever one of us needed the other. We never questioned whether we were right or wrong, nor did we worry about morality. To us, the purest form of love was one given freely, without conditions, giving to each other with no expectation of anything in return.

A lightning flash jolted me from my reverie, momentarily turning my thoughts to Michael and our first encounter. It's easy to forget how quickly fascinations fade once the intensity of a moment passes. As we navigate daily life, today's impressions replace yesterday's, relegating memories to mere recollections. I briefly considered contacting Michael but couldn't locate his card. I knew I had it recently, but its whereabouts eluded me.

I recalled his assertion, coincidences don't exist, and everything happens for a reason. Perhaps misplacing his card was one such 'coincidence.' I shrugged, realising thoughts of Melissa and the past had distracted me from work. I promised myself I'd call her tomorrow, though I doubted I would. Heading to the bathroom, I decided a shave and a hot shower might clear my mind. Another lightning flash and thunderclap seemed to affirm my decision.

By late afternoon, the storm had subsided, and I'd worked without pause. After five, the phone rang. Grateful for the interruption, I reached for it, accidentally knocking over a half-filled coffee mug. Stifling a curse, I answered, and a swimming pool salesperson launched into their sales pitch. When I could speak, I politely suggested they check potential customers' residences before trying to sell their product. I explained it would save time, especially for apartment dwellers lacking pool space. The sales-person thanked me and wished me a nice day before hanging up. 'Have a nice day,' I mimicked under my breath while cleaning the carpet. 'It's already dark outside, or had this fact escaped his notice?'

Finishing the clean-up, I was in a foul mood. As I stood, a book caught my eye: 'Chances and Coincidences,' which I had started to read weeks ago. Flipping through it, a card fell out, Michael's card.

I remembered using his card as a bookmark when I bought the book. Coincidence? I doubted it. Logic dictates there's no such thing, and I've always prided myself on being logical and practical. But then again, as Michael had said, life rarely follows logic or practicality. Maybe he was right after all.

Until recently, I'd never contemplated my life's purpose. We are conceived, born, nurtured, and grow. Some have it easy, others struggle. Eventually, we die, some peacefully, others not as peaceful. To me the existence of gods or devils seemed irrelevant. I believed I controlled my destiny, not some unseen deity. For me, there's no heaven or hell, nor is there retribution and reward.

Faced with moral dilemmas, I'll decide my actions. No authority, religious or governmental, will compel me to kill or commit crimes against humanity. It's easy to justify self-serving actions, even when lives are lost, but much of today's world defies justification. I live in my reality because, ultimately, I answer to myself. Still, I sometimes ponder alternate paths. The past is immutable, but does it shape the future? Perhaps someone else holds the answer.

With this in mind, I called Michael the next evening. Our lengthy conversation covered many topics. He listened intently before offering calm, thoughtful responses. Though I asked many questions, he never gave direct answers, explaining it was better for me to reach my own conclusions.

"After all," he pointed out, "it's your life and reality you're dealing with, not mine." I accepted this, but my curiosity was aroused.

As we concluded, he invited me to his house the following Tuesday for a group discussion on these topics. I eagerly accepted, noting his address. As I was about to hang up, he said, "By the way, don't misplace my address like you did my card." I froze. How could he have known? I hadn't mentioned it.

Puzzled, I marked my appointment book in bold red: Michael's Place, 7:30 pm. There was no way I would miss this meeting, not even for Melissa.

The week passed uneventfully, and I was jubilant. My conversation with Michael had energised me to progress on my novel, leaving the final chapter to be written. As I prepared for Michael's gathering, many thoughts raced through my mind. It took some effort on my part to stay focused as my mind was running in circles about the weekend when I first met him. It seemed so long ago but the thought of going to his place and listening to his philosophies and views on life excited me.

It took some effort on my part to silence the constant voice in my head, but I did manage to, as I departed.

CHAPTER 2

MICHAEL'S PLACE

'Three things cannot hide for long: The Moon, the Sun and the Truth.' – Gautama Buddha

Michael lives on several hectares in a semi-rural area outside the city. Although off the main road, I anticipated no trouble finding it. The drive was pleasant, a welcome change after days of confinement. Nearing his property, I stopped briefly to savour the fresh, clean air, a rarity in the city. I've always been a city dweller, feeling rooted there, but someday, I'd like to escape the rat race and settle in the countryside. The peace, quiet, and unpolluted air of open spaces could easily become my new norm.

I found Michael's house without difficulty, but I was the last to arrive. After introductions and small talk, we moved to a large sunroom and settled in. As the newcomer, Michael addressed me first.

"Peter," he began, "what motivated you to come tonight?"

Besides his invitation, I wasn't entirely sure of my motives.

"I'm not certain," I stammered, feeling flushed. "I was impressed by your explanations of life, its aspects, and curiosity got the better of me. I wanted to know more."

He smiled, sensing my discomfort. "You're among friends then," he said gently. "Many of us started in the same way, curious, seeking answers, unwilling to accept life lacks purpose. Do you have any specific questions?"

"Many," I admitted, "but I'd rather observe for now. This is new territory, and I'd hate to ask something foolish and embarrass myself."

"Of course," Michael replied, smiling. "Speak as much or little as you like, and never fear asking questions. Often, the one you think foolish is precisely the one needing an answer. We've all been there."

The group murmured in agreement, and I relaxed.

"Francine," Michael turned to her, "you mentioned having a question?"

"Yes," she replied. "I'd like to know what 'metaphysical' means."

We all looked to Michael, expecting his explanation, but he wasn't making it easy.

"Anyone care to answer Francine's question?" he asked casually.

After a brief silence, Mark raised his hand. "From what I understand, it comes from the Greek words 'meta' and 'physical.' Meta means beyond or among, and physical refers to the material world, the body within the universe, or the universe as a whole."

"Anything to add?" someone asked, but Mark shook his head.

"Peter," Michael said, turning to me, "you're a writer. What does the term mean to you?"

"I agree with Mark," I said, "but isn't it used today to describe the mind-body connection?"

"Exactly," Michael said, smiling. "Wasn't to disturbing, was it?"

"No, not at all," I replied, sheepishly.

The group laughed good-naturedly. Michael had broken the ice by putting me on the spot, but he did it gently. As a child, I'd been shy, finding social interactions challenging. I wondered if Michael knew this about me, as he'd somehow known about the misplaced card. I made a mental note to ask him later.

"Both answers are correct," Michael stated. "The word is used in many different ways and has many meanings. Time erodes many things, language included. English has diverse origins and sometimes it lacks precision in translating phrases from other languages. Does the explanation answer your question, Francine?"

"Yes, it does," she replied. "But how exactly does the mind affect the body?"

Michael continued, "Many alternative health practitioners believe our thoughts shape us. Healthy thoughts often result in a healthy body. The mind can't exist without the body, and the body relies on the mind to function."

"Does it make them dependent or interdependent?" Francine asked.

"Both," Michael said. "One can't operate without the other. Science hasn't found a way to separate them and likely never will."

"What about when the body is immobilised due to disease or accident?" I asked.

"Because the body is immobilised doesn't mean the mind stops functioning," Michael replied. "Some people's bodies don't respond to brain signals, but their minds remain aware and active."

"Isn't the mind, the brain?" Simon asked.

"Not exactly," Michael replied. "The mind is connected to the brain, but the brain isn't the mind. Some brain areas can be damaged without affecting mental abilities, while damage to other parts could be fatal. Someone who loses mobility can still live relatively normally. Their body might be immobilised, but their brain and mind continue functioning. You can lose many body parts without impacting the mind or brain, but the body needs both to function. The mind is intangible, invisible, and untouchable, while the brain and body are physical, visible, and operable if necessary." Michael paused briefly, then plunged into his explanation. "Each action springs from a thought, our mind conceives, and the brain commands the body. You could say every achievement began as a mere spark in someone's mind. The mind resides within the brain, which acts as the body's control center.

When we conjure an idea or solve a puzzle, the brain signals the body to act, if an action is needed. Not every thought demands action, but its memory endures. Evidence suggests the brain stores all thoughts, even those we don't act upon. The mind can access these memories, making every thought a permanent part of our mental landscape."

Michael took a breath before diving deeper. "Imagine this scenario: Someone feels a persistent pain in their leg. They might seek medical advice or ignore it, hoping it'll vanish. Some might fear the worst, like a serious illness, and avoid action altogether. If a person starts envisioning a malignant tumour requiring surgery, they're crafting a mental scenario which could impact their physical well-being. What began as a simple muscle ache could spiral into a grave issue, all because they underestimated the power of their mind."

"Are you suggesting we create our diseases?" I asked, intrigued.

"We can," Michael confirmed.

"I find your statement a bit hard to swallow," I admitted. "What about birth defects and childhood illnesses? Surely, the mind doesn't create those?"

"It can," Michael countered. "We exist in a dual reality: the tangible Earth and its many facets, and the reality we each craft as individuals."

"How do you mean?" I probed, my curiosity piqued.

"The Earth and Universe are concrete; we can see, map, and photograph them. They're real in the physical sense. But the human mind is different. It's intangible, indefinable, invisible, unmeasurable, and unique to each person. The mind wields the power to create and destroy. Remember, every creation begins as a thought."

"But surely," I persisted, "we can't create diseases with our minds?"

Michael's eyes sparkled with excitement as he continued. "I once read a report by a world-renowned cancer specialist. He emphatically stated every form of cancer has, at some point, been cured by the power of the mind. It's a case of 'think healthy, be healthy.' If the mind can cure a disease, it stands to reason it can also create one."

"Perhaps," I conceded, "but it's still challenging to accept we're our own worst enemies."

"Is it hard to believe, Peter?" Michael challenged. "Consider wars. Aren't they human creations?"

"Yes, they are," I admitted, realising I was venturing into uncharted territory. I urged him to continue, eager to explore this new frontier of thought.

Michael's words flowed like a river, carrying us through a journey of ancestral legacies, genetic mysteries, and the intricate dance between mind and body. He painted a vivid picture of how our thoughts, our ancestors' lives, and even the environments we inhabit all contribute to our physical well-being.

As we delved deeper into the discussion, exploring childhood illnesses, parental influence, and the untapped potential of the human brain, I felt like an explorer charting unknown waters. Each revelation was a new island of knowledge, waiting to be discovered and understood.

Michael's final words resonated like a call to adventure:

"Our minds interact with our bodies, why can't they interact with the Earth we live on? Nature has much to offer which some ignore because of our modern lifestyles. When we finally learn to harness the free and abundant energy around us, we'll stop tearing the Earth apart and start a new journey of discovery and living in harmony."

As the conversation drew to a close, I realised we had embarked on an extraordinary expedition into the realms of mind, body, spirit, and nature. The path ahead was challenging, but the promise of unlocking our true potential made it an adventure worth pursuing.

A hush fell over the room as we absorbed Michael's words, captivated by their weight.

"Children have an immense capacity to learn, absorbing far more than adults realise. At birth, the physical connection with the mother breaks, but not the mental one. It's akin to telepathy. A child can communicate with their mother through this mental link. Have any parents here ever sensed their child misbehaving, to find you were right?"

Several people nodded and murmured in agreement.

"Exactly," Michael continued. "We possess this ability, but it atrophies when unused. A mother senses when something's wrong with her child, and vice versa. Fathers can have the same effect. Anxious or overprotective parents might transmit a double dose of those feelings. Conversely, distant parents can create emotional and mental issues which surface later. We're complex beings, each unique. Many childhood illnesses stem from parental fear or the belief their child will fall ill."

Michael paused before resuming. "A mother who labels her child 'sickly' prolongs the issue rather than healing it. Some parents discuss their children's illnesses with anyone who'll listen, perpetuating the cycle. Most children prefer playing with friends to being stuck at home, with some feigned illness for attention. When successful, this behaviour becomes ingrained, easily accessible whenever they seek attention again."

Simon, visibly unsettled, interjected. "Do you believe the mind causes disease? It seems oversimplified. Surely other factors are at play. What if an illness is part of someone's fate? What if they're destined to experience sickness?" His voice was tense, struggling with the concept.

Michael paused, sensing Simon's agitation. When he spoke, his tone was measured, as it always was when addressing someone's discomfort.

"As I mentioned earlier, numerous factors are always involved. I'm sharing my beliefs. Life is intricate, with countless aspects. There's no 'book of life' we can consult for all answers. If there was, we could turn to the right page, read the solution, and move on. Each of us must find our answers. It took me years to release the chaos in my life and find peace. I had to confront many difficult questions and discard the irrelevant. I believe many of us unnecessarily complicate our lives, creating self-inflicted misfortune and drama."

By the time Michael finished, Simon's tension had eased. His voice was calmer when he spoke again.

"I apologise if I came across harshly," Simon said. "I meant no offense. Your words are new to me, and I'm struggling to process them."

"No need to apologise," Michael reassured him. "I fought against it for a long time, too. Eventually, I cleared away the old to make room for the new. Humanity is experiencing a shift in awareness, and adapting won't be easy for many. But those willing to try will find their efforts rewarded, not materially, but with inner peace. Feeling peaceful is far more valuable than any material gain."

"You sound like you've been on a quest, searching for the Holy Grail," I joked, "Are you Sir Lancelot reincarnated?"

Michael laughed, and we all joined in. "No, of course not," he said smiling. "But I like the analogy. I'm not Sir Lancelot reincarnated, but your Grail remark is closer to the truth than you think. Legends tell of brave knights searching for the Holy Grail, sometimes never returning. In other words, the unwise searched beyond themselves and were disappointed, while the wise found the answer within and ceased seeking. For them, the quest ended. They had found The Knowing."

"Do, you believe the Holy Grail stories were fabricated to conceal a deeper meaning?" I asked.

"In a way... yes," Michael replied. "In the Middle Ages, when these stories originated, few could read or write. Religious fervour was sweeping across Europe, and anything contradicting Church doctrines was branded heretical. Dissenters faced persecution and possibly death if they dared go against the Church's teachings. Consequently, much of The Knowing was lost or destroyed. The Grail stories became a way to circumvent the stranglehold religious leaders had imposed on free thought. Over time, even though people didn't fully grasp the deeper meaning, they accepted the stories as fact. The tales survived because they were acceptable to the Church."

He paused before continuing, "The search for the cup, supposedly used by Jesus at the Last Supper, became the symbol of the knight's quest for the Grail."

"What is this Knowing you speak of?" I asked.

"Many things, Peter, many things." Michael grew quiet as if lost in thought. "At its core, it's about knowing yourself and your beliefs intimately, and you no longer need to defend or justify them. You quietly achieve results through understanding. You attain inner peace, and your new-found knowledge frees you from suffering. Truth has always liberated people, and The Knowing is part of the Universal truth... the true reality we exist in."

"Sounds like you're describing yourself," I remarked.

"Not me, not yet," he protested. "I still have much to learn before fully understanding The Knowing."

I was puzzled by his humility. I'd never met anyone like him; his compassion and dedication were evident, yet he claimed he didn't fully grasp The Knowing. Maybe he didn't, but I'd settle for what he already knew.

I glanced at my watch. It was 9:15. Close to two hours had flown by.

"Surprised time has passed as quickly, Peter?" Michael asked.

"Yes, I am. It feels like I arrived minutes ago."

"Good. I'm glad you're enjoying yourself. We'll have refreshments soon, but first, I'd like to add to our discussion."

We all turned toward Michael as he paused, gathering his thoughts. "We are nearing the millennium's end, and many aspects of life are being questioned. Humanity is multiplying rapidly, polluting and poisoning its habitat to the point where the current state of affairs risk collapse. The Knowing is part of a new awareness, but each person must seek it for themselves. It can't be bought, sold, or bartered, and no one can lead you to it. Finding a road without a map is never easy, but once you've found the way, the journey becomes easier. The challenge lies in finding the way. Often, we encounter people who seem to have part of the answer, to discover they were brought into our lives to test our resolve. The path to The Knowing isn't simple. Some will move beyond current relationships; others will question if it's worth continuing. But our times demand we keep moving. To stop is to die, not necessarily physically, but a stagnation of the soul. If we don't grow within ourselves, we'll be left behind. We're all equipped for this journey of self-discovery. Everything we need is already within us. All we need is to start the search. What we've discussed tonight points the way, but each of you must decide what to keep and what to discard. I assure you, it's worth the effort. It leads to an inexplicable inner peace and ends suffering."

We sat silently, absorbing his words. It felt like both a warning and a promise of better things to come.

Margaret broke the quiet. "I've known you a long time, Michael, and I know you're careful with your words. Is the situation dire? After all, there have been many doomsday predictions, yet here we are."

"I don't believe we're headed for Armageddon, Margaret. But I sense something major on the horizon. Humanity won't change overnight; even if the sky fell tomorrow, many wouldn't react. It'll take something drastic to shake humanity from its apathy. There's more information available now than ever, but only a small percentage of the population is aware of it. Everyone is free to choose their reality. Part of The Knowing is living with and harmonising with reality; acting with it, rather than reacting to it. Some will ignore the obvious and continue viewing life through rose-coloured glasses. Others will believe a Messiah is coming to save humanity from itself. And some will take responsibility for their lives, and be ready for whatever may come. Being calm and stress-free in any situation isn't easy, but it's attainable. Awareness of The Knowing helps one find ways to overcome life's difficulties."

"Michael, you often talk about leading a simpler life and not letting stress control us, but you never tell us how to do it," Simon complained.

"It's not my place to tell you how, Simon," Michael replied, his voice filled with compassion. He was well aware of Simon's struggles and the journey which had led him here.

"Every experience in life is personal. Each discovery contributes to one's growth. Showing you or anyone else how to progress would deprive you of the experience and joy of discovery. The simple truth, Simon, is no one has the right to dictate how another should live. I'd be doing you a disservice by telling you how to reduce your stress. These are discoveries you'll make on your own, and trust me, the joy you'll feel will be worth the effort."

"Thank you," Simon said, smiling.

I noticed Michael's firm yet gentle tone as he spoke to Simon. It was a rare kindness I'd seen in few people, and Simon responded well to it.

"What's the first step one should take?" I asked.

"There isn't one, Peter," Michael replied.

"Then where do we begin?" I pressed.

"You already have," he answered.

I didn't push further, unsure of his meaning. Wisdom often lies in silence, I've been led to believe, and I gladly followed this advice.

"Be patient, Peter," Michael added with a reassuring smile. "Everything will become clear as you progress."

I immediately felt more at ease.

"Well, I think we've covered enough for tonight," Michael said. "Those who'd like to stay for refreshments, please help yourselves."

We moved toward the refreshment table while Michael bid farewell to those leaving. I wandered into the adjacent room, a cosy library. Michael found me there when he returned.

"Checking if I have one of your books, Peter?" he asked, grinning.

"Not my intention, no," I replied. "You have an impressive collection, though. Is this how you discovered The Knowing?"

"Thank you, Peter. I'm glad you noticed, not many do. To answer your question, I've always been an avid reader. While not everything I've learned came from books, they have helped. Occasionally, you find wisdom in unexpected places, making the journey a little easier."

As we chatted, others came to say goodnight. Excusing himself, Michael walked them to the door. I finished my coffee and was about to leave when Michael offered to walk me to my car.

"Did you enjoy yourself tonight, Peter?" he asked as we stepped outside.

"I did. Thank you for inviting me."

"Would you like to come again next week?"

"Yes, I would. Thank you."

"Good. I thought you might. Curiosity often leads us into unexpected situations."

I nodded, feeling peaceful in the surrounding stillness. The quiet, misty night felt worlds away from the city's rush. The mist swirled around us, evoking memories of a younger, less cynical me, ready to take on anything. Despite the late hour and brisk winter air, I felt warm and invigorated.

As I opened my car door, I turned to Michael. "How did you know I'd misplaced your card?"

"You told me," he said.

"But I'm sure I didn't mention it," I replied, puzzled.

"You did, but not in the way you are thinking."

"Then how?" I asked, intrigued.

"It's simple to explain because you were thinking about it while we were talking."

"For you, maybe," I said, smiling. I slid into the car and started the motor. "I suppose you're going to tell me it's part of The Knowing."

"Could be, Peter, could be. You'll find out, be patient." He waved as he turned back toward the house. "See you next Tuesday."

As I closed the door, my mind lingered on the night's discussions. The evening's revelations provided some answers but left me with more questions, heightening my excitement.

I had stumbled upon something fresh and unfamiliar. Concepts I hadn't considered before were now before me, sparking deep curiosity. Michael had said the joy of discovery is the true reward for effort, and now I understood. Unconsciously, I had unearthed a part of myself I hadn't known existed. The thrill of this realisation filled me with unexpected elation, a joy which resonated beyond the moment.

The mist had thickened into fog as I headed home, the road barely visible. But I knew I would return. Next Tuesday, 7:30 pm. I'd be back.

CHAPTER 3

My Journey Begins

'Do not dwell in the past, do not dream of the future, concentrate the mind on the present moment.' — Gautama Buddha

The morning sunlight filtered through the window as I poured my first cup of coffee. The warmth of the mug offered little comfort as my mind raced with unanswered questions. Last night's conversation with Michael echoed in my thoughts, his cryptic words stirring something within me. 'I had already started?' What exactly had I begun? This uncertainty was unfamiliar territory. Usually, when I wanted something, I pursued it relentlessly. Patience was never my strong suit. Now, I stood on the brink of something elusive, something which wouldn't come easily. Should I chase it down, or would it find me?

I sipped the coffee, letting its bitterness rouse me. The day was pristine, with clear skies and wispy clouds drifting lazily. I decided to work on my balcony, hoping the fresh air would clear my head and help me progress on my book. My ninth novel was proving to be the most challenging yet. Writing has always been my way of making sense of the world. Though I didn't consider myself a literary genius, it paid the bills and afforded me some luxuries. I didn't need much more to be content.

As a child, writing was my refuge, an escape from the loneliness of being without brothers or sisters. No siblings and no playmates, all I had was my imagination, and the stories I crafted to fill the void. I always cast myself as the hero, a small consolation for never feeling like one in real life. My parents were distant, more caretakers than nurturers. I knew they loved me in their way, but I couldn't recall a single moment of affection. No hugs, no kisses, and no warmth. I had this ever-present sense, I was a responsibility to manage rather than a child to cherish.

Perhaps this is the reason why I've always needed to control, to make things happen on my terms. Yet here I was, on the edge of something intangible, feeling more lost than I had in years. I glanced at the blank page before me, wondering if the words would flow as they always had, or if something had shifted inside me.

I was never lonely; I was alone. There's a difference. I didn't crave company, but isolation was my constant companion. School was a special kind of hell, every hallway and classroom, a maze which I had to navigate. Making friends seemed a chore, and whenever I connected with someone, they inevitably moved away. It became a pattern which left me questioning the worth of my efforts. Eventually, I stopped trying. Instead, I built my world, populated with imaginary friends who would never abandon me.

Around my eleventh birthday, I made a quiet but firm decision: I couldn't trust anyone, anymore. Life has taught me people always leave. It was then I learned to rely on myself. I reasoned I was the one constant in my life, the one person who would never leave me behind. Strangely, I became my own best friend and found comfort in this realisation. It wasn't a grand epiphany; it was a simple truth which guided me through my early years.

This philosophy became my armour as I navigated the awkward maze of adolescence. Whenever things got messy or uncomfortable, and they often did, it was this inner resolve which pulled me through. I didn't need anyone else. I had myself, which was enough.

My attitude shifted when I discovered girls had more to offer than I had previously thought. I sometimes think I lost my innocence by default rather than by any effort on my part. I hadn't set out to discover what it was all about; but it happened. A wry smile creeps up on me whenever I think of my first time, I was damn awkward. It was a good thing my amorous partner knew what she was doing, because I didn't. But I learned quickly. For days after, I walked around in a daze, but the euphoria quickly faded as I realised there was more to learn, and I was determined to find out as much as I could, as quickly as circumstances would allow.

It wasn't until my mid-twenties I met the woman I would eventually marry. The moment I met Annette, I fell 'in love.' I can't recall where we first met, but I remember thinking she was the woman I wanted to marry. In the beginning, all was well, but I never expected living together to be as challenging as it was. Sharing the same space strained our relationship in ways I hadn't anticipated. Marriage involved changes, and at times I had to compromise to maintain peace, which I resented. Having to modify my behaviour seemed ludicrous. Why couldn't she accept me as I was, rather than trying to mould me into what she thought I should be?

I've often thought control can be exerted in many forms within a relationship, and love is sometimes an excuse to manipulate others. Maybe I'm cynical when I say falling 'in love' is for starry-eyed teenagers, not adults. If a person falls 'in love,' it follows they may eventually fall 'out of love,' and then the recriminations begin. I've come to believe I fell 'in love' with the idea of 'being in love' rather than loving unconditionally.

Now, I easily admit, I could spend the rest of my life as a bachelor, free from accommodating another person's needs. Perhaps I'm selfish, but I cherish my independence and wouldn't give it up. A few years of trying to make the impossible possible was more than I could handle. I couldn't bring myself to fit into the niche of domesticity which some claimed would bring me happiness.

After the divorce, I vowed not to be foolish again, not to let romantic ideas cloud my judgment. I don't know where Annette is today, and when thoughts of the time I spent with her enter into my mind, it's with regret rather than fondness. We spent over five years together, and now it's as if it never happened. Even when we parted ways, I knew we wouldn't remain friends or keep in touch, as we had little in common. But it could have been worse. At least we parted with a smile and a polite kiss on the cheek before disappearing from each other's lives forever. I've always maintained if I can't solve a problem, I'll ignore it; it will go away... eventually.

My study's balcony overlooks a park where I do some of my work, weather permitting. The park is an oasis of green among the drab red tile roofs and cream brick buildings which dominate my suburb. Often, I find myself daydreaming, my thoughts wandering among the leaves and branches of this mini-forest. As I free my mind from its constraints, I venture back to a time when I was king and nature welcomed me. There, I was free to roam and do as I pleased, where my imagination could invent anything and sustain it as if it were real. Everything was my friend, the birds, the bugs, even things which slithered and crawled paid me homage, and it all was mine to command. This wasn't your average fantasy land; it was a slice of reality created by a small boy longing for love and approval. Within its boundaries, there was no sadness, no anger, and no hurt. This make-believe home was my refuge when all other avenues were exhausted. The magic kingdom I created still exists, and I retreat to it now and again. It serves as a sanctuary of calmness, sanity, and security when frustration and pressure overwhelm me.

A gentle breeze rustled the branches as I sipped my coffee, the warmth of the sun on my face heightening my senses. My thoughts kept drifting to the previous night and what I had heard. I know our minds are capable of much more than many realise, but could we cure ourselves naturally? The idea disease can be passed from generation to generation isn't new, but how can it be stopped? Drugs seem to offer temporary solutions, delaying the inevitable. While I don't advocate abandoning modern medicine, I wonder if there might be a better way. I believe there's truth to the idea we're responsible for our thoughts, words, and deeds. If we can create and destroy, it seems logical we can do the same to ourselves. Disease might be a form of self-destruction, especially when there's no apparent cause for a person's condition. We are what we think we are, and if we believe we'll get sick, perhaps we will.

Until Michael mentioned it, I had never considered our ancestors might be partly responsible for our physiological profile. It's a reasonable assumption, after all, none of us appeared out of thin air. We all have biological parents, as they did. The more I ponder it, the more logical it seems. I don't know who my great-great-grandfather was, and he could have had an illness which was passed down the family tree. The same applies to my great-grandmother. With my parents gone, I doubt if I'll ever know. I wonder if some of my mannerisms are inherited from my deceased ancestors. It's possible, and the idea mannerisms and diseases can be passed on intrigues me.

Work first, I told myself as I attempted to write, but concentrated thought eluded me. My mind kept returning to the previous night's conversation. Eventually, I abandoned my efforts and decided to act on my curiosity. There's a well-stocked bookshop near my home, and I headed there, unable to contain my interest any longer. Several hours later, I returned to my apartment with my purchases tucked under my arm. It was too late to resume work, and I didn't give it a second thought. Besides, I was too excited about the books I'd bought to worry about what I should have been doing. Sometimes I let myself be distracted too easily, and this was one of those times. I know eventually, the piper must be paid, but he can wait, my inquiring mind can't.

I spent the rest of the day and the next reading, without satisfying my curiosity. Rather than providing hoped-for answers, it left me puzzled. Perhaps I had bought the wrong type of book, despite the bookstore clerk assuring me the titles were all 'new age'. The contradictory information in the books made me question their validity. Reading about 'spirit guides' and 'divas' made me wonder if believers in this 'new age' philosophy might need help with their mental state. One thing was certain: an individual didn't need to be an expert to claim awareness. They could 'channel' an 'entity' or two, label them 'higher beings', and write a book about it. Who would question their beliefs? I began to wonder if I had made the right decision by indulging my curiosity. It's one thing to be curious about life, but another to start believing in 'spirit entities.'

However, all was not lost. I bought one book on self-healing which I found fascinating. Written by a medical specialist, it impressed me with its simple explanation of how our bodies can regenerate and how disease can be overcome by positive thought. The doctor pointed out research had established we inherit many of our attitudes, characteristics, and diseases from our parents. If I ever needed proof of what Michael had been discussing, I had found it. This doctor also advocated a holistic approach to health, treating both causes and symptoms. Disease can manifest on many levels, he explained, and by treating the symptoms and ignoring the causes is like showering without soap. Several chapters were devoted to the body's ability to regenerate, which fascinated me and warranted multiple readings. The mind-body approach to medicine was new to me and gave me much to contemplate. My trip to the bookstore hadn't been in vain after all!

CHAPTER 4

BACK TO MICHAEL'S PLACE

'Every morning, we are born again. What we do today is what matters most.'
— Gautama Buddha

The drive to Michael's property hadn't taken as long as the previous week. Earlier he had phoned, and invited Melissa and I to spend a few days at his place. I gladly accepted as I had completed and sent off my novel for proofreading and editing.

My car tyres crunching on the gravel made a lone sound which disturbed the stillness as I turned into the lane which led to Michael's place, and after several turns of the tree lined driveway, his house finally came into view.

I parked, grabbed our bags, and we headed for the front door. The warm glow from the windows contrasted with the stark trees, casting surreal shadows. A full moon began its ascent over the horizon, and in the distance, I heard a truck labouring up a hill on its way out of the valley. The beauty of the scene made me wonder if I could adjust to this lifestyle. Sudden laughter broke my concentration, and with a sigh, I dismissed the thought and approached the front door where Michael greeted us.

"Good evening, welcome. How are you both?" Michael asked.

"Fine, thanks," I replied. "I hope you don't mind us being a bit early."

"No, of course not. Come in. There are some here already." Michael stepped aside. "Give me your bags and go through to the back room. I'll join you shortly."

The house was warm and cheerful, filled with laughter and animated conversation. I greeted familiar faces from the previous week and was introduced to new ones. The warmth and friendliness immediately put us at ease, and their relaxed interaction made me feel as if I had known them for some time. It was a stark contrast to my city's social circles; here, everyone seemed to accept each other, interacting in a way which was new to me.

"Hello Peter, nice to see you again," Janette smiled at me, "would you like a coffee?" "Yes, thank you, I would," I replied.

"May I have one too," Melissa asked.

"Of course, you can. Two cups of coffee coming up."

Tall, and slender, Janette had deep blue eyes, and long auburn coloured hair which fell loosely about her shoulders.

"White with sugar?" she asked, and I replied with a nod.

"How would you like yours?" She asked Melissa.

"Black, thanks." Answered Melissa.

I took the offered cup, and although her hands were steady, she seemed a little unsure of herself. It's never been easy for me to make small talk with a person I did not know, but her good looks attracted me, and I wanted to get to know her a little more. My shyness must have been obvious to her as she took the initiative, and asked about my work, and my plans for the future. Fortunately, she had read several of my books, and her easy manner of conversing helped to relax me, and I was able to warm up to our conversation. Her love of life was reflected in her eyes, and it didn't take long for me to realise she was more than a pretty face.

"Would you like a copy of my latest book?" I asked her.

"Yes, thank you," she replied, "What's it about?"

"I'd rather not say much about its content as it hasn't been published yet, but it will be soon. I'll send it to you as soon as it is."

"Terrific, thank you, I'll look forward to receiving it"

We moved to the back room and made ourselves comfortable. I was pleased she chose to sit next to me, as I felt relaxed in her presence. Melissa took the chair by my left side and made herself comfortable. Being a published author has its benefits at times, I thought to myself.

Michael was the last to sit down and immediately asked if anyone had any questions.

"I have," replied James, "I have been thinking about the direction my life has been taking, and was wondering what the point of it all is. I mean if heaven is the goal, it seems such a waste of time."

Michael took a few moments to reply, "Living is never a waste of time, James. At times, life may seem pointless, but there's always a purpose to it. Every moment of our lives has meaning, even if it doesn't seem like it at times. The individual who is you has many facets, and all of those facets are what make you unique. Your life has meaning and purpose, it's because, as yet, you haven't discovered, what the meaning and purpose is. I've used the word discovered because I believe we all know what our purpose is deep within ourselves. Finding this inner knowledge, and accepting it as it opens to us, is part of growing, and becoming aware."

"Aware of what?" came the blunt reply.

"Yourself and the reason for your existence," replied Michael.

"My point is I don't see any reason for my existence," James stated aggressively.

"I understand your point, but I ask you to reflect on your statement. Allow me to suggest you haven't yet found your reason for existing, rather than making such a broad statement. You have as much reason to exist as I do, and there is purpose for both of us. I see in you a reflection of myself when I was searching and asking why I'm here. However, I'm not saying the quest for finding the real you will be easy, because it isn't. You've already started the process by asking, and it will become clearer as you open yourself to the answers."

"Currently, what you say is about as clear as mud," James said. "If there's a reason and purpose for life, why aren't we given it at birth or as we become of age? Anytime would have suited me."

"You make a forceful point, but let me ask you who you think would be qualified enough to provide such information."

"I don't know, maybe there should be people trained in this sort of thing," retorted James.

"When you think about it, you may find this beyond the capabilities of any government or organisation to provide. Inner knowledge is for the individual to access in their own time. Nobody can teach or show you how to do this, as everybody is different. What may seem important to you may not seem important to others. Inner knowledge is a nebulous thing. Some will not care or want to know about it, and there will be others who access it but won't trust their intuition enough to be guided by the information provided."

"Is it part of The Knowing you've talked about?" I asked.

"Yes, it is, Peter."

"You say all I need to know is within me. Can I ask where in me is it?" Asked James.

"What an excellent question, and it's difficult to answer because it doesn't reside in any one location within you. It's with you from the time you're conceived and stays with you until you depart. Liken it to the mind; we know it's there, but we can't touch, taste, or see it. To my way of thinking, it resides within the strands of DNA which determine who we are. Scientists working on The Human Genome Project are expecting to produce a sequence of DNA representing the functional blueprint and evolutionary history of our species. In my opinion, within the genes contained in the DNA strands, the evolutionary memory is stored. I prefer to think of it as one of the mysteries of life, rather than understanding the mechanics of it."

"Could you elaborate on what you mean by meaning and purpose?" asked Janette.

"As you all know, I believe we have many lifetimes, reincarnating time and again until we reach a state of bliss; Nirvana, it's called in Eastern philosophies. What I believe goes against the traditional view of Christianity as I don't have a belief in heaven and hell; I believe these are concepts which enslave mankind, they then can be manipulated and controlled by whoever wields enough power to enforce this belief system. I believe we are free to choose our path, make our own decisions, and be responsible for them which gives our life meaning and purpose. To illustrate this point, let me give you an example; I can't be specific and you need to bear with me and don't take what I say as gospel. Let's use Peter; you don't object do you Peter?" he enquired of me.

He turned my way as he asked me and noticed the bemused expression on my face.

"Don't be alarmed," he reassured me, "you have nothing to fear."

I chuckled slightly at this and shifted uneasily in my chair. "I know I have nothing to fear, please continue."

"We all know Peter is a writer and a successful one. We can assume he didn't attain this status without a lot of work. It's not difficult to grasp he had a purpose, and he strove to become the writer he is by applying himself to his craft. Peter, can you explain the meaning of your life based on your purpose?"

Warming to Michael's obvious intent, I accepted the invitation to elaborate.

"I've always been attracted to books as long as I can remember," I started. "I remember as a child many stories were read to me by nannies before bedtime. I loved them all, and I remember saying to one of them I was going to grow up and be a writer of storybooks. I must have been about seven or eight at the time, but it was there, forming inside me, but I still had to do the work to achieve the goal."

"Thank you, Peter, and it's as I had thought it was. From an early age, he had the idea he wanted to be a writer, and a writer he became. As you can see for yourselves, his life means something, and he has a purpose to it as well. Now, I'm not saying life is the same in all cases, but one has to do a bit of searching of the inner self to find the meaning and purpose behind our reason for existing."

"But," interrupted James, "the example you used is of a successful person; what about the less fortunate, and the derelicts who sleep on park benches at night? How does their life have meaning and purpose?"

"It's not for us to know what another's life purpose is. A derelict has as much purpose as all of us. On the surface, it may not seem this way but think outside the square. The sight of a derelict sleeping on a park bench has affected you. How you reacted to the impression it created in you, and your subsequent feelings, may have been what was needed by you to produce a desired result."

"What do you mean?" challenged James.

"What was your reaction when you saw this gentleman on the bench?"

"I wouldn't exactly call him a gentleman, and I felt disgusted a person could live this way," answered James.

"And why wouldn't you call him a gentleman, do you have a preconceived idea men who don't live on park benches are gentlemen?"

"No, not at all; It's… he was a derelict, a bum if you like, and I was appalled they are allowed to bed down wherever they want, and I think something should be done about it."

"Did you allow yourself to see the beauty in the situation?" asked Michael.

"What was beautiful in a derelict asleep on a park bench? He was dirty, rubbish was all around him, and he smelled awful."

"Do you think there is something you could have learned from the experience?"

"No," was James's firm reply.

"I'm not as adamant as you," Michael stated. "We can all learn something from every experience if we keep an open mind. I have known you long enough to know you are not a heartless person, and I have experienced firsthand your compassion for your fellow beings. What was it about seeing this gentleman on the park bench which upset you? Search your feelings; allow the inner voice to deliver its message."

James sat in silence, and the rest of us allowed him his space. Michael sat with his eyes half-closed, his breathing steady and even. Time was irrelevant, and the serenity of those present added a surreal atmosphere which couldn't be ignored. I hadn't experienced this sort of peace with a group before, and I was keen to observe the reactions of the others. As I glanced from face to face, I couldn't help wondering what was going on in their minds; were they also listening for their inner voice to speak, or maybe they were wrestling with long forgotten feelings also.

James unexpectedly broke the silence, "I think, it was an event I witnessed when I was a youngster. I had an uncle who meant the world to me. He was my mother's brother, and he lived with us for some time. He was always making up games for us to play, and I looked upon him as my bigger brother rather than an uncle, but he had a drinking problem; a bad one, and on occasions, we wouldn't see him for days. He was always dirty, unshaven, and looking terrible when he returned home. It was many years later I found out from my mother, my uncle was an alcoholic, and his drinking binges were his way of coping. I was about eight when it happened, it was wintertime, and because of the weather we were confined indoors, my uncle had been gone for days, and I was distressed thinking about him.

My mother had asked me to run to the corner store to get some groceries, and on the way there, to my horror, I found my uncle prostrate on the bench in the bus shelter. He was dead. I was devastated, and it took me ages to get over him not being around anymore. My big brother, who could do no wrong, was gone, and I mourned his passing for weeks. I cried myself to sleep every night and asked over and over again, why, why did he have to die? I guess I'll never know why, but as soon as I was old enough to understand, my mother told me about his troubled life. Now, every time I see a derelict, I think about my uncle, and how angry and hurt I was. Maybe I projected my anger onto those poor unfortunate souls in a vain attempt to make myself feel better."

In the silence which followed, I did a little inner searching of my own. I remember times I had taken out on others my feelings of anguish and pain, and I related to what James was saying. I realised why Michael had pursued the subject and eagerly waited for him to speak.

"I asked you earlier if you had seen the beauty in the situation," began Michael. "Maybe now you can see it."

"Sort of," replied James. "By being still and listening, I was able to discern my inner voice over the mind chatter. I got the feeling it was my anger I had to notice, and to acknowledge the pain I carried with me."

"Precisely," said Michael, without any hint of smugness or satisfaction. "Quite often a situation will present itself because we can gain insights into what is troubling us. If it hadn't been for this gentleman, you may have taken a lot longer to deal with the anger and resentment which was in you. Life is full of such miracles, and all we have to do is find them and become aware as they are presented to us. The Knowing is ever-present, and all we have to do is accept and embrace it. It is truly a miracle unto itself, and we all can share in its magnificence. How are you feeling now you have experienced some part of The Knowing for yourself?"

"I'm relieved and awestruck at how easy it was," he replied. "Relieved I've got it out into the open, and awestruck at how simple it was to do. To be honest with you, I was starting to think what you were saying about The Knowing was a fantasy on your part, but I'm convinced now it's everything you have said it is."

"And it's a lot more, there's much more to it than what you have experienced tonight. As you wander the path of life, many such examples will present themselves to you, and as you grow and become more aware you'll know how to recognise them for what they are, and when they happen, you'll say, like I do, it's all part of The Knowing."

"You have made a believer of me, Michael. I'm truly grateful to you. I now see how I was presented with the solution to what was pulling me down. I have never known what it's like to be intoxicated, because I have never drunk alcohol. I swore I'd never drink after my uncle had died, and I never have. Tonight, I finally faced the anger I had locked away inside myself, and I now can see it for what it is. Thank you, Michael, for persevering with the why of what I was feeling. If you hadn't asked the right questions of me, I could have struggled with this dilemma for a lot longer."

"It's always a pleasure to assist another to hear their inner voice," replied Michael. "The more you listen, the more you grow, and then life becomes a little less complicated. The majority of people spend ninety percent of their time trying to please others, which leaves ten percent for themselves. In my opinion, there's not a lot of time left for working through personal issues, and every one of us has issues which need to be resolved."

I thought to myself how true his statement was, and Michael, with his knowledge, seemed able to zero in on the issue and help the person resolve it. There's something remarkable about him, something worth exploring, and I marvelled at his extraordinary mental strength. I resolved to ask him more about his abilities over the next couple of days.

"I think we've had enough for this evening," stated Michael. "I'll see to the refreshments if you care to join me." Nobody moved for several minutes; it seemed as if everybody was lost in their thoughts. Janette was the first to speak, "Care for a cup of coffee, Peter?" she asked.

"Thank you, I will," I answered. "What did you make of tonight's revelations?" I asked her.

"Enlightening," she replied. "Michael never ceases to amaze me. I wasn't getting what he was probing for, but when it all came out, I could understand his point. I know we can receive messages at any time, but this was a bit different. Who would have thought a situation as told to us could have had such an important message?"

"Yes, I know what you mean. I'm amazed and impressed by him," I answered.

"Michael told me you and Melissa are staying for a few days."

"Yes, we are," I replied.

"Good for you. You city folk need the country air to clear all the polluted gunk you breathe from your lungs."

"Maybe you're right," I said, "but living there has many advantages over country life."

"Name one?" she challenged.

"Well, I think more to do is one thing which comes to mind."

"You have never lived in a rural setting. There's always something to do or see, and there's never enough time in the day to accomplish everything."

There was a sparkle in her eye and a slight smile on her lips as she said this which warned me not to take this last statement too much to heart.

"Have you travelled overseas?" I asked her.

"Yes, quite a bit," she replied. "My former husband was a Civil Engineer, and he travelled extensively. Fortunately, I was able to join him on many of his trips, and I got to see a lot of the world."

"What is your favourite city?"

"London," she replied.

"Good choice," I said, impressed. "Sydney is mine."

"It figures," she laughed.

"What do you mean?" I asked.

"Easy to work out. You love city life. What city in our land is bigger than Sydney? Living there would suit you."

Janette, you're one smart lady, I thought to myself. She had outplayed me, but I didn't feel she did it to put me down. I felt it was more to let me know she was in control and not to be trifled with.

After helping ourselves to coffee, we found some vacant chairs in the corner of the room.

"Peter," Michael's voice broke in, "how did you find tonight's discussion?"

"Enlightening comes to mind, as does interesting and surprising," I replied.

"How about you, Melissa?" he asked.

"I would say much the same as Peter, but I'd add it was also a beautiful experience, one I was pleased to be part of," she answered.

"And you, Janette, what were your impressions?" he asked.

"I was amazed at how you brought him out to face what truly disturbed him," Janette replied.

"Good. I thought as much. Everybody has a role to play, and we all can learn from every situation." He turned and walked away.

"I have to say, he is an enigmatic man," I remarked to Janette.

"Yes, he is," she agreed. "It's getting late, and time for me to go. I hope I'll meet you both again. It's been a pleasure meeting you, Melissa."

"Lovely to have met you as well," Melissa replied with a warm smile.

After she left, Melissa busied herself clearing away the supper things. A few moments later, Michael entered the room.

CHAPTER 5

THE VEIL IS LIFTING

'If you do not change direction, you may end up where you are heading.'
– Gautama Buddha

"You and Melissa make yourselves comfortable on the lounge. I'll make a fresh pot of coffee," his voice calm and measured as always.

A few minutes passed, and when Michael returned, balancing cups of coffee on a tray, he remarked with a grin, "Here you are, Peter, and also for you, Melissa."

"Thanks," I replied, accepting the cup.

Melissa smiled. "Thank you, Michael."

Melissa shifted closer to me on the lounge, tucking her legs beneath her as she sipped her coffee.

The room felt warm, peaceful, and filled with quiet anticipation. Michael sat across from us, his eyes thoughtful, as if he was preparing to dive deeper into conversation.

"Peter, you said you found tonight's discussion interesting. May I ask in what way?"

I took a moment, glancing at Melissa, who nodded encouragingly. "It was the way everything unfolded," I began. "How you know exactly what questions to ask... It felt like you were drawing something out of James which even he wasn't aware of.

Michael smiled, leaning back slightly. "Therein is the beauty of conversation, Peter. It's not about having all the answers. It's about asking the right questions, questions which can guide someone to find what's already within them."

"I understand," I said, pausing to collect my thoughts. "But there was something more. It wasn't casual conversation. It was as if you sensed something in him, something specific which needed addressing."

Michael took a slow sip of his coffee before responding.

"Perhaps, but it's not about sensing mystically. It's about listening, not to the words, but to the spaces between them. People often reveal more in what they don't say."

Melissa, who had been quietly listening, now chimed in. "I've noticed with you, Michael, you have a way of making people feel like they're understood, even when they can't quite express what's going on."

Michael chuckled softly. "I don't know if it's quite as profound. It's more about creating a space where people feel safe to explore their thoughts, and wait for the answers to come."

I nodded, feeling the weight of his words. "It's interesting because, for me, in a sense, writing is similar. I don't always know where a story is going, but if I ask the right questions, of myself, and the characters, it reveals itself."

"Yes," Michael agreed, his eyes lighting up. "Writing and conversation aren't much different. They're both journeys into the unknown, guided by curiosity and the willingness to explore."

Melissa rested her head on my shoulder, adding softly, "Maybe this is why you have always been drawn to deeper conversations. You are searching for something beneath the surface."

I smiled, feeling a warmth in her words. "I suppose, but what fascinates me is how Michael seems to guide the process naturally. Do you think it's something which can be learned, or is it... you?"

Michael's gaze softened. "It can be learned, Peter. It's not about having some rare gift; it's about being present. When you're truly present with someone, without an agenda or a need to control the outcome, you create room for them to reveal themselves. It's as much about patience as it is about curiosity."

There was a pause as we all sat with this thought. The quiet hum of the night outside seemed to fill the room, making the conversation feel even more intimate.

I glanced at Michael, then at Melissa. "Do you think it's the reason why tonight's conversation had such an impact on James? Because you were fully present with him?"

Michael considered the question, then nodded. "I'd like to think it was. People respond to being truly heard. It's a rare thing in today's world, with many distractions and much noise. When someone feels truly listened to, it can be transformative."

Melissa shifted slightly; her voice thoughtful. "It's funny, but I think Peter's writing resonates with his readers because he explores these feelings. He's not telling stories; he's listening to them, too. The characters, their struggles, their inner worlds... it's all connected to something deeper."

I felt a sudden rush of gratitude for her insight. She had always understood me, often better than I understood myself. "Maybe you're right. Maybe it's why I've always been searching for meaning and connection."

Michael smiled, a glimmer of understanding in his eyes. "The search never truly ends, Peter, but in searching, we find the moments which matter. Tonight, was one of those moments, for James, and perhaps for you as well."

I looked at him, then at Melissa, and realised he was right. Tonight, had been more than an evening of conversation. It was part of my journey toward something deeper, something more profound than I had ever imagined.

"It was the way everything unfolded, and how you knew what questions to ask. I wouldn't have thought there was a message there for James, but then, I don't have your faculties. It was fascinating to observe."

"What makes you think you don't have the same abilities as I do?" asked Michael.

"I would think it's obvious," I said. "It didn't occur to me at all James seeing a derelict on a park bench could trigger his anger about something which happened when he was young."

"You didn't answer my question, Peter. You seem to think you don't have the same abilities I have, but I don't agree. Remember, I said The Knowing is in all of us, waiting to be accessed, and it is with you, also. I'm certain there are times you have tapped into it, but you probably weren't aware you were doing it."

"You are giving me something to think about," I said.

"We are capable of much more than many realise. What you have witnessed is a small part of it. There's nothing special about it, and in my opinion, it's our unacknowledged heritage. The human animal is a fascinating species, and we have abilities which have atrophied in most because they are not used. This doesn't mean, though, they can't be accessed."

"Is it the same as intuition?" I enquired.

"Intuition is a part of it, but it's a small part. As you would know, many indigenous cultures have telepathic abilities, and this has been studied. Many also claim they see the ghosts or spirits of their ancestors. The question here is: is it real or a myth? Because we are talking about an intangible aspect of our being, it's difficult to prove or disprove. I know it to be a fact because of my experiences, and I accept it as a part of my reality."

"Are you saying you can see ghosts and you are telepathic?" I asked.

"Yes, I am, and much more," answered Michael.

I sat in silence for a time, taken aback by Michael's statement. I was comfortable believing there was no such thing as spirits or ghosts, and I wasn't prepared for what I had heard. I knew Michael was different, possibly the most unique person I had ever met, but alarm bells were going off in my head. For a moment, I contemplated leaving, but he had asked me to give him the courtesy of proving to me what he had to say was true, and I couldn't find a good enough reason not to do this.

Breaking the silence, Michael stated, "You seem at a loss for words, Peter."

"Yes and no," I replied, my voice trailing off as I searched for the right words. "I had certain fixed ideas about what's real and what isn't, and what you've said... it's more than I can cope with right now.

You're full of surprises."

Michael gave me a measured smile, the kind which made me feel both challenged and reassured.

"I make no apologies for my beliefs, Peter. I'm comfortable with them. All I ask of you is to suspend your current belief system, for a while, then new concepts can be presented to you. Let them reside within you. Don't try to analyse anything right now. The more you allow these ideas to exist without judgment, the more open you'll become to new possibilities."

I stared at him, feeling a strange mix of intrigue and unease. He was asking me to step away from everything I'd built my understanding on, to let go, at least temporarily, of my rational, structured mind. It felt daunting, but something about the way he spoke, with such calm certainty, made me want to trust him.

"OK," I agreed, the words feeling heavier than I intended. "I'll do as you ask."

"Excellent," Michael said, standing and placing a hand on my shoulder. His grip was firm, but there was a gentleness in his eyes. "Our journey together holds much promise, and I think you'll find it more interesting than you could ever imagine."

He glanced at Melissa, who had been observing the exchange with a look of quiet understanding. Then, he motioned for us to follow him. "Come, I'll lead you to your room. I'll wake you around six for breakfast."

Melissa and I exchanged glances as we followed him down the hallway. There was a strange energy in the air, a weight which hadn't been there before. As we entered the room, I felt a knot forming in my stomach. This wasn't another conversation, I realised. It was the beginning of something far more complex than I had anticipated.

"Good night, and don't stay awake too long analysing the events of tonight," he said with a knowing smile.

We prepared for bed and when the light was off, I stared at the ceiling, the shadows from the moonlight flickering across the room. 'How did he know I analysed everything?' The thought unnerved me. It was as if Michael had peered straight into my soul, effortlessly dismantling the walls I had carefully built around my mind.

'Maybe there are such things as ghosts and spirits,' I thought, surprising myself. 'And if there are, I hope they don't come calling tonight.' I shook my head, dismissing the idea as ridiculous, but the unease lingered.

'No, what a stupid thought,' I scolded myself, trying to laugh it off. But the more I tried to push the thought away, the more it seemed to creep back in, like an itch I couldn't scratch. I rolled over, trying to settle my racing thoughts, but they wouldn't stop. I couldn't shake the feeling. Maybe I'd bitten off more than I could chew.

Melissa stirred beside me, her breathing soft and steady. She had a way of calming me without saying a word. I looked over at her, wondering if she could sense the turmoil inside me. If she did, she didn't show it.

'I can always go,' I told myself, clinging to the idea like a lifeline. 'If it gets too strange, I can leave.' But deep down, I knew it wasn't about leaving. Something about this, about Michael, about the conversation tonight, had pulled me in, and part of me would rather not let go.

I tossed and turned in the dark, unable to quiet my mind. Each time I closed my eyes, fragments of the conversation with Michael replayed in a loop, as though my subconscious refused to let go. Michael's words echoed through the silence: 'Suspend your present belief system, allow new concepts to reside within you, don't analyse.' Yet, analysing was all I could do.

The room was eerily quiet, save for the rhythmic sound of Melissa's soft breathing. Even her presence, which usually grounded me, couldn't stop the flood of thoughts swirling in my head. Every shadow in the room seemed to take on a strange shape, every creak of the house felt like something, or someone, lurking beyond the edges of my perception. 'Was it my mind playing tricks, or something more?' I wondered.

'Ghosts and spirits...' The thoughts surfaced again, unbidden. I squeezed my eyes shut, trying to dismiss them. But then, a flash of an image appeared behind my eyelids, a shadowy figure standing in front of the bed, indistinct, but undeniably there. My heart raced, and I bolted upright, my eyes darting around the room. Nothing. There were shadows cast by the moonlight filtering through the curtains, but no-one standing there.

I exhaled, long and slow, trying to steady my breath. 'It's nothing. You're imagining things,' I said to myself. But the unease lingered, like a heavy weight in my chest which wouldn't go away.

I lay back down, once again staring at the ceiling. My mind felt like a tangled knot, one which tightened the more I tried to unravel it. 'Why had Michael's words shaken me in such a way?'

It wasn't like me to be affected by something spiritual or other-worldly. I had always prided myself on being grounded in logic, in reason. But tonight, something had shifted.

I thought back to Michael's serene confidence, the way he spoke as if the answers were already known to him, waiting for me to discover them on my own. It unnerved me, how easily Michael had slipped beneath the surface of my defences, revealing parts of me I hadn't even realised were there. 'He knew about my constant need to analyse, to pick everything apart,' I thought. 'How could he have known?'

As the minutes dragged on, my restlessness grew. My thoughts became more fragmented as if my rational mind was losing its grip. A nagging feeling gnawed at me, a sense something was shifting within me, something I couldn't quite put into words. I tried to silence it, to bury it under the weight of my usual logic, but it kept rising to the surface, persistent and unyielding.

A cold breeze swept through the room, brushing against my skin like icy fingers. I shivered, pulling the blanket tighter around me. The window was closed, the air still. What happened? I glanced toward the corner of the room, where the shadows seemed darker and denser than before. For a split second, I thought I saw movement, something stirring in the blackness. My heart leaped into my throat.

'It's nothing,' I told myself again, but the words felt hollow, like a weak shield against the rising tide of fear. My imagination. And yet, I couldn't shake the feeling. Something, someone, was there, watching. I squeezed my eyes shut, trying to block it all out, but the feeling of being observed grew stronger. The silence of the room seemed to thicken, pressing in on me. My pulse pounded in my ears, and I could feel my breathing quicken. 'This is ridiculous,' I thought, frustrated with myself. You don't believe in any of this nonsense.

But Michael's words had planted a seed, and now the seed was growing, its roots twisting deep into my subconscious. A faint sound caught my attention, like a whisper, barely audible, but unmistakable. It seemed to come from nowhere and everywhere at once, drifting through the room like a ghostly breeze. I strained to listen, my heart pounding. The words were unintelligible, a soft murmur, but they sent a chill down my spine.

I sat up again, my body tense, scanning the room. 'Nothing… there's nothing here,' I repeated to myself, but my mind wasn't convinced. I glanced at Melissa, who was still sleeping peacefully beside me, unaware of the inner storm which raged within me. I envied her calm, the way she could let go and rest. But for me, sleep seemed impossible now.

'What if Michael's right?' The thought came unbidden, breaking through the walls of my resistance. 'What if there's more to this than I have ever allowed myself to believe?' I had always dismissed such things, spirits, the supernatural, the unseen forces which others claimed to feel or understand. But tonight… tonight felt different. Something in the air, in Michael's presence, had shifted my perspective, whether I liked it or not.

I lay back, staring once again at the ceiling, feeling the weight of the unknown pressing down on me. My mind raced through the possibilities, trying to find an anchor in the storm of uncertainty. But there was no anchor tonight. My pulse pounded in my ears, and I could feel my breathing quicken. 'This is ridiculous,' I thought, frustrated with myself. 'You don't believe in any of this nonsense. But for me, sleep seemed impossible. 'What if Michael's right?' The thought came unbidden, breaking through the walls of my resistance. 'What if there's more to this than I've ever allowed myself to believe?' I had always dismissed such things, spirits, the supernatural, the unseen forces others claimed to feel or understand.

As my eyelids grew heavier and exhaustion finally started to take hold, I allowed myself one last thought before sleep claimed me:

'What if I've been wrong all along? What if there's more to this world than what I've always believed?' I drifted into a restless, dream-filled sleep, haunted by images of shadows, whispers, and the unsettling feeling my journey had only just begun.

CHAPTER 6

FEELING THE PAIN

'A man is not called wise because he talks, and talks again; but if he is peaceful, loving and fearless then he is in truth called wise.' — Gautama Buddha

The morning light filtered gently through the curtains, casting a soft glow across the room. I blinked against the brightness; my mind sluggish as I slowly regained consciousness. There was the sound of peace and the quiet sounds of the early morning with the distant call of birds, and Melissa's steady breathing beside me. But as the fog of sleep lifted, memories of the previous night came rushing back.

I groaned inwardly. My head felt heavy, not from lack of sleep, but from the weight of thoughts which had kept me awake. 'What had I started?' The question from the night before echoed again, and a deep unease settled in my chest. I rolled over, glancing at the clock. It was five-thirty. Michael had said he would wake us at six.

Melissa stirred beside me, yawning softly as she stretched. She opened her eyes and gave me a lazy smile. "Good morning darling," she murmured, her voice thick with sleep.

I managed a weak smile in return. "Morning," I replied, though it felt anything but ordinary.

Melissa propped herself up on her elbow, studying me. "You look as if you didn't sleep well."

"I didn't," I admitted, running a hand through my hair. "I couldn't stop thinking about last night. Everything Michael said, it was all to unsettling."

She nodded; her eyes soft with understanding. "I could feel it too. There's something about him, isn't there? Something which makes you question everything."

I sighed, rubbing my temples. "Yeah, exactly. And I don't like it. I mean, I'm a writer, I'm used to exploring different ideas, but this... this is different. It feels personal like he's peeling back layers I didn't even know I had."

Melissa placed a hand on my chest, her touch warm and grounding. "Maybe he's helping you see things from a new perspective."

I didn't respond right away. I wanted to resist, to push back against the idea Michael might be leading me somewhere I wasn't ready to go. But deep down, I knew Melissa was right. Last night had opened a door in my mind I couldn't easily close.

I felt a jolt of surprise at how composed Michael sounded when he called us, as though last night's conversation hadn't stirred anything in him at all. It was as if, for him, this was perfectly normal, while my mind had been spinning. He had likely slept peacefully, knowing exactly where he was leading us.

Melissa got out of bed first, wrapping a robe around herself. "Come on, let's see what he's got for us. Maybe some food will help clear your head." I reluctantly followed, though my mind was still clouded by unease. We made our way down the hall and into the kitchen, where the smell of freshly brewed coffee and warm bread greeted us. Michael stood at the counter, stirring something on the stove, looking perfectly at ease, as though the events of last night had never happened.

"Morning, Peter," Micheal said, as he handed me a cup of coffee. "I trust you slept well?"

I couldn't help but let out a dry chuckle. "Not exactly," I admitted, taking a sip of the coffee. It was rich and strong, and for a moment, I savoured it, hoping it might help shake off the remnants of my restless night. "I couldn't stop thinking about everything we talked about."

Michael raised an eyebrow, his smile widening slightly. "Not surprising. Big ideas often take time to settle. Did you manage to make peace with any of it?"

I shook my head, feeling a little foolish. "No, I didn't. If anything, I feel more confused. You talked about suspending my beliefs, but it's challenging when I'm wired to question everything."

Michael nodded thoughtfully, turning down the heat on the stove. "You've spent a lifetime building a framework to understand the world, and now I'm asking you to step outside of it. It's uncomfortable, I know, but discomfort is often the first step toward growth."

Melissa, who had been quietly sipping her coffee, spoke up. "I think what Peter's struggling with is you seem sure of everything, Michael. It's like you already know the answers, and we're playing catch-up."

Michael's gaze softened as he turned to face us fully. "It's not because I have all the answers. It's because I've learned to trust the process of discovery. What we discussed last night isn't something you can understand all at once. It takes time, patience, and openness."

I leaned against the counter, staring into my coffee. "But what if I'm not ready for it? What if I can't let go of the way I've always seen things?"

Michael walked over to me, placing a hand on my shoulder, his expression kind but firm. "You don't have to be ready, Peter. You have to be willing. Willing to question, to explore, to sit with the unknown without trying to control it. This is what I'm asking of you."

I looked up, meeting Michael's gaze. There was something there, something steady and reassuring, but also challenging. It was as if he was offering me a path, but it was up to me to decide whether to walk it.

"I don't know if I can," I admitted, my voice quiet.

Michael smiled gently. "You've already started. Last night was the first step. Now it's a matter of continuing the journey."

I didn't respond right away, the weight of Michael's words settling over me. I felt both pulled and resistant, a strange duality left me feeling raw and exposed. But beneath the surface, there was a flicker of something else, a curiosity, a small but growing desire to see where this journey might lead.

"I'll try," I finally said, though the words felt tentative, as though I wasn't entirely sure what I was agreeing to.

Michael nodded, satisfied. "Let's eat. We have got a long day ahead."

As we settled around the breakfast table, the smell of freshly baked bread and sizzling eggs filled the air. Michael had set the table with a simple but inviting spread: eggs, toast, and fruit. There was a calmness in his movements as he served the food, a contrast to the restless energy still swirling inside me.

Melissa poured herself another cup of coffee, her eyes flicking between Michael and me as if anticipating the conversation which was bound to unfold. I took a bite of my toast, chewing slowly, my mind still churning. Michael seemed content to let the silence linger, sipping his coffee thoughtfully. Finally, I couldn't take it anymore. I put down my fork and spoke, my voice tinged with frustration.

"Michael, I've been thinking about what you said last night, about suspending my beliefs. But here's the thing: I don't know how to do it. My whole life, I've relied on understanding the world through logic and reason. You're asking me to... let it go?"

Michael looked up, his expression calm but attentive. "I'm not asking you to abandon logic, Peter. Logic has its place, and it's served you well, but sometimes, it's not enough. There are things in this world, things within yourself, which can't be grasped with logic alone."

I frowned, stirring my coffee absentmindedly. "But how can I trust something, I can't explain or understand?"

Michael placed his cup down, leaning forward slightly. "It's not about trust in the conventional sense. It's about openness. Presently, your mind is a fortress, built to protect you from uncertainty. Which is perfectly natural. But what if I told you some of the greatest discoveries, both in the world and within ourselves, are made when we step outside our fortress?"

I shifted uncomfortably in my chair. "You're saying I should accept things blindly?"

Michael smiled gently. "No, not blindly. Curiously. There's a difference. Blind acceptance means you're surrendering control completely. But curiosity allows you to explore without needing immediate answers."

Melissa chimed in; her voice is soft but thoughtful. "It's like when you're writing, darling. Now and again, the story unfolds in ways you don't expect, and you have to follow it, even if it doesn't make sense right away. Maybe life is similar."

I considered her words. "But in writing, I'm still in control. I'm the one crafting the story."

Michael nodded, but there was a glimmer in his eyes as if he were about to challenge my perception. "Are you? Or is the story crafting itself, and you're merely its vessel?"

I froze, caught off guard by the question. It was something I had thought about before but had never fully acknowledged. There had been times, in the middle of writing, when the words seemed to flow from someplace beyond me, moments when it felt less like I was creating and more like I was uncovering something which already existed.

"I..." I started, but the words faltered. I didn't know how to respond.

Michael leaned back, his expression kind but probing. "What if the same thing is happening with your life? What if, instead of constantly trying to shape it, you allowed yourself to be shaped by the experiences which unfold?"

I stared down at my plate, my appetite abruptly gone. My mind was a battlefield, logic on one side, this strange, unsettling notion on the other. The idea I might not be in full control of my life and there were forces at work beyond my understanding, both terrified and intrigued me.

"But how do I even start?" I asked, my voice quieter now, more vulnerable. "How do I let go of control?"

Michael's eyes softened. "By taking one small step at a time. You don't need to dismantle everything you believe all at once. Start by noticing. Notice the moments when life takes you in unexpected directions. Notice how you feel when something happens which you didn't plan, and most importantly, notice your resistance. Growth is in understanding what you're resisting and why."

Melissa reached out, gently placing her hand on mine. "You don't have to do this alone," she said softly. "We're in this together."

I squeezed her hand, grateful for her presence. But there was still a gnawing uncertainty inside me, a voice which whispered I might be getting in too deep. I glanced at Michael, who seemed to sense my hesitation.

"You're not being asked to commit to anything, Peter," Michael said, his voice gentle but firm. "All I'm asking is for you to be willing to explore. Suspend judgment for a while. Let the questions live inside you without needing immediate answers."

I looked at him, feeling the weight of the unspoken challenge. Part of me wanted to retreat into the safety of familiar thought patterns, but another part, small yet persistent, was curious about what might happen if I let down my guard.

"I'll try," I said slowly, with more conviction. "I will be open."

Michael smiled, the lines around his eyes crinkling.

"Remember, Peter, you're not alone on this journey. We're all walking it together, each in our way."

As we continued eating, the conversation shifted to lighter topics, but the undercurrent of our earlier discussion lingered in my mind. The words hung there, like shadows in the corners, waiting for acknowledgment. Despite my attempts to push them aside, they kept returning, reminding me something inside had already begun to shift.

For the first time in a long while, I felt on the cusp of something unknown. Though uncertainty still made me uneasy, a quiet excitement was building inside me, a sense maybe there was more to this journey than I had imagined.

After breakfast, the air felt lighter yet charged with the unspoken weight of our discussion. We cleared the table in comfortable silence, each lost in thought. Michael remained calm and steady, while I felt a growing sense of anticipation.

Once the dishes were cleared, Michael suggested a walk through the woods behind the house. "It's a good place to think, to clear the mind," he said.

Melissa smiled. "I'm happy to, it sounds perfect."

Though still uneasy, I nodded in agreement. The idea of being outdoors seemed like the reset I needed after the intensity of the morning.

We grabbed our coats and stepped outside. The morning air was crisp, the sky pale blue with low-hanging clouds. As we made our way toward the wooded trail, leaves crunched beneath our feet.

Michael led the way at an unhurried pace, hands tucked into his pockets. Melissa and I followed closely behind, our footsteps falling into rhythm. For a while, no one spoke, and I found myself focusing on the forest sounds, rustling branches, occasional bird calls, and the clean, crisp air. The simplicity of it all was soothing, and for the first time since waking, my mind began to quiet.

The trail wound through dense trees, sunlight dappling the path ahead. Michael finally broke the silence. "Nature has a way of showing us things we can't always see when surrounded by noise and distractions."

I looked at the towering trees, their leaves trembling in the light wind. I had always appreciated nature casually, but now there was something different about it. I felt more aware of the subtle details, the way the forest seemed alive with invisible energy.

"I've never thought about it much," I admitted.

Michael nodded, his gaze moving over the landscape. "In some ways we are trained to see the world in a particular way. Our minds filter out most of what's happening around us to function in daily life. But when we step out of the framework, when we slow down and observe, we start to notice things we hadn't before."

We walked further in silence, the crunch of leaves blending with the soft rustle of the wind. I could feel the tension in my body easing as the quiet of the forest worked its way into me.

"What exactly are we supposed to notice?" I asked, glancing at Michael. "What are we looking for?"

Michael smiled softly as if expecting the question. "It's not about looking for anything specific. It's about being open to whatever presents itself. Sometimes it's a feeling, a thought, or a memory which surfaces. The forest can be a mirror, reflecting what we need to see."

I frowned slightly, still feeling the itch of my analytical mind. "But how do you know when you've seen something important? What if it's random thoughts?"

Michael paused, turning to face me. His eyes held a calm intensity. "You'll know. When something resonates deeply, you feel it. It's not something we can explain with logic. It's an understanding which comes from within, something you recognise without needing to analyse."

I felt a flicker of frustration mixed with curiosity. Despite my resistance, I couldn't deny Michael's words stirred something inside me, something half-formed and elusive.

Melissa, who had been quietly listening, spoke up. "It's like intuition, right? Like a gut feeling you get when something clicks, even if you don't fully understand it."

Michael nodded, a pleased look in his eyes. "Exactly. Intuition is often dismissed because it doesn't follow the same rules as rational thought. But it's a powerful guide, especially when exploring things beyond the surface."

We continued walking, the forest growing denser. I felt a strange sense of anticipation building, as though on the verge of some revelation, though I had no idea what it might be. I tried to relax, to let go of the need for answers, but it was harder than expected.

As we rounded a bend, the trees opened to reveal a small clearing bathed in soft sunlight. A wooden bench sat at the edge, facing a large, ancient tree which towered over the rest of the forest. Its roots stretched deep into the earth, and its branches extended high into the sky, swaying gently.

Michael stopped and gestured toward the tree. "This is one of my favourite spots," he said quietly. "There's something about this tree, its age, its presence. It has a wisdom all its own."

I stared at the tree, feeling a strange pull toward it. There was something majestic about it, something ancient and still. Standing before it made me feel small in a way which wasn't unpleasant. It was humbling, like being in the presence of something far greater than myself.

Michael sat on the bench, motioning for us to join him. "Sometimes, all we need is a quiet place to reflect," he said softly.

"This tree has been here for centuries. It's seen the seasons come and go, the world changes around it, yet it remains, steady and rooted."

I sat down, feeling the weight of Michael's words. The tree's roots twisted and turned, some breaking through the surface, gnarled and weathered. I could feel its strength, its patience. For the first time, I didn't feel the need to fill the silence with questions. I sat, letting the stillness of the clearing wash over me.

Melissa leaned into me, resting her head on my shoulder. "This feels good," she whispered. "Sitting here in the stillness."

I nodded, unsure how to put my feelings into words. The tension which had gripped me since last night was starting to loosen, replaced by something quieter, more peaceful. For a moment, I allowed myself to be, with no questions or analysis, with the soft rustle of leaves, the steady presence of the ancient tree, and Melissa's warmth beside me.

Michael glanced at me, his eyes filled with quiet understanding. "This is the first step," he said softly. "Learning to be still, to listen, not to the world around you, but to yourself. The answers you seek are already within you. You have to make space for them to emerge."

I didn't respond immediately, unsure what to say. But as I sat there, surrounded by the forest and the quiet wisdom of the ancient tree, I felt something shift within me. It wasn't a revelation, not yet, but it was a beginning. A softening of the walls I had built around my mind. And for the first time, I felt a small sense of peace as if maybe, I was starting to understand.

As I sat on the bench, staring at the massive tree, something shifted inside. I couldn't pinpoint what it was, but for the first time in a long while, I felt... still. Not the stillness of exhaustion or resignation, but something deeper, like I had stopped running from the questions swirling in my mind. The tree, ancient and rooted, seemed to exude a patience I couldn't help but feel.

Michael had talked about intuition, about letting go of control, and I had resisted every bit of it. My whole life, I've relied on reason, logic, things I could measure and grasp. But sitting here, in the presence of something which had likely stood in this forest for centuries, it felt like maybe there were things I'd been missing. Things I'd never considered because I was too busy trying to make sense of everything. Melissa was right beside me, her head resting on my shoulder, her body's warmth grounding me. I've always known she's more open than I am, more willing to trust her gut feeling, to let things unfold without questioning every little detail. I envy this in her.

I want the same kind of peace. But I'm not sure I know how to get there.

Would it be possible to let go of control? I've spent many years defining who I am through my thoughts, through the stories I write, through the careful, measured way I approach life. It feels like giving up a piece of myself to loosen its grip. But sitting here, something about the stillness, the presence of this tree, and the way the light filters through the branches makes me wonder if I've been holding on too tightly.

Michael had said the tree was a mirror, reflecting what we needed to see. At the time, it sounded like mystical nonsense to me, but now, I'm not sure. As I watch the leaves tremble in the breeze, the roots twisting in and out of the ground, I can't help but feel a strange connection. Not in some grand, spiritual sense, but in a way, which speaks to something simpler, something I've ignored for too long. The tree's there. It's not asking anything of the world. It's not trying to prove itself. It's as it is. 'Can I ever be like the tree?' I asked myself.

My mind, always racing, always seeking the next question, the next answer, it's exhausting. I think back to all the nights I've stayed up, dissecting every little thought, every decision, every fear. Trying to control the narrative of my life the way I control the characters in my stories. And for what? Has it brought me any closer to peace? To understanding? Or has it kept me locked in a never-ending loop of questions which can't ever be answered?

I'd rather not admit it, but maybe Michael's right. Maybe it's not about figuring everything out. Maybe it's about noticing, about making space for the questions to exist without needing to solve them. This is hard for me. It goes against everything I've built myself on. But something is comforting in the idea, too. The thought is I don't have to have all the answers right now. "Be open, and stay open." Michael had said to me.

I glance at him out of the corner of my eye. He's sitting there, calm as ever, watching the tree like it holds some secret. Maybe it does. Maybe it doesn't. But Michael looks at the world in a way I can't yet, and which unnerves me. It's like he's operating on a different level, one which doesn't need to tear everything apart to understand it. Maybe it's the reason why I've been resistant to him. Because deep down, I know he's seeing something which I'm not.

I take a deep breath, letting the air fill my lungs, then release it slowly. The tension in my chest loosens a little. Maybe I don't need to fight this. Maybe I can let it unfold.

I turn my gaze back to the tree. It's there, standing tall, weathered by time, but still strong. It doesn't need answers. It doesn't need control. It's existing, in its quiet way as it has done forever.

'Could I, do it?' Could I exist without needing everything to make sense all the time? The thought both scares and excites me. There's a part of me which is afraid of what I might lose if I let go of control. But there's also a part of me which is curious about what I might gain.

I don't know what this journey with Michael will bring or what I'll discover about myself along the way. But for the first time, I'm willing to admit, maybe I don't need to know. Perhaps it's enough to sit here in the quiet and let the questions exist without rushing to answer them.

I feel Melissa's hand slip into mine, and I squeeze it gently, grateful for her presence. I can feel her quiet support, her under-standing. She's always been more accepting of these things than I am. Maybe she's been trying to show me this all along, in her way.

The wind picks up, rustling the leaves overhead, and I close my eyes, for a moment, letting the sound wash over me. I don't have any answers yet, I'm still conflicted, and still questioning, but maybe it's okay to be open, to be free. Maybe this is what it feels like to start letting go.

As I sit there, surrounded by the quiet strength of the forest, and I realise something; I'm tired of fighting. Tired of trying to control everything, of holding on to tightly to the way I think things 'should' be. I don't know what comes next, but for the first time in a long while, I'm fine with not knowing. There's a small sense of peace in a flicker of something new. I open my eyes and look at the tree again. It's still there, steady and rooted, and for the first time, I think I understand what Michael meant.

After what felt like hours, but could've been minutes, Michael stood up from the bench, stretching slightly. "Shall we head back to the house?" he asked, his voice gentle, but breaking the stillness of the moment. He didn't rush us, though. It was like he knew we needed to ease back into the world, into reality.

I took one last look at the tree, its roots twisting into the earth like an anchor which had been there far longer than I could comprehend.

'I wonder what it's seen,' I thought, before shaking off the strange sense the tree somehow knew more than I ever would.

Melissa slid her hand out of mine and stood up, stretching her arms above her head and taking in a deep breath.

"I feel terrific." she said quietly, her eyes meeting mine for a brief moment.

There was warmth there, and understanding. She always seemed to get it, whatever 'it' was, before I did. I envied her for her stability, but I also took comfort in it. She made this journey feel less foreign, less daunting.

I stood as well, and we began the walk back. The path seemed less heavy this time, lighter in a way which mirrored the shift in my mind. The forest was still, but it felt more welcoming now. The sounds of birds chirping in the distance, the soft rustle of leaves overhead, it all felt like part of the same quiet rhythm.

As we walked, I found myself glancing at Michael. He didn't speak, didn't offer any profound insights. He walked ahead, leading us back toward the house with the same steady pace he'd had when we left. It made me wonder how long he had been on this path, and how many people he had guided through these same steps. How many minds he had asked to let go, to be open?

Melissa walked beside me, our hands brushing occasionally as we made our way down the path. She was quiet too, but there was no tension in the silence. It was the kind of silence which felt comfortable like we were all absorbing what had happened in our own way. I felt more at ease with it now, more okay with not having all the answers.

As the house came into view, I realised I was hungry. The knots which had tied themselves in my stomach during the restless night had loosened, and now I felt a gnawing emptiness which needed filling. I glanced at Melissa and caught her smiling slightly.

"I'm starving," she said, like she could read my mind.

I laughed, the sound surprising me. It had been a while since I'd felt as light. "Yeah, me too."

Michael glanced back at us, a small smile tugging at the corner of his lips. "Lunch should be about ready by the time we get back to the house. I thought something simple, a few sandwiches, maybe some soup. Nothing fancy."

"Sounds perfect," Melissa chimed in.

I nodded, though my mind drifted again, still caught between the peace I had felt at the tree and the lingering sense of uncertainty which hovered on the edges. The walk back had given me time to reflect, but now, as the house came into view, I wondered if the questions would come rushing back once we stepped inside. Would I be able to hold on to this feeling, or would the old patterns start creeping in again?

As we approached the house, I could smell something warm and familiar. Michael had been right, it wasn't anything fancy, but the scent of freshly made soup and bread filled the air as we stepped inside. It was comforting, and grounding. It made the surrealism of the morning feel a little more tangible.

"Take a seat," Michael said, gesturing to the table. "I'll bring everything out."

Melissa and I sat down, the warmth of the house settling around us. For the first time since we had arrived, I felt a sense of normalcy. No heavy conversations, no deep philosophical questions, the simple act of sitting down to lunch.

As Michael busied himself in the kitchen, Melissa looked over at me. "How are you feeling?" she asked, her voice soft, but curious. I hesitated, not because I didn't know how to answer, but because the answer felt more complicated than usual.

"I don't know," I finally said. "Better, I think, lighter in a way, but I'm still not sure what any of this means."

Melissa smiled knowingly. "I don't think you're supposed to know yet. Michael seems like the kind of person who lets things unfold in their own time."

"I don't like not knowing," I admitted, running a hand through my hair. "It's hard for me to sit with it."

She nodded; her eyes filled with the same understanding I had come to rely on. "I get it. But you did today. You let it be. It's a start, right?"

I looked at her, and realised she was right. I had let go, it was a start. The restless need for answers, the constant analysing, it had quieted, at least for a little while. Maybe it was something, and maybe it was enough for now.

Michael stepped out from the kitchen balancing a tray with bowls of steaming soup and a plate of sandwiches. "Here we go," he said cheerfully, setting everything down on the table. "Nothing like a good meal after a walk through the woods."

I picked up my spoon, the smell of the soup filling my senses. It was simple, some kind of vegetable broth, I guessed, but it was undoubtedly what I needed. The warmth of the first mouthful settled into me, and for the first time since we had arrived, I felt myself relax fully.

As we ate, the conversation stayed light. Michael asked about my writing, our lives, and what we feel about the strange spiritual journey he was leading us on. He was curious, but not probing, like he wanted to get to know us beyond the big questions. And I found I enjoyed it, talking about the ordinary, the everyday. It made the surrealism of the past twenty-four hours feel more grounded.

After a while, Michael leaned back in his chair, a contented look on his face. "You know," he said, his voice thoughtful, "sometimes the most profound moments happen in the quiet spaces between the big revelations. It's not always about finding answers or uncovering deep truths. Occasionally, it's about being present, whether you're walking through the woods or sharing a meal with friends."

I glanced at him, surprised by the simplicity of his words. Maybe it was the advice I needed to hear right now, not everything had to be a grand discovery.

As we finished lunch, I found myself feeling something I hadn't expected, peace, deep peace. Not because I had figured everything out or because I was rapidly enlightened, but because, for the first time in a long while, I was okay with being here, without needing to know what came next.

After lunch, the warm satisfaction of the meal lingered, and for a while, we sat around the table, basking in the quiet sense of contentment which had settled over us. But as the plates were cleared, I could feel a shift in the air, like something new was about to unfold.

Michael stood up and stretched, his movements unhurried as always, but there was a sense of purpose in his eyes now. "There's something I'd like to show you both," he said, his voice calm, but inviting. "It's part of why I asked you here in the first place."

Melissa and I exchanged glances. I could see the curiosity sparking in her eyes, and though I was hesitant, I couldn't deny I wanted to know what Michael had been hinting at ever since we arrived.

"What is it?" I asked, my voice a little wary, but intrigued.

Michael smiled, a knowing look in his eyes. "Come with me, and I'll show you."

We stood up, following him out of the dining area and through a narrow hallway which led to the back of the house. The air felt cooler here, as though we were moving toward something more secluded, more hidden. My pulse quickened slightly, a mix of curiosity and anxiety. Whatever Michael was about to reveal, it felt important, like a step deeper into the journey he had invited us on.

We passed through a door which led outside, into a part of the property I hadn't noticed before. It was different from the forest path we'd taken earlier; this area felt more enclosed, like a secret garden. The trees grew denser here, and the sunlight filtered through the canopy in thin, golden beams, casting long shadows on the ground. There was a stillness in the air, but it wasn't the peaceful kind I'd felt earlier by the ancient tree. This was different. It felt charged, like the air before a storm.

Michael led us down a narrow stone path, our footsteps muted by the soft earth beneath. Ahead, partially obscured by trees, stood a structure I couldn't yet identify.

"What is this place?" Melissa asked, her voice filled with wonder.

Michael remained silent, his pace deliberate, until we reached a small clearing. In the centre stood an old stone building, no larger than a small chapel, its walls weathered and moss-covered. It exuded an ancient, timeless aura, the kind of place you might stumble upon in the middle of nowhere and wonder how long it had stood untouched by the modern world.

"This," Michael said, turning to face us, "is a place of reflection. A place for you to confront the questions you've been avoiding."

A chill ran down my spine, though the air wasn't cold. Whether from Michael's words or the strange energy of the place, something felt deeply significant. I stood at the threshold of an experience I wasn't sure I was ready for.

Melissa, always more attuned to these things, stepped forward, her eyes wide with curiosity. "It's beautiful," she whispered reverently. "How long has this been here?"

"A long time," Michael replied, his gaze resting on the stone structure. "Longer than I've been here. It's been a place of reflection for generations. People come here to face themselves, to ask the questions they've been too afraid to ask. And sometimes, if they're open enough, they find the answers they didn't know they were seeking."

A lump formed in my throat, my mind racing. 'Face myself?' The idea unsettled me more than I cared to admit. I had spent a lot of time running from certain questions, from the darker corners of my mind. The thought of confronting them in this strange, quiet place was more than a little unnerving.

Melissa stepped closer to the structure, running her hand gently along the moss-covered stones. "What do we do?" she asked, her voice soft but filled with wonder.

Michael smiled, though his eyes held a seriousness now. "You go inside. There's a space for reflection, for meditation. You'll be alone in there. It's not about anyone else, it's about you. You'll stay as long as you need, and when you are ready, you'll know."

I swallowed hard, my nerves kicking in. This wasn't what I had expected when we had set out this morning. I thought we were on a simple retreat, maybe some light spiritual exploration. But this felt different. It felt heavier.

"I don't know if I'm ready for it," I admitted, my voice sounding small in the clearing's stillness.

Michael turned to me, his gaze steady but compassionate. "No one ever feels ready, Peter. The answers you're seeking, the clarity you're looking for, are already within you. You have to make space for them to come through. This place will help you realise it if you're willing."

I stared at the building, my stomach churning with unease. Part of me wanted to turn around and leave. I wasn't sure I could handle whatever this place might reveal. But then I felt Melissa's hand on my arm, a gentle squeeze of reassurance. I looked at her and saw in her eyes the same calm, quiet support she had always given me. She wasn't pushing me, but she wasn't running from this either.

"I'll go first," she said softly, stepping toward the entrance.

I watched her disappear inside; the old wooden door creaking shut behind her. My heart raced as I stood there, staring at the building, feeling the weight of whatever was pressing down on me. Michael stood beside me, silent but present, allowing me space to make my own decision. I could feel his eyes on me, but he didn't say a word.

CHAPTER 7

REVELATIONS

'Your mind is a powerful thing. When you start to filter it with positive thoughts your life will start to change.' – Gautama Buddha

The stale air felt heavy, as if on the brink of change. It reminded her of the electric tension before a storm, filled with anticipation, yet oddly tranquil. Melissa tiptoed further into the room, her eyes locking onto a plain wooden bench in the center. Nothing else adorned the space, no distractions, no clues to guide her next steps.

She hesitated briefly. Always more open to such experiences than me, she trusted her intuition and she believed in inexplicable forces. Yet even in this intimate space, a slight tremor of uncertainty coursed through her. 'What am I supposed to find here?' she wondered, though something deep inside whispered, 'You already know.'

Sitting on the bench, Melissa folded her hands in her lap and closed her eyes. Silence enveloped her like a blanket. Her mind briefly wandered to thoughts of her morning walk, the conversation with Michael, and Peter's unease. She worried about him but understood he also had his personal journey.

'Let go,' she reminded herself, taking a deep breath. Focusing on her slow, steady breathing, she allowed her thoughts to drift away. As the silence deepened, she slipped into a meditative state, the outside world fading into the background.

Gradually, like a soft ripple in still water, something stirred within her. It wasn't a vision or a voice, but rather an awareness rising from her core. She focused on it, letting it expand, and with it came a flood of emotion. Long-buried memories surfaced gently as if asking to be acknowledged.

She saw herself as a child in her mother's garden, the scent of flowers in the air, the feel of dirt between her fingers as they planted seeds together. She recalled her mother's words about life, how everything which grows needs both light and darkness. The memory was tender yet tinged with sadness. Her mother's early passing had profoundly shaped Melissa's identity.

She allowed the memory to wash over her, embracing it fully. She hadn't reflected on her mother in this way for a long time. In the tranquil atmosphere, her mother's presence seemed to envelop her, whispering softly from beyond the veil of memory.

'You're still growing,' the memory echoed. 'You're still planting seeds, even when you don't realise it.'

Tears welled in Melissa's eyes, not of sorrow, but of profound understanding. She realised her mother's teachings had remained with her, subconsciously. Melissa had always sought connection, growth, and nurturing, in relationships, and in her approach to life itself. The seeds her mother had planted weren't confined to the earth; they flourished in the heart of Melissa. 'You've been nurturing him, too,' she mused, her thoughts drifting to me. Though I might not always recognise it, Melissa knew she had been a steady presence in my life, guiding me subtly, much as her mother had once guided her. However, Melissa now understood a crucial truth: she couldn't always be the nurturer. Sometimes, she had to allow others to grow independently. She needed to let me confront my darkness and questions, even if witnessing my struggle was painful.

Melissa inhaled deeply, feeling the air in the small room lighten. She opened her eyes slowly, allowing the newfound peace to settle within her. While she didn't have all the answers, she felt she had received what she needed: a reminder of her identity and the quiet strength she possessed.

Rising to her feet, Melissa gave the room one last glance and smiled. The earlier burden had lifted, replaced by a sense of calm. She felt prepared to face whatever lay ahead, not merely for herself, but for me as well. With a final breath, Melissa exited the building, leaving the quiet space behind.

Michael waited outside. Their eyes met, and though no words were exchanged, she could tell he understood. She smiled softly and nodded towards Peter.

"It's your turn now," she said quietly.

When Melissa emerged from the building, her face serene and composed, I experienced a mixture of relief and apprehension. Relief because she was alright, having navigated whatever this place demanded of her, but apprehensive because now it was my turn. I was uncertain about what I would discover inside. Or worse, what might discover me.

I took a deep breath, attempting to calm my nerves. 'You don't have to do this,' I thought, though the words rang hollow. Deep down, I knew I had already crossed the threshold. I was committed to this journey, ready or not.

After what seemed an eternity, I nodded slowly. "Alright," I said, my voice quiet yet determined. "I'll go in." Michael gave me a reassuring nod as I stepped forward. My heart raced as I reached for the handle, the cool metal sending a shiver through my skin.

The door creaked open, and cool air hit my face as I entered. The building greeted me with soft, muted light. It wasn't dark, but it wasn't bright either. Enough light filtered through the small windows to reveal a simple stone floor and a lone wooden bench in the room's center. The space was small and intimate, on the brink of claustrophobic, yet it exuded a certain peace. A deliberate quietness hung in the air.

'I'm here,' I thought, closing my eyes briefly. 'Now what?'

I stepped forward, the space feeling smaller and more focused now I was alone. Dim light cast shadows across the floor, and the silence was deafening.

I approached the bench, my mind racing. 'What am I supposed to do?' I wondered, anxiety building in my chest. Unlike Melissa, I didn't trust my intuition or believe answers would come if I waited. I craved structure, logic, something tangible. But here, there was nothing to grasp. Silence and stillness were my companions.

I sat on the bench, its cool wood grounding me. Closing my eyes, I tried to breathe slowly, to calm the storm in my mind. It didn't work. Questions came rapid-fire: 'What if I find nothing here? What if there's nothing inside me worth confronting? What if I'm running in circles, trying to cope with the incomprehensible?'

Frustrated, I gritted my teeth. This was why I despised such exercises, no clear instructions, no definitive answers, and vague notions of 'reflection' and 'inner truth.'

Yet as I sat there, fighting the silence, something shifted within me. It was subtle, like a whisper at the edge of my consciousness. I tried to ignore it, but it persisted, growing louder until it demanded attention.

It wasn't exactly a voice, but more a presence, a weight which had always been there, one I had never wanted to acknowledge.

'Why must you understand everything?' it seemed to ask. 'Why do you always need control?'

I swallowed hard, my throat tightening. I had no answer. Or perhaps I did, but wasn't ready to voice it.

'Because if I don't control it, everything will fall apart.'

The thought hit me like a punch to the gut, and the room felt alive. My heart pounded, and my hands clenched into fists. I had spent my entire life trying to control everything, my writing, my career, and even my relationship with Melissa. I had built walls around myself, believing if I could keep everything in order, nothing would hurt me. Nothing could break me.

Sitting in this quiet, ancient place, I realised something: I wasn't in control. I never had been.

'You're scared,' the presence seemed to say, its voice growing clearer. 'You're scared of what will happen if you let go. Scared of what you'll find if you stop running.'

My chest tightened, a wave of panic rising. 'I'm not scared,' I wanted to shout. But the truth was, I was terrified.

Terrified of letting my walls down. Terrified of what lay buried beneath my need for control. Terrified of the loneliness and emptiness which had haunted me for years.

The silence pressed in, and for the first time, I didn't fight it. I let it wash over me, filling the spaces I had tried hard to keep hidden. But then, something broke. Not violently, but in a soft, quiet release. Like a door gently opening. The fear remained, but it wasn't all-consuming. It was there, a part of me, and for the first time, I didn't push it away.

I opened my eyes, the dim light now less oppressive. The air felt lighter, easier to breathe. I wasn't sure what had happened, but I knew something had shifted. Something had opened up inside me, and though I didn't fully understand it, I knew it was important.

I stood up slowly, my legs shaky, and made my way to the door. The room now felt less like a place of confinement and more like a space which had offered something valuable, something unexpected. My hand hovered over the door handle for a moment, needing one last breath before stepping back into the world outside.

When I pushed the door open, the air hit my face, refreshing in its simplicity. The forest seemed brighter, sunlight breaking through the leaves in soft patches of gold. Michael and Melissa stood a few feet away, watching me with calm, patient expressions.

Melissa's eyes were soft, filled with understanding, as if she knew exactly what I'd experienced. Michael, as always, was unreadable, his gaze thoughtful but without judgment.

I walked toward them, feeling a mix of relief and vulnerability. There were no words to explain what had happened, no neat summary to make sense of it. But I knew something inside me had shifted, something had been let go, or at least loosened.

"How was it?" Melissa asked quietly, her voice gentle, as if she understood I might not be ready to talk about it yet.

I hesitated, running a hand through my hair. "I... I don't know yet," I admitted, my voice rough from the weight of the emotions I had confronted. "But it was... something."

She smiled knowingly. "Yeah, I felt it too. It's like you're not quite the same, but you don't know why."

I nodded; grateful she understood without pressing me for more. This was one of things I loved about her; she never pushed me when I wasn't ready. She let me be, let me process things in my own time.

Michael stepped forward; his gaze steady yet kind. "You both did well," he said, his voice low and even. "Facing yourself isn't easy, but it's necessary, especially for where you're headed."

"Where are we headed?" I asked, frowning slightly. "What do you mean?"

Michael's eyes met mine, revealing a depth of understanding which suggested he had already walked the path I was beginning to see.

"Your journey is about more than this moment. This was an important step, but the real work comes after. It's about integrating what you've experienced and allowing the shifts to take root."

I swallowed, absorbing the weight of his words. 'Integrating' sounded long-term, ongoing. Part of me had hoped for closure, a tidy resolution. But Michael was telling me this was the beginning. The real work lay ahead.

Melissa seemed to grasp this better than I did. She nodded thoughtfully.

"It feels like something's shifted in me already," she said softly. "Like I've released something I didn't even know I was holding onto."

I glanced at her, feeling a flicker of envy at her quick understanding. Then I reminded myself: 'this wasn't a race. We were each on our journey.' Michael turned his gaze toward me, his intensity palpable.

"Peter, you've begun to loosen your grip on control," he said calmly yet firmly. "But it's not an instant change. There's more to uncover, more to face. But you've taken the first step."

I exhaled slowly, acknowledging the truth in his words. I had started to understand how my need for control had shaped my life. Now, I had to learn to live without it. It wouldn't be easy, but it felt necessary.

Melissa took my hand, squeezing it gently. I squeezed back, grateful for her anchoring presence.

"What happens now?" I asked, my voice quieter but more confident. I didn't know the next steps, but for the first time, I wasn't afraid of the unknown.

Michael smiled knowingly. "Now, you rest. Let today settle within you. The next steps will reveal themselves when you're ready."

I nodded, feeling the weight of the moment start to lift. There was still much I didn't understand, but for the first time, I wasn't rushing to figure it all out. There was freedom in not needing to control every piece of the puzzle.

Michael gestured toward the house. "Let's head back. The day is young, and there's time for reflection in simpler ways."

We turned and began walking back. The forest felt different now as if it had witnessed our transformation. The once ordinary path now felt like an essential part of the journey.

As we walked in silence, I felt Melissa's warmth beside me and Michael's steady presence. There was no urgency, the quiet rhythm of our footsteps, the soft rustle of leaves, and the understanding our journey was beginning.

The forest welcomed us back with a quiet reflection. Sunlight filtered softly through the trees, and birds calling to each other in the distance. Everything seemed clearer, more vivid as if the morning's intensity had given way to a peaceful awareness.

Melissa stayed close, our hands occasionally brushing. The comfortable silence between us gave me space to process the experience. Instead of feeling shaken, I felt oddly calm, as if something had clicked into place.

Michael walked ahead; his quiet presence steady. He didn't rush us, knowing we needed time. The gentle crunch of leaves beneath our feet was a comforting sound, and I felt grateful for the stillness after the emotional weight of the morning.

When the house came into view, I felt relief and anticipation. It stood like an anchor, offering safety and comfort amidst uncertainty. I could already picture myself in one of the old chairs, cradling a warm cup of tea, letting the experience work its magic within.

Michael turned to us as we approached the door, his expression serene. "Before we enter, take a moment," he said softly. "You've both experienced something significant today. Let it settle before you step back into the day's rhythm."

I paused, glancing at Melissa. She offered a small, under-standing smile and nodded. We stopped outside, enveloped by the forest's quiet. I took a deep breath, closing my eyes briefly, letting the cool air fill my lungs. The morning's weight lingered in my chest, but it no longer felt heavy. It was there, like an old companion I was finally ready to acknowledge.

'It's okay to let go,' I reminded. 'It's okay not to have all the answers.'

Melissa squeezed my hand gently, and I opened my eyes to find her looking at me with her usual warmth and quiet understanding. Her presence alone reassured me she was there, fully present, ready to face whatever came next.

I nodded to Michael, who smiled slightly and opened the door. We followed him inside, immediately wrapped in the house's warmth. The faint aroma of herbs and something sweet wafted from the kitchen, reminding me how long the day had already felt.

Inside, the house seemed alive with its own energy, calm and grounding. The walls, lined with books and old photographs, exuded a sense of history and familiarity. The worn wooden furniture and soft rugs underfoot created a lived-in warmness which invited relaxation and deep breathing. "Make yourselves comfortable," Michael said, gesturing toward the sitting area near the fireplace. "I'll brew some tea, a blend I use for reflection, gentle and calming."

Melissa and I sank into the plush, worn couch. She curled her legs beneath her, and I found myself mirroring her posture, releasing the day's tension for the first time. The fire crackled softly, adding to the peace of the room. I hadn't realised how much I needed this moment of stillness after everything which had transpired.

"Tea sounds perfect," Melissa said softly, her voice matching the room's peacefulness. I nodded in agreement, still processing the events in the small stone building. But there was no urgency to figure it all out. The experience would unfold in its own time, and for now, it felt okay to be me.

As Michael prepared the tea, my gaze drifted to the window. Afternoon light bathed the forest, and I could see the path we had taken winding through the trees. Hours ago, I had felt uneasy and uncertain about Michael's guidance. Now, I felt different. Not fixed, not fully sure of my direction, but calmer. Like I had taken a step in the right direction, even if the next one remained unclear.

Melissa shifted beside me; her eyes soft as she studied my face.

"You seem more at peace," she said gently, her hand resting on mine.

"I think I am," I admitted, surprised by the truth in those words. "I may not fully understand what happened out there, but something's different. I feel different."

She nodded, her smile widening slightly. "I understand. It's as if the whole world has slowed down, enough to make room for something new."

I squeezed her hand, feeling the warmth of her presence anchor me even more. She had been with me through much, always steady and patient. I couldn't imagine navigating this journey without her by my side.

Michael returned with a tray holding a steaming teapot and three small cups. He set it down on the low table before us, pouring the tea with his characteristic deliberate calm. The scent of herbs and flowers filled the room, soothing and familiar, like a drink for unwinding after a long day.

"This tea is special," Michael said as he handed each of us a cup. "It's made from herbs which promote reflection and clarity. A blend of chamomile, lavender, and a few other ingredients which help to settle the mind."

I took a sip, feeling the tea's warmth spread through my chest. The taste was delicate and floral, with a hint of earthiness. It invited savouring each sip slowly. I could feel my body's tension easing further, my mind quieting as the tea worked its magic.

We sat in comfortable silence, sipping our tea and watching the fire crackle softly in the hearth. I felt the day's events settling deeper into my bones, the weight of the experience becoming more manageable with each passing moment.

Michael, knowing when to speak and when to remain silent, finally broke the silence.

"You've both done well today," he said quietly, his voice filled with calm certainty. "Today was the beginning, but you've made important strides. The journey ahead will reveal itself as needed."

I nodded, feeling the truth of his words, even if I didn't fully grasp the scope of what lay ahead. Melissa smiled softly, her gaze meeting mine, and for the first time since we had started this journey, I felt a quiet sense of peace, not because everything made sense, but because it was enough to let things unfold in their own time.

As we finished our tea, I thought whatever came next, I wouldn't face it alone.

We were in this together, and this was enough.

CHAPTER 8

THE ROCK

'Change is never painful. Only resistance to change is painful.'
— Gautama Buddha

As the afternoon wore on, the warmth of the tea and the quiet ambiance of the house lulled us into a peaceful rhythm. The weight of the morning's intensity seemed to lift, leaving behind a sense of calm and clarity. As I was beginning to relax into stillness, Michael leaned forward, his hands resting on his knees, and spoke softly.

"I'd like to take you both somewhere else," he said thoughtfully. "The day isn't over yet, and there's another part of this journey which I believe you're ready for."

Melissa and I exchanged a glance. Part of me wanted to stay in the comfort of the house, letting the day settle in a way which felt safe. However, there was something in Michael's tone, gentle yet purposeful, which made me realise this next step was important. There was still more to uncover, more to face, and I wasn't sure if I was ready for it.

"Where are we going?" I asked, feeling uncertainty rise in my chest again.

Michael smiled, a calm but enigmatic expression crossing his face. "Not far, to another part of the forest. It's a place of deeper reflection, offering clarity when you're ready to see things from a different perspective."

Melissa nodded; curiosity evident in her eyes. At times it made me feel uncomfortable but I admired her for it.

I admit, I hesitated, feeling the pull of both curiosity and resistance. But something about Michael's quiet confidence, the way he seemed to know exactly what we needed even before we did, made me trust him. Trust wasn't something I was used to giving easily, but at this moment, it felt right.

"Okay," I said finally, my voice steadying. "Let's go."

Michael rose from his seat, his movements as deliberate as ever, and gestured for us to follow him. We put our cups down, and we both stood. The house felt like a safe cocoon, and as we stepped outside, the coolness of the afternoon air contrasted sharply with the warmth we'd left behind.

The sun had shifted lower in the sky, casting shadows over the landscape as we made our way toward a different path through the forest. This path wasn't as well-trodden as the one we had taken earlier. The undergrowth was thicker, the trees closer together, and the sounds of the forest seemed more muted here, as though the world was holding its breath.

We walked in silence, and as we ventured deeper into the forest, the air seemed to change. It wasn't the physical environment; something felt charged, as if the forest were alive with unseen energy. I glanced at Melissa, wondering if she felt it too, and from her expression, I could tell she did. After a long walk, we arrived at another clearing, smaller and more intimate than the one with the ancient tree. At its center stood a large, smooth rock, perfectly round and reflective, as if shaped by something other than nature.

Michael stopped at the edge of the clearing and turned to face us. "This is a place where clarity often comes," he said quietly, his eyes resting on the rock. "It's where the veil between what you believe and what's possible becomes thinner, allowing you to see things which might have been hidden before."

I frowned, unsure of his meaning. "How does it work?"

Michael smiled. "It's not about how. It's about being open to what comes. This isn't a place where you seek answers. It's a place where answers find you if you're ready to accept them."

Melissa stepped forward first, her eyes locked on the rock. Something about it seemed to draw her in, calling her without words. She glanced back at me, and I saw calm resolve in her eyes. She was ready.

She approached the rock with slow, deliberate steps. Placing her hand on its smooth surface, she closed her eyes and breathed deeply. I watched as her body relaxed into the moment as if merging with the stillness of the place.

I stayed back, feeling the weight of the moment but unsure what to do next. Part of me wanted to step forward, to experience whatever she was feeling, but I held back, still wrestling with the discomfort of not being in control. What if I felt nothing? What if nothing happened?

After a few minutes, Melissa opened her eyes and looked back at me, her expression soft yet intense.

"It's like everything slows down," she whispered, "and in the stillness, things become clear. You don't have to force it. It comes of its own accord."

Michael nodded, pleased with her experience. He turned to me, his gaze steady.

"Peter, it's your turn."

My heart raced as I took a deep breath, trying to shake off my nerves. I stepped forward, feeling the air grow cooler as I approached the rock. I hesitated, my hand hovering over the surface.

I glanced at Michael, who gave me a small nod of encouragement, then at Melissa, who smiled gently. They were both waiting, not pressuring me but giving me space to proceed at my own pace. Finally, I placed my hand on the rock.

The surface was cool and smooth, seemingly unnatural. As soon as my fingers made contact, I felt a subtle shift, a sensation hard to describe. The world around me faded, and I stood in suspended silence. My mind, buzzing with thoughts moments ago, quieted, and for the first time, I wasn't trying to analyse what was happening.

I closed my eyes and breathed deeply, letting the stillness settle over me. The longer I stood there, the more I felt like I was sinking into something deeper, an awareness which wasn't entirely mine but wasn't foreign either. It was like tapping into a current of energy which had always been there, beneath the surface, waiting for me to reach out to it.

It was then, something happened. It wasn't a vision or a voice, but a realisation, a knowing which emerged from deep within me. It was simple, startlingly: 'You don't have to figure it all out right now. You have to let it unfold.'

The thought hit me like a wave, washing over the fear and uncertainty I had within me. I didn't have to have all the answers. I didn't have to control every outcome. I had to trust the process, trust things would reveal themselves in time, as they needed to.

I opened my eyes, my hand still resting on the rock, and felt a deep sense of peace settle over me. It wasn't the peace which came from understanding everything, but the kind came from accepting I didn't need to.

I turned to Michael, who was watching me with his usual calm expression. He nodded, as if he knew exactly what had happened, and said softly, "You have it now, Peter. It's the clarity you asked for."

Melissa smiled at me, her eyes full of warmth and under-standing. "You look lighter," she said quietly.

I took a deep breath, feeling the truth of her words. I did feel lighter, not because I had found all the answers, but because I was finally starting to let go of the need to find them all at once.

We stood there for a few moments longer, the quiet of the clearing wrapping around us like a protective embrace. Then, slowly, we began to make our way back toward the path, the forest welcoming us back into its fold.

As we walked, I realised something important: This journey wasn't about reaching a final destination or uncovering some grand truth. It was about the moments in between, the quiet realisations, the small shifts, the subtle clarity which came when I stopped trying to control everything. The journey wasn't over, but I was ready for whatever came next.

CHAPTER 9

The Heart Tree

'Quiet the mind, and the soul will speak.' – Gautama Buddha

As we left the clearing and ventured back into the dense forest, the air felt lighter and more breathable. The path ahead seemed less daunting, though I knew challenges still lay ahead. Michael remained quiet after we left the rock, but I sensed we were moving towards something more significant, even if I didn't fully grasp what it would be.

The forest grew quieter, with muted bird songs and rustling leaves, as if nature itself held its breath, anticipating the next phase of our journey. My earlier apprehension had transformed into a sense of anticipation, a feeling something important was about to unfold.

We walked for what seemed like hours, though time was difficult to gauge. The sun hung lower in the sky, casting long shadows and bathing everything in a warm, golden light. As we delved deeper into the forest, the landscape transformed. Trees towered above us, their branches intertwining to form a natural cathedral. The air grew fresher and cleaner, as if the forest was becoming wilder and more ancient with each step.

Eventually, the path opened into a new clearing, unlike any we had encountered before. At its center stood an enormous tree, its gnarled trunk thick with age and its massive branches stretching high into the sky. The tree's roots seemed to merge with the earth, as if it had always been there, predating everything else.

Michael halted at the clearing's edge and turned to face us. "This is the Heart Tree," he said softly, his voice filled with reverence. "It's a place of deep connection, where the boundaries between self and the world become thinner."

I stared at the tree, feeling an inexplicable pull towards it. Its presence radiated power, age, and serenity, commanding attention without uttering a word. Glancing at Melissa, I saw the same awe reflected in her eyes.

"The Heart Tree?" I whispered. "What does it do?"

Michael smiled gently. "It doesn't 'do' anything, Peter. It's a presence, a reminder of our connection to the world around us. People come here to remember, to reconnect with themselves, each other, and the earth."

Melissa stepped forward; her gaze fixed on the tree. "It feels... alive," she murmured. "Like it's more than a tree."

Michael nodded. "In many ways, it is. People often feel the connection deeply here. It's not something which can be explained, you have to experience it."

I stood there, absorbing it all, feeling both drawn to the tree and unsure of what to do. Unlike the rock from earlier, which had given me clarity, this tree felt different. It made no demands; it existed in its quiet power.

Michael approached the tree, beckoning us to follow. "Come closer," he said calmly but encouragingly. "There's something I'd like you both to do."

Melissa and I exchanged glances before slowly walking towards the tree. As we neared, I could feel its energy, like a subtle hum in the air. The tree was more than wood and leaves; it was a presence, an ancient force which had witnessed centuries of change.

At the tree's base, Michael motioned for us to place our hands on the trunk. After a moment's hesitation, I pressed my palm against the rough bark. The tree felt cool and solid, but beneath it, something pulsed faintly, like a heartbeat deep within the wood.

Melissa placed her hand next to mine, her face serene. Her slow, steady breathing suggested she was already attuning to the tree's energy. I closed my eyes, following her lead, and focused on the sensation beneath my hand.

When I first touched it, all I felt was the rough texture of the bark. But as I stood there, something shifted. A subtle vibration ran through my fingertips, not a sound or voice, but an awareness. I sensed the tree was part of something larger, something I was connected to, even if I didn't fully understand how.

Then, like a wave, a profound feeling washed over me. I felt grounded, held by something far greater than myself. I wasn't standing in a clearing, touching a tree. I was connected to the earth beneath my feet, the sky above, and the breath moving through my body. It was an overwhelming sense of unity, with the tree, and with everything. The boundaries I had always perceived between myself and the world blurred, for a brief moment.

I opened my eyes, my heart pounding, not from fear but from something deeper. Melissa stood with her eyes still closed, her hand on the tree, looking peaceful, as if she had found something in the stillness she had long sought.

Michael observed us with his characteristic calm. "This tree reminds us we are never separate from the world around us," he said softly. "No matter how disconnected we feel, no matter how lost, a deeper connection always awaits us if we're willing to listen."

His words sank in as I stood there. I had spent much of my life feeling separate, believing I needed to control everything to feel safe. But here, in the presence of this ancient tree, the sense of separation dissolved, even if it was for a moment.

Melissa opened her eyes and looked at me, a quiet smile on her face. "Did you feel it?" she whispered.

I nodded, not trusting myself to speak yet. I had felt it, some-thing deeper, something unexpected. It wasn't a revelation or a vision, but a feeling, a knowing I was part of something much bigger than I had ever realised.

We stood there for a few more moments, the three of us, the quiet forest wrapping around us. I didn't know what came next, but for now, it didn't seem to matter. I had found something which went beyond words, beyond understanding. For the first time, I didn't need to explain it.

Michael stepped forward, also placing his hand on the tree.

"This is a place you can return to whenever you need," he said softly. "Not physically, but within yourself. The connection is always there; you need to feel it."

I looked at him, feeling a strange sense of gratitude. He had led us here, but the journey had been ours to take. Somehow, through it all, I had found something I hadn't even known I was searching for.

We stepped back from the tree, letting the moment settle within us. As we turned to leave the clearing, I felt a peace I hadn't experienced in a long time. The journey wasn't over, but I had discovered something important, something which would stay with me long after we had left the place.

Standing before the Heart Tree, I felt its presence transcend mere sight. The surrounding air seemed charged with an energy both ancient and alive as if the tree held within it the memory of centuries. The gnarled, twisted bark felt like the skin of the earth itself, weathered yet indestructible. Its thick, serpentine roots weaved in and out of the ground like veins connecting the tree to everything around it.

This tree was more than a tree; it was something eternal. As I looked up, its branches stretched high into the sky, forming a vast canopy which seemed to breathe with the forest. It was rooted in the earth, but more, it was part of it, inseparable. Somehow, by standing in its presence, I felt the connection extending to me as well.

Melissa and I, once more, placed our hands on the bark. It was rough and cold to the touch, but beneath the initial sensation was a warmth, a pulse of life which hummed quietly like a steady heartbeat. I could feel it reverberating up through my fingertips, gentle but persistent. As I stood there, I began to feel lighter, as if the weight of all my doubts and fears was being absorbed into the tree, becoming part of something much larger than myself.

Michael stood a few steps back, watching us with his usual calm, but even he seemed different here. There was a quiet reverence in the way he looked at the Heart Tree, as though he, too, was a student in its presence. The energy of this place seemed to humble everyone who came near it.

"This tree," Michael began, his voice low and filled with deep reverence, "has been here for longer than we can imagine. People have come here for centuries, maybe even longer, to connect with something beyond themselves. The Heart Tree reminds us, no matter how isolated we feel, we are never truly alone. We are always part of something greater."

As he spoke, I let his words settle into me. They felt right, like something I had always known but had forgotten. There's a deep truth in the idea we are never separate from the world around us, even when it feels like we are. The Heart Tree embodied this truth. It was rooted in the same earth we walked on, breathing the same air, part of the same cycle of life.

I closed my eyes, letting my hand remain on the bark, and focused on the quiet rhythm beneath the surface. The pulsing energy, subtle but unmistakable, seemed to echo within me, matching my heartbeat. For the first time in a long while, I felt connected, and grounded to something much larger than the earth beneath me.

Images flickered in the back of my mind, unbidden but welcome. I saw roots, deep and tangled, spreading out beneath the ground. They stretched far and wide, intertwining with other roots, connecting trees, plants, and even the soil itself. It was as if the whole forest were one giant organism, each part supporting the other in a quiet, invisible way. And somewhere in the network of roots, I felt myself, my life, my struggles, my fears, woven into the same fabric, not separate, but part of the complete forest.

I felt Melissa's presence beside me, her energy quiet and steady. She, too, seemed absorbed, her breath deep, as if she were drawing something from the tree. The connection wasn't about us as individuals; it was about us together, as part of this living, breathing world. For the first time, I truly felt what it meant to be connected, not to another person, but to the earth, to life itself.

And with this connection came a peace I hadn't expected. It wasn't the kind of peace which comes from having all the answers, but rather the kind which comes from realising I didn't need to have them all. It was enough to know I was part of something larger, something would continue long after I was gone. The tree had been here for centuries, perhaps millennia, and it would remain long after I had moved on.

I opened my eyes slowly, taking in the sight of the Heart Tree once more. The bark, the roots, the immense canopy above, it all felt like it was breathing in sync with me as if the boundaries between us had dissolved. There was no rush to leave, no urgency to move on. Time felt different here, slower, less linear. I could have stood there for hours, and it wouldn't have mattered. The tree was patient. It had seen lifetimes pass, and it would see countless more.

Michael stepped closer, his voice breaking the quiet but not disrupting the peace. "The Heart Tree teaches us the greatest wisdom often comes not from seeking, but from listening, from being still, and allowing the world to speak to us in its time."

I glanced at him, feeling the truth of his words. The whole time I'd been there, I hadn't sought any answers. I hadn't tried to analyse or understand what was happening. I had listened, to the tree, to the quiet, to the rhythm of life which moved through everything. And by listening, I had found a sense of clarity I hadn't realised I was searching for.

Melissa opened her eyes as well, her hand still resting on the bark. "It feels like home," she whispered, her voice full of wonder.

I knew what she meant. This place, this tree, wasn't a physical location. It was a reminder of something deeper, something we all carry with us, even when we don't recognise it. It was a reminder we belong, we are part of the earth, and part of each other.

Michael nodded. "Many people describe the feeling as you have. The Heart Tree connects us to the essence of who we are, to the part of ourselves which knows, unquestionably, we belong."

I took a deep breath, feeling a sense of belonging settle deep into my bones. It was a strange but comforting feeling, like I had been carrying the weight of separation, and didn't even realise it. Here, in the presence of this tree, the weight had lifted, replaced by a quiet acceptance. I didn't have to struggle to belong; I was accepted as I was.

After what felt like an eternity, but really was no time at all, Michael gently stepped back, signalling it was time to leave. "You can return here whenever you need," he said softly. "Physically or in your mind. The connection is always there, waiting for you to remember."

Melissa and I slowly pulled our hands away from the tree, and I felt a pang of reluctance, as if part of me wanted to stay, to remain in this quiet sanctuary forever. But as my hand fell to my side, the sense of connection didn't disappear. It was still there, like a quiet pulse beneath the surface of everything. The Heart Tree had shown me something important, the connection wasn't confined to this place. It was within me, within all of us, wherever we went.

As we turned to leave the clearing, I cast one last glance at the Heart Tree, its vast branches reaching toward the sky like a guardian of the forest. I knew I would carry this moment with me, this sense of belonging would be something I could return to whenever I needed it. The Heart Tree had given me this gift, and I was grateful for it.

We walked back in silence, the path winding through the forest as the sun began to set, casting the world in a soft, golden light. But something was different now. The world didn't feel as separate or distant as it had before. I felt connected to everything, the trees, the earth, the sky, even the air I breathed. It was all part of the same web of life, and I was part of it too.

As we walked back through the forest, the sun low in the sky, I knew whatever came next, I was ready.

CHAPTER 10

PETER TALKS ABOUT HIMSELF

'When it hurts, observe. Life is trying to teach you something.' – Gautama Buddha

I've spent most of my life unravelling the layers of my identity, seeking to understand what drives me, holds me back, and propels me forward. At 43, with a successful career and stable relationship, one might assume I've figured it all out. However, the reality is more complex.

I'm still the solitary child who grew up in a house too vast for a single occupant, with parents too preoccupied to notice the deafening silence. My childhood, while not overtly traumatic, left me with an insatiable longing for connection and belonging.

Even now, amidst the acclaim my writing has garnered, a void persists. While I can eloquently express my thoughts and emotions on paper, face-to-face interactions remain challenging. My childhood shyness, once a protective armour against rejection, still my behaveiour, causing me to retreat when situations become overwhelming. Books and imagination were my steadfast companions in my youth. I found solace in stories, living vicariously through characters and experiencing emotions I couldn't process. Writing became my voice, when I struggled to use my own, evolving into my primary means of connecting with the world.

My literary success is a testament to the universality of themes like loneliness, longing, and self-discovery. Yet, despite this achievement, I'm still searching for inner peace, the kind which silences the persistent noise in my mind. The weight of my childhood experiences, the loneliness and uncertainty, continues to influence me.

Melissa has been instrumental in my personal growth. Her vivaciousness and self-assurance complement my reserved nature. She sees beyond my protective layers, gently drawing me out of my shell without overwhelming me. In her, I've found a safety I never knew existed. Our relationship has deepened over time, transforming from initial passion into a solid, comforting foundation.

However, even with Melissa's unwavering support, I grapple with my past. On challenging days, my childhood insecurities resurface. I've come to recognise this vulnerability is integral to my identity as a writer, allowing me to create relatable characters who, like me, are flawed and searching for meaning.

The prospect of starting a family with Melissa both excites and terrifies me. While part of me yearns to create the loving family environment I lacked, I fear repeating my parents' mistakes. The idea of fatherhood fills me with both anticipation and dread.

Recently, I've found myself contemplating life's bigger questions. My writing has become more introspective, exploring themes of purpose, meaning, and spirituality. While I may never find definitive answers, I'm committed to the journey of self-discovery and understanding.

As I age, I'm acutely aware of time's relentless march. I'm striving to make peace with my past, to forgive my parents' absence, and accept my imperfections. Melissa helps ground me in the present, teaching me to appreciate the here and now.

Ultimately, I seek wholeness, a state where I no longer question my worth or succumb to long-standing insecurities. I aspire to find peace not with my past, but with myself. I've learned vulnerability is not a weakness, but a vital part of my story, a story I continue to write.

I am a complex, introspective individual whose desires are deeply rooted in my past and my quest for meaning. I yearn for connection, love, and understanding, while simultaneously seeking inner peace. This journey requires me to confront my fears, embrace my vulnerabilities, and accept all facets of my identity.

My inner world is a labyrinth of complexity, shaped by a childhood marked by emotional neglect. Despite my professional accomplishments, I continue to grapple with deep-seated insecurities and an ever-present longing for belonging and inner tranquillity.

I've come to understand external validation cannot fill the void within me. True fulfillment lies in self-acceptance, meaningful connections, and the ongoing pursuit of personal growth and understanding.

There's a part of me which craves something more profound, emotional, and spiritual. As a child, I built walls around myself, using shyness as protection against rejection. Even now, these walls persist, hindering my full engagement with life and those closest to me. Melissa's warmth and vibrancy have helped me feel more secure in ways I never thought possible, yet insecurities still emerge, pulling me back into old emotional patterns.

I yearn to create the family I never had, to fill an emotional void with a child's love and connection. However, a deep-seated fear of failing, of repeating my parents' emotional absence, holds me back. The prospect of fatherhood both excites and terrifies me, it's not about having a child but confronting the possibility of not being enough for them.

As I get older, I'm drawn to life's bigger questions about purpose, meaning, and spirituality. My introspection has become more urgent and present. I can't help but wonder about existence and the soul's journey. My writing, always personal, now grapples with these existential questions.

Melissa has been crucial in this process. Her confidence and self-assurance ground me, complementing my hesitancy and introspection. Our relationship has deepened beyond initial passion to something solid and homely. I've found safety and stability with her, though my past still surfaces unexpectedly. Ironically, this vulnerability enhances my writing, allowing me to create flawed, searching characters which resonate with readers.

Ultimately, my journey is about self-acceptance. I may never have all the answers, but I'm beginning to understand the search for meaning in relationships, spirituality, or writing is what matters. As I explore life's questions, I'm not reconciling with my past but seeking my place in the larger narrative of existence.

Recently, I've delved deeper into spirituality and philosophy, attending talks and studying ancient wisdom. I find solace in connecting with fellow seekers. During quiet moments, I often feel on the cusp of a profound realisation, frustrating, yet motivating. My curiosity has led me to explore various belief systems, meditative practices, and philosophical ideas. While hesitant to fully commit to any single path, I'm drawn to something deeper, beyond the intellectual. I yearn to experience life more fully on emotional and spiritual levels.

This shift is evident in my writing. My characters now seek deeper self-connection, grappling with inner conflicts and external realities. My stories probe existence, purpose, and the soul's journey, serving as a form of personal therapy. I've also begun practicing mindfulness and meditation. Despite this growth, I sometimes question if I'll ever feel truly whole. I acknowledge the scars of my past will remain, and healing is an ongoing process. The search for meaning, connection, and peace isn't a weakness, it's intrinsically human.

I may never have all the answers, but the questions themselves are part of the journey, they define what it means to live.

CHAPTER 11

MICHAEL AND MELISSA

'Better than a thousand hollow words, is one word which brings peace.'
— Gautama Buddha

In the soft twilight of the day, the forest around them was alive but hushed, like it too was listening. Michael and Melissa walked side by side down a narrow, winding path, their footsteps barely disturbing the silence. Melissa had been quiet for most of the walk, her thoughts circling the concept which had brought them together, the elusive, ever-changing 'Knowing.' Michael's calm presence beside her made it easier to sink into the questions swirling in her mind, questions she had long wanted to voice.

Finally, as the trees thickened and the light dimmed to a muted amber, Melissa spoke.

"Michael," she began, her voice soft but tinged with curiosity, "The Knowing... what is it? I mean, I feel it sometimes, but then it slips away, and I wonder if I ever understood it at all. It's like trying to grasp smoke."

Michael smiled, not in a condescending way, but with the kind of understanding which comes from having walked a similar path to himself.

"It's the paradox of The Knowing," he said, his tone gentle yet firm. "It isn't something to grasp. It's not something you can hold or control. The moment you try, it vanishes. The Knowing is more like... letting go. Allowing yourself to be, without needing to define or contain."

Melissa's brow furrowed. "But how can you manage to live? Without definition? Without control? It seems like we need structure, something to guide us."

Michael nodded as if her question was one, he had expected.

"We do need structure, yes. But the structure is not The Knowing itself. It's more like the framework which lets you experience it. Think of it as a canvas. The canvas is important, but it's not the painting. The Knowing happens in the spaces in between. It's in the flow of life, not the framework we impose on it."

Melissa let his words sink in, feeling the weight and the lightness of what he was saying. It was both complex and simple, an idea which seemed to change shape even as she tried to hold onto it. "It's not about certainty?"

Michael's gaze softened as they walked. "No, certainty is a trap. It's a false sense of security. Certainty closes you off from poss-ibilities, from the unexpected, and The Knowing thrives in the spaces where things are uncertain. It's like the forest around us, Melissa. Look at these trees. They don't fight to grow in a straight line. They bend, twist, and grow in whatever direction they need to. It's about being in the flow of life, not trying to control it."

Melissa glanced at the trees, their thick trunks and wild branches rising haphazardly into the dusky sky. They seemed to embrace the chaos of their existence, growing without question, without a plan, responding to what was around them.

"Is The Knowing like... acceptance?" she asked, her voice soft but intense.

Michael smiled again, this time with a quiet depth behind it. "I wouldn't say acceptance. It's much deeper. It's trusting even when you don't understand, even when everything feels uncertain, you're still exactly where you need to be. And the universe is unfolding as it should, even if you can't see the whole picture yet."

Melissa stopped walking for a moment, turning to face him. "But how do you get there? How do you stop needing to understand? How do you stop needing control?"

Michael paused as well, looking at her with a kind of compassion which comes from experience. "You don't stop needing it," he said gently. "You learn to live with it. The desire for control, for understanding, it doesn't go away. But you learn to let it sit beside you, like an old friend, without letting it rule you. You listen to it, acknowledge it, but you don't give it the steering wheel."

Melissa exhaled slowly; her breath visible in the cooling evening air. "Sure sounds... hard."

"It is," Michael agreed. "But it's also liberating. When you realise you don't have to control everything, you don't have to have all the answers, a kind of freedom opens up. You start to trust life, to trust yourself, this is when The Knowing becomes clear. It's not about knowing in the intellectual sense. It's a deeper kind of Knowing, an intuitive understanding you're connected to everything around you, and everything is connected to you."

They began walking again, the path now dappled with shadows as the light faded into dusk. The trees loomed larger, their branches like outstretched hands, guiding them forward. Melissa was silent for a while, letting Michael's words settle into her, their meaning twisting and turning in her mind like the roots of the trees they passed.

"But Michael," she said after a time, "what happens when life feels like it's pulling you apart? When everything around you feels disconnected and chaotic? How can The Knowing help then?"

Michael stopped and turned to her, his eyes reflecting a deep calm which came from years of wrestling with the same questions she was asking. "The Knowing doesn't stop the chaos, Melissa. It doesn't make life neat, and it doesn't give you easy answers. What it does is remind you even in the chaos, even when everything feels like it's falling apart, there's still a thread of connection running through it all. You may not see it in the moment, but it's there. You are still part of the whole. You're never truly lost."

Melissa looked down at her hands, feeling the coolness of the evening settling in. "It's hard for me to grasp. I want to feel it all the time. I want to feel the connection, the sense of being part of something bigger. But most of the time, I feel... separate."

Michael reached out and placed a hand gently on her shoulder.

"A feeling of separation is part of the journey. It's part of being human. But the more you practice The Knowing, the more you realise the separation is an illusion. It's like looking at the surface of a lake and thinking it's separate from the sky. But when you look deeper, you realise the lake reflects the sky. They're always connected. The Knowing is about learning to see beneath the surface."

Melissa's breath caught in her throat, the metaphor sinking into her like the sun dipping below the horizon. She had always felt like she was standing on the shore, looking out at life from a distance. The idea she was already part of it, already connected, was too much to take in.

"I want to see beneath the surface," she whispered, more to herself than to Michael.

He nodded, his hand still resting on her shoulder, his voice low and full of understanding.

"You already do, Melissa. It's about remembering."

They stood there for a moment, the forest around them seeming to grow stiller, quieter, as if it too was part of their conversation. Melissa felt the weight of her questions, but also a lightness, as though a door had opened inside her, a door which led to something she had always known but had forgotten.

"The Knowing isn't a destination," Michael said softly, as they began walking again, the path now dark but familiar. "It's a journey one never ends. And there's the beauty of it. The more you walk it, the more you see, the more you realise you don't have to understand everything. You have to be present. To listen."

Melissa smiled a quiet, thoughtful smile. "I think I'm beginning to get it," she said, her voice filled with something deeper than certainty. It was filled with trust.

Walking beside Michael in the gathering darkness, Melissa felt The Knowing stirring within her, not as something to be held, but as something to be lived.

Chapter 12

More About Melissa

'One moment can change a day, one day can change a life and one life can change the world' – Gautama Buddha

Melissa is captivating. Every time I look at her, my heart races and my breath catches. At 39, she exudes a confidence which comes from self-awareness. Standing at 168 cm, her figure is graceful yet alluring, every curve a testament to her natural beauty. Her thick, luxurious brunette hair frames a face both striking and gentle. But it's her deep, mesmerising brown eyes which truly draw me in. They hold warmth, mischief, and life, making it impossible not to be caught in her orbit. When she looks at me, it's as if she sees through to my core, understanding things I haven't yet grasped.

From our first meeting, an undeniable attraction pulled us together. Her movements and speech feel effortless yet deliberate. I'm drawn to her not for her beauty alone, but for her energy as well.

Melissa has a vibrancy and passion for life which is infectious. She's fully present in every moment, whether laughing at my jokes or sitting quietly in thought. Her laugh is music to me, lifting me from my darkest moods and brightening the world. And her smile, it's like sunlight breaking through clouds, warm and inviting.

When we're together, I can't keep my hands off her, but it's more than physical attraction. There's an intensity, a connection beyond the surface. I feel it in every touch and kiss. It's not desire; it's a conversation between our bodies, an unspoken language which we understand. Every moment with her is charged, alive with the tension of wanting and being utterly lost in each other. In her arms, I rediscover myself repeatedly.

The way she looks at me when we're alone, her eyes darkening with desire, makes me feel like I'm the one man in the world she wants. I crave the look, the feeling of being desired. When we're close, the world disappears. I lose myself in her, the feel of her skin, the soft gasp when I kiss her neck, the way her body fits perfectly against mine. It's more than lust. It's a profound connection which ties us together, making each touch feel like a revelation, each kiss an affirmation of something deeper.

Melissa and I have an unspoken understanding and a shared respect for each other's boundaries. We both need space and moments to ourselves, and this is part of what makes it work well. She never tries to hold me to close or attempts to make me something I'm not. She lets me be me, even when I'm lost in my thoughts or wrestling with my demons. She's there, steady and unwavering, always ready to welcome me back into her arms when I'm ready.

The freedom we give each other strengthens our connection. We don't need to be together every second to feel close. In fact, the time apart deepens the anticipation, making every moment together more intense. When we reunite, it's like no time has passed, the chemistry between us as fiery and alive as ever. There's a sense of belonging with Melissa, as if we were always meant to find each other, and every interaction reaffirms the fact.

She understands me without words. She can read my mood with one glance, knowing exactly what I need. Whether it's a quiet night together or something more heated, our intimacy is about more than physical pleasure. It's about the deep sense of trust and vulnerability we share. She makes me feel alive in ways I didn't think possible, reminding me of the man I used to be and still am, deep down.

Melissa, with all her passion, knows how to draw me out, how to reignite the fire inside me. Her confidence and experience are intoxicating. She's a master at this dance we share, always knowing when to be gentle and when to be wild, when to let things simmer, and when to let them burn. It's a kind of power, not about dominance, but about sharing something raw and real which makes us both feel more alive.

Even when apart, I can't stop thinking about her and how we fit together perfectly. There's a constant undercurrent of desire between us, even in the smallest moments. It's like electricity crackling beneath the surface, always ready to spark into something more.

Yet, despite the intensity, there's tenderness too. A softness in the way we hold each other after the passion has ebbed, in the quiet moments when words aren't necessary. In these moments I realise how much she means to me, how much this connection goes beyond the physical. She is my confidante, my partner, the one person who knows me better than anyone. She accepts me, flaws and all, something I've never had before.

Melissa and I have built something rare, a relationship where passion and respect go hand in hand. We're free to be ourselves, to explore the depths of our desires without losing who we are, and it's in such freedom our love thrives, growing stronger with each passing day.

In her, I've found something I didn't even know I was looking for, a connection which is as exhilarating as it is grounding. With Melissa, I feel like I can finally breathe, finally let go of all the doubts and insecurities which have haunted me for too long. In her arms, I'm home, and there's no place I'd rather be.

CHAPTER 13

MICHAEL'S ADVICE TO MELISSA

'Kindness should become the natural way of life, not the exception.'
– Gautama Buddha

Michael began, "Melissa, I can see how deeply you're concerned about Peter," his voice a soothing balm amidst the stillness of the garden. The air was thick with the fragrance of Jasmine, a distant hum of nature wrapping around them like a comforting cocoon.

"You've been his rock, steady, unwavering. You've stood by him as his confidante, his lover. Your care is undeniable, but Melissa, helping someone through their pain requires a delicate balance. You want to be there, but you must also protect your well-being."

Melissa nodded, her gaze drifting to the ground as if trying to make sense of her own emotions.

"I love him, Michael. I want to be the one who helps him heal, but sometimes... sometimes I feel like I'm not enough. Like I can't reach him when he's lost in those memories, those dark places."

Michael's expression softened, his wisdom echoing in his words. "I completely understand your fears. Peter's journey is deeply personal, and though you can walk beside him, you can't walk it for him. What you can offer is a sanctuary, a space where he feels safe, loved, and accepted. No matter what storm he's caught in."

"How do I create such a space?" Melissa asked, her voice carrying the weight of both determination and confusion. "How do I support him without getting swallowed by his pain too?"

"Boundaries, Melissa. It starts with boundaries," Michael replied, his tone gentle but firm. "Loving someone doesn't mean losing yourself in their struggle. You must preserve your emotional health if you're going to be strong, for both yourself and Peter. Take time for your own needs. Step back when you need to. Supporting Peter doesn't mean you carry the entire weight of his burden on your shoulders. He needs to know you're there, yes, but also you trust him to navigate his way through the darkness."

Melissa sighed; her gaze distant as if looking into the memories she shared with Peter.

"Sometimes I feel guilty for needing space or wanting time for myself. Like... I'm abandoning him when he needs me most."

"You're not abandoning him," Michael said, his voice more resolute now. "In fact, taking care of yourself is the opposite, it's necessary. If you're drained, how can you give him what he truly needs? Think of it like this: On an airplane, they tell you to put on your oxygen mask before helping others. It's not selfish, Melissa. It's survival."

Melissa blinked, a new understanding softening her expression.

"But what if he pushes me away? What if he gets lost in those memories and doesn't want me near?"

Tilting his head slightly, Michael considered her fears. "This could happen or it may not. When people wrestle with their pain, they sometimes retreat, not because they don't need you, but because they don't want to burden you. If he pulls away, give him space, but gently remind him you're there. Even if words aren't exchanged, your presence alone can be enough to ground him. A silent reassurance."

Melissa's nod was small, her internal conflict palpable. "I want to help him. I don't always know how or what to say or do."

"Sometimes," Michael said, lowering his voice as if speaking the truth of the universe, "the most powerful thing you can do is be there. No solutions, no perfect words. Your presence is enough. The quiet comfort of sitting beside him, listening when he's ready to talk, holding him when he feels overwhelmed, those things carry immense healing. Let him know he's not alone, but also, it's okay for him to take his time. Healing doesn't follow a timeline."

Melissa's eyes filled with the fears she had been trying to keep hidden.

"I'm... I'm afraid of losing him, Michael. Afraid he'll get lost in those memories and they'll take him away from me."

Michael paused, choosing his next words with care.

"I understand your fear, but remember, Peter's love for you is deep, enduring. He may be struggling, but your love is an anchor for him. Even when he's lost, your bond can guide him back. Keep showing him patience, understanding, and love, and he'll find his way. Stronger. More whole."

A slow breath escaped Melissa's lips, and with it, a small wave of relief seemed to wash over her.

"Thank you, Michael, I needed to know how to navigate this without getting lost myself."

"You're doing better than you realise," Michael reassured her with a smile. "Remember always not to forget to take care of yourself. You both deserve the best."

Melissa smiled faintly, feeling a new clarity settle within her. She knew the journey ahead would not be easy, but Michael's words had given her a compass. She could support Peter without losing herself.

"It's easy to forget," she murmured after a moment of reflection. "When you're focused on helping someone else, it's easy to forget we're not alone in this."

"Exactly," Michael said, his voice encouraging. "You do have your support system, friends, family, me. Peter needs you, but you need people too. Don't hesitate to lean on them when the weight gets too heavy. You don't have to carry it all on your own."

Melissa hesitated, chewing on her thoughts. "But sometimes I feel like I have to be the strong one, like if I show any cracks, it'll make things harder for him."

"Melissa," Michael said, his tone patient, "strength isn't about never feeling weak. It's about knowing when to ask for help. When to be vulnerable. Being honest about your struggles doesn't make you weak; it makes you human. It might even help Peter realise he doesn't have to hide his pain. Sometimes, by sharing your vulnerability, you create a space where he can feel safe sharing his."

"Do you think it's okay for him to see when I'm struggling?" she asked, her voice soft but laced with newfound hope.

"Of course, it is," Michael replied. "Relationships are partnerships. By showing him, you trust him enough to be vulnerable, you're telling him it's okay for him to do the same. Building mutual understanding is how you grow stronger together. It's not about being perfect; it's about being real."

Melissa's smile grew warmer, fuller this time. "I guess I've been focused on being his strength. I forgot we're supposed to share this. I need to let him be there for me too."

"Exactly," Michael said with a knowing nod. "Let him see your strength, but let him see your humanity too. It could help him feel less alone. Sometimes knowing someone else is struggling, albeit in a different way, can be enough to open the door to sharing."

"I hadn't considered those options," Melissa admitted, her brow furrowing slightly. "I've been focused on protecting him... maybe I need to open up more."

"It's all about balance, Melissa. Protecting Peter is important, as is letting him be part of your world. Love, openness, vulnerability, they're all forms of healing, for both of you. It's yours and Peters journey together. And as a couple, every challenge can either pull you apart or strengthen your bond. It all depends on how you choose to walk through it."

"I want us to come through this stronger," Melissa said, her voice firmer now. "Not as individuals, but as partners."

"And you will," Michael said, his tone brimming with quiet certainty. "With patience, communication, and love, you and Peter will find your way through this, side by side. There will be rough patches, but it's the moving forward together which counts."

Melissa's heart felt lighter. "Thank you, Michael. Your words make a lot of sense. I feel like I finally understand how to be there for him, without losing myself."

"You're doing an incredible job, Melissa," Michael said warmly. "Always remember to be kind to yourself. Doubts and fears will come, but don't let them overshadow the strength and love you already have. Let your love be your guide."

As Melissa walked away from Michael, a quiet but persistent strength bloomed within her. His words had given her the clarity she needed, the confidence she hadn't realised was there. She understood the road ahead wouldn't be easy but knew she wasn't alone.

Together, she and Peter would navigate the past, heal the wounds, and step into a future where their love, stronger, tested, and real, could truly thrive.

CHAPTER 14

THE KNOWING

'Drop by drop is the water pot filled. Likewise, the wise man, gathering it little by little, fills himself with good.' – Gautama Buddha

The Knowing is a profound and elusive concept, more an experience than a doctrine, more a way of being than a set of beliefs. It represents a deep, intuitive understanding of life which transcends the limitations of traditional knowledge and conventional wisdom. Unlike religious dogma or philosophical teachings, The Knowing cannot be easily articulated in words; it must be felt, lived, and integrated into one's essence.

At its core, The Knowing is about a connection to the fundamental truths of existence, universal, yet uniquely experienced by each individual. It is the awareness life is interconnected, everything and everyone is part of a greater whole. This understanding brings a sense of peace and acceptance, releasing the need to control outcomes. Those who have embraced The Knowing often describe it as a state of flow, where they are in harmony with the world around them, guided by an inner compass rather than external pressures.

The Knowing is not tied to any specific religion or spiritual practice, though it can complement and deepen them. It transcends religious labels and boundaries, recognising truth is not confined to any one path. For some, it might be akin to enlightenment or awakening, but it's less about reaching a final state and more about an ongoing journey of deepening awareness.

In practical terms, it manifests as a deep trust in life's processes. It is the realisation everything has its place and every experience contributes to the wholeness of one's being. This perspective brings quiet strength and resilience in the face of adversity, as those who live in The Knowing understand they are an integral part of life's flow.

The Knowing also fosters compassion for oneself and others. When one understands the interconnectedness of all life, it becomes impossible to see others as truly separate or different. This leads to natural empathy and a desire to alleviate suffering and act for the greater good. However, The Knowing also teaches the importance of balance and boundaries, recognising true compassion includes self-care.

Those who seek The Knowing often find it is not something to be pursued in the traditional sense. It comes not through striving or effort, but through surrender, letting go of preconceived notions, and being open to what life offers. It often reveals itself in moments of stillness, in nature, or during deep contemplation, offering insights which feel like they come from beyond the mind.

In conversation, Michael might describe The Knowing as a 'quiet wisdom' which guides him. It's a source of inner peace, a confidence which comes from understanding his place in the world without needing to define it rigidly. He might compare it to the difference between reading about love and being in love, the former is intellectual; the latter is an all-encompassing experience.

The Knowing is not static; it evolves with the individual. As one's understanding deepens, The Knowing does too. It's a lifelong journey which invites continuous exploration and discovery. While challenging to describe fully, those who have experienced it know it is real, powerful, and transformative, offering a way of living aligned with the deepest truths of existence.

It's an ever-evolving state of consciousness, a journey rather than a destination. It's both the question and the answer, the search and the discovery. It doesn't demand adherence to rigid rules or beliefs; instead, it encourages a fluid, open approach to life, where every experience is a teacher.

Michael's relationship with The Knowing began as an intellectual pursuit rooted in his early religious studies. As he grew older, he realised structured religious teachings, while valuable, were one piece of a larger puzzle. Religion offered him a foundation to understand the world and his place in it, but over time, he began to feel constrained by its boundaries, sensing something more which couldn't be fully captured by scripture or doctrine.

This yearning for something beyond set him on the path to discovering The Knowing. Unlike religion, which often focuses on the external, rules, rituals, and a defined concept of the divine, The Knowing turned Michael's gaze inward. It was about self-exploration, peeling back the layers of ego, fear, and conditioning to reveal a deeper truth. This truth couldn't be taught; it had to be experienced, felt in quiet moments of reflection, connections with others, and the stillness of nature.

Michael often describes The Knowing as an inner compass. It doesn't provide detailed maps or clear instructions but gives a sense of direction, a feeling of what is right and true at any given moment. It's a way of navigating life, relying on intuition and a deep trust in oneself and the universe. This trust doesn't mean life becomes easy or free from challenges; rather, it means challenges are seen as part of the journey, opportunities for growth, and learning.

One of the most profound aspects of The Knowing is its emphasis on presence. In Michael's view, the past and future are important, but life truly happens in the present moment. The Knowing teaches the importance of being fully engaged in the moment, whatever it may bring. This doesn't mean ignoring the past or neglecting the future, but rather not allowing them to dominate or detract from the richness of the present.

The Knowing also emphasises acceptance of oneself, others, and life as it is. This doesn't mean passivity or resignation, but a deep, compassionate understanding everything is as it needs to be at this moment. It's about letting go of resistance and the need to control or change things to fit preconceived ideas. Instead, The Knowing invites a state of flow, where one moves with life rather than against it, responding to each situation with clarity and grace.

For Michael, it's a way of being which transcends dualities of right and wrong, good and bad. It's about seeing the underlying unity in all things, recognising every experience, person, and emotion is part of a larger whole. This perspective brings peace, releasing one from constant judgment and comparison. In The Knowing, there is no need to prove oneself or compete in the conventional sense. There is the unfolding of one's true nature, moment by moment.

Michael's understanding of The Knowing has deepened his relationships. He no longer sees others as separate from himself but as reflections, mirrors showing different aspects of universal truth. This has brought a profound sense of connection, a love which is not possessive or dependent, but free and unconditional. He loves others for who they are, not for what they can give him or how they make him feel. This love is an expression of The Knowing, a natural outflow of his understanding we are all part of the same whole.

In his conversations, Michael often speaks of The Knowing as a path of liberation, not from the world, but within it. It's about being fully engaged with life, not retreating from it. The Knowing doesn't promise escape from pain or suffering; instead, it offers a way to transcend them, to see them as part of the greater tapestry of existence. This perspective allows Michael to approach life with curiosity and wonder, always open to what the next moment will bring.

Ultimately, The Knowing is a mystery which can never be fully explained or understood, but lived. It's a journey without end, an ever-deepening spiral into the heart of existence. For Michael, his journey is the greatest adventure of all.

The Knowing is a profound inner recognition, a sense of truth which comes not from the mind, but from a deeper place within. It's not the result of reasoning or analysis; it bypasses these. It's like a quiet, unwavering certainty. Think of it as a moment when everything clicks into place effortlessly. It's when you realise the answers you've been searching for were always within you, waiting for the right moment to surface.

It's not loud or forceful; it often arrives as a calm, gentle presence. You might not even notice it, because it's not about thinking harder or working through a problem step by step. Instead, it feels like a subtle shift, a sudden flash of clarity. In a way, it's like being tuned into a frequency where all distractions fall away, and what's left is pure understanding. It's beyond words, beyond logic; it's experiential, felt rather than thought.

The Knowing is deeply personal and unique to each individual.

It could manifest as a sense of peace amid chaos or as a guiding force when you're unsure of what to do next. When it comes, it doesn't require proof or validation from the outside world. You trust it because it feels undeniably right, aligned with your true self.

To give it more texture: imagine standing at a crossroads in life, full of uncertainty. You could weigh the pros and cons, seek advice, or try to logically map out the best path. But then, out of nowhere, comes The Knowing, an unshakeable sense this is the direction you're meant to go. There's no questioning it, no back and forth in your mind. You know. And in Knowing, there's relief, because you no longer need to search for answers outside yourself.

It could be spiritual, or it could feel like a deep connection to intuition. For some, The Knowing is linked to a higher consciousness, the universe, or even a divine source, while for others, it might be seen as an awakening of their inner wisdom. Either way, it's a powerful and transformative experience which guides you toward truth and authenticity.

In essence, The Knowing transcends ordinary understanding. It's a moment when you realise the answers are already within you, waiting to be acknowledged. Once you do, the world around you feels a little clearer, a little lighter, and far more aligned with who you are. It's not about facts or logic, but more like an instinctive recognition of what's real or right in a given moment. The Knowing might be a gut feeling, a spiritual insight, or a sudden realisation which cuts through confusion, offering a direct path forward.

It's something you feel on a core level, like when you know something is true, even if you can't quite explain how or why. It's like tapping into a deeper layer of consciousness, where things make sense without needing to be examined or broken down. In essence, it's a connection to truth or understanding which comes from within, something which resonates deeply and offers certainty or guidance. It's intuitive, personal, and powerful.

At its core, it provides access to an inner compass, a guide which doesn't rely on outside validation or external sources of truth. In today's world, we are bombarded with information, opinions, and expectations. It's easy to get lost in the noise, feeling pressured to follow others' ideas of success. However, The Knowing offers an escape from this chaos, focussing you and helping you tune into your voice. It allows you to act with clarity and confidence.

Imagine feeling empowered to trust your decisions whole-heartedly, without second-guessing yourself due to outside influence. We have all experienced situations where we are overwhelmed by choices or conflicting emotions. When you access The Knowing, it cuts through the fog, simplifying everything. You intuitively know what feels right, even if you can't explain it logically. This can save countless hours of overthinking and worrying, as you're guided by a deeper truth rather than getting tangled in analysis.

Imagine for a moment you are at a career crossroads. Everyone around you has opinions: your boss wants one path, friends suggest another, and family yet another. It's easy to feel lost in their well-meaning advice. With The Knowing, you'd filter through the noise and feel confident about what's right for you. This clarity is invaluable, leading to fulfillment which is aligned with your true self, not external expectations.

Often, we make decisions based on logic, societal expectations, or perceived safety. While these factors have their place, they often drown out our inner voice. The Knowing helps you reconnect with the voice, empowering you to make choices which resonate with your authentic self. When you operate from The Knowing, your decisions feel more aligned with your values, passions, and desires. Living in alignment with your true self improves relationships, strengthens your sense of purpose, and makes everyday challenges more manageable.

Reflect on a time when you followed expectations rather than your intuition. Perhaps you took a job which looked good on paper but left you feeling drained. Now imagine if you had tapped into The Knowing. It would have steered you toward a decision which felt right for you, saving frustration and providing a deeper sense of fulfillment.

Life is full of unknowns, but The Knowing instills self-trust you'll find the right path. This trust is incredibly valuable as it reduces anxiety. Instead of worrying about the unknown, you learn to navigate challenges with clarity and purpose. This self-trust builds resilience and reduces the fear of failure, allowing you to embrace opportunities you might otherwise avoid.

Many people live in constant stress, worrying about the future or second-guessing past decisions. The Knowing offers peace by silencing inner turmoil. When you truly know something deep inside, mental chatter quiets. You stop questioning your choices because you trust your path, regardless of others' opinions. This inner peace is invaluable, providing stability to handle whatever comes your way and allowing you to be more present in daily life.

The Knowing also improves relationships. When you're in tune with your authentic self, you interact with others honestly and sincerely. You communicate more distinctly, set healthier boundaries, and express yourself without fear. This deepens connections because you're showing up as your true self. You also become more empathetic and understanding of others, approaching relationships with calm, grounded energy which invites openness and trust.

The value of The Knowing lies in its ability to transform how you navigate life. It simplifies decisions, connects you with your authentic self, reduces anxiety, and helps you trust your inner wisdom.

By embracing The Knowing, you open yourself to a life of greater fulfillment, peace, and alignment with your true self.

CHAPTER 15

MICHAEL AND PETER TALK

'You are the community now. Be a lamp for yourselves. Be your own refuge. Seek for no other. All things must pass. Strive on diligently. Don't give up.'
— Gautama Buddha

I awoke around 5:00 am with a start, my mind immediately focusing on the previous day's events. I distinctly felt someone had called my name. Listening intently, the only sound I heard was my own short, rapid breathing. 'Get a grip on yourself,' I whispered, 'there's nothing here which can harm you.' I lay back and closed my eyes; and then I heard it again! A long, drawn-out sound, like someone exhaling, but the name was unmistakable...

'Peter,' the voice whispered, 'Peter, pay attention.' The curtains moved slightly as if disturbed by a breeze, but the window was closed and the air still. Then silence. My heart pounded as I pulled the covers over me, shivering. I scanned the room, finding nothing out of place. What was I looking for anyway? There's no such thing as ghosts or spirits... or is there?

Melissa was still asleep, but I couldn't rest. I dressed and went to the kitchen. Michael was already preparing breakfast and greeted me warmly.

"Morning Peter, did you sleep well?" he asked, his face slightly quizzical.

"It wasn't my best night," I admitted.

"Something bothering you?"

"Not at all... but I'm certain something or somebody was in the room around five and woke me up. I thought you, Melissa, and I were alone here."

"We are, Peter," he said. "What do you think troubled you?"

"I don't know, but something did. My name was called, and I distinctly heard a voice telling me to pay attention."

"Will you, Peter?" Michael asked.

"Will I what?"

"Will you pay attention? You know listening to others and following your feelings isn't one of your strong points," Michael replied.

"I agree, but hearing a voice did get my attention. Maybe I imagined it; maybe I was dreaming!"

"A lot of maybes, Peter. What if the voice you heard was real? What would you say then?"

"Not much. I tend to think it was my imagination; there's a lot of new information I haven't fully processed. It wouldn't be the first time my mind has played tricks on me."

"Our minds never play tricks on us, Peter, despite what you may think. Is your mind a separate entity from you?"

I responded with a firm no, still unsure of his point. By now, however, I was well aware of his ability to get to the point. I listened intently.

"Then why say your mind plays tricks on you? You are your mind and your mind is you, it stands to reason the only person who can play tricks on you is yourself!"

He said this in such a matter-of-fact way I was taken aback and said nothing for a moment.

As Michael continued to prepared breakfast, Melissa joined us in the kitchen.

Michael greeted her first, "Good morning, Melissa, did you sleep well?"

Smiling, Melissa replied, "Sure did, thanks for asking. How are you, darling?" she asked me.

I replied without looking up, "Not good, I didn't have a restful night."

"Anything you want to talk about?" Melissa inquired.

"Not yet, not now," I replied.

Melissa knew me well enough to understand although I wasn't forthcoming at the moment, I would be later.

"Sit down, both of you, and enjoy your breakfast," Michael gestured towards the chairs.

"Later, Peter, we'll go for a walk. I'm sure Melissa won't mind. At least I have you thinking, and it is the best way I know to over-come a cynical mind."

As we sat, he continued, "Many things surround us which go unnoticed because we choose not to make them part of our reality. You don't accept the idea of spirits and ghosts; the result is you limit what you can perceive. When one comes calling, you're blind to it. All it takes is to allow all possibilities and accept realities exist beyond your conscious senses."

"And a liberal dose of The Knowing," I added.

"Which helps, but first, its accepting other realities exist. To access The Knowing, an open mind is essential."

"Okay, I understand what you're saying. I'll try, but I find it hard to believe ghosts exist," I replied.

"Even after your experience this morning? Hasn't it made you think?" he asked.

"Yes, it has," I admitted. "I have a feeling you're leading me to something."

"I think it's more likely you're leading yourself. The obvious can be ignored for a while before it must be noticed. You received a visitor this morning who brought you a message, and try as you might, you cannot ignore it. You're fortunate to have received such a wake-up call. If my advice is worth anything, I suggest you take notice and acknowledge it. There's a reason behind everything, including your visitor."

"It's not easy for me to understand the reason or see the purpose behind it, Michael. Yes, I know I have preconceived ideas and find it

105

hard to admit mistakes, but this is something I never expected."

"Seek the wonder of it, Peter. You've been given something many people search for their entire lives. I can still remember the sensation of wonder, even though it was long ago, I felt when I was first visited. I was at a crossroads in my life, young and thinking I had all the answers and was invincible. How wrong I was. My visitor changed something in me. I became more conscious of life and more aware of other possibilities. I went from being a strict churchgoer and believer in heaven and hell to a seeker and questioner. The quest I embarked on led me to The Knowing, all because of one question asked of me. For the next week, I asked myself the question repeatedly. I got an answer, deep from within, it was crystal clear, and I've never forgotten it. From there on, I became free… free to think my thoughts, to pursue avenues previously closed to me, and to grow exponentially because of it."

"Will you tell me what the question was, Michael?" I asked quietly.

"No, Peter, not yet. You have much to learn, and the time isn't right. I will someday if you don't find it yourself, but my journey was for me. You have a different path, and the message you carry will need to be spread. Come now, let's walk. The morning is beautiful, and walking here is invigorating."

We stepped into the cool, crisp air and had gone a few paces when the phone started to ring, halting our progress.

"I'll have to answer," Michael said, pointing to a path. "Go ahead, follow the path, and it'll take you to some bench seats in a clearing. Wait for me there; I'll join you shortly."

He returned inside, and I took a moment to look around. The house was larger than I thought, with a veranda running around three sides. The gardens were neat and well-tended, and the house was positioned for the morning sun to highlight the kitchen and patio area at the back. I made a mental note to ask Michael about the design and positioning because it fitted perfectly into the surrounding setting. As if by divine design, I mused as I started walking.

The sun was warm, and I slowed my pace to absorb the sensations assailing me. Various insects buzzed by, and several birds called to each other high in the trees. The well-trodden path was easy to follow, and the sweet scent of timber and cracking of fallen twigs under my feet reminded me of Melissa. We both enjoyed taking long walks, especially early in the morning.

I found the clearing easily and sat down. The area had several benches around a circular fire pit. The ash from the last fire seemed reasonably fresh, and I wondered how long since it had been used. I closed my eyes, and my mind drifted back to when the voice woke me, telling me to 'pay attention.' Could it have been a spirit, as Michael said? What did he mean by a message to be spread? If spirits exist, why can't everyone see them? What did he mean by The Knowing? How does he manage to know as much as he does about others? Once again, there were many questions but few answers. A crunching underfoot stirred me, and I opened my eyes to see Michael walking towards me.

"I see you were deep in thought, Peter. Any questions?" he asked as he sat beside me.

"Are you kidding me?" I answered rather flippantly. "Which one do I ask first?"

He chuckled softly before answering, "It can be taxing when you become a seeker. You asked the question but didn't take notice of the answer."

"What answer and which question?" I shot back.

"One thing at a time. Remember a wedding dress a silkworm did not make." Seeing my quizzical look, he expanded, "It means to be patient, Peter. In time, it will all come together. You are the reality you have created for yourself, and within your reality are the answers you seek. It's all there, my boy, but be patient and pay attention."

To say I was starting to get frustrated would be an understatement. I contemplated my options, which weren't many. I could get up and leave or take his advice and pay attention. Not much of a choice, but I decided on the latter. Michael's voice broke the silence.

"A wise decision. Congratulations, you learned one of the most important messages The Knowing has, and it is to keep seeking, it couldn't be simpler."

My mouth dropped open, and he must have seen my amazement, for he added, "Don't act so surprised. I'm no different than you; I listen and hear things others don't. Some call it telepathy, others clairvoyance, but I don't give it a label. It's part of My Knowing and will become part of yours, too."

"You are full of surprises." I replied weakly.

"Thank you," replied Michael with a bemused smile. "Life is wonderful when you go with the flow. Everything is energy, and when we learn to live with the energy, all things are possible."

"I have read about it somewhere," I said. "I can accept the idea, but I don't fully understand it."

"You will, Peter. Maybe not today, but soon."

"Can you explain what you think spirits are?" I asked.

"They are energy, like everything else, but of a different vibration. To see them, you must feel the vibration, tune your senses, and believe they exist."

"But I don't believe they exist, and yet I know something or someone woke me. If, as you say, it was a spirit, who was it?"

"Who it was isn't important. The point is you were contacted, and it made you take notice. I'd say mission accomplished for your entity. I don't expect you to accept everything I say, and I anticipate you'll question much of it which is fine with me. But I want you to keep an open mind and let my words sit within your being. If you have doubts about my sanity, it's understandable, but please accept what I'm saying, for the time being anyway. When the time is right your higher self, some call it the superconscious mind, will feed it back to you. Do we have a deal?"

I thought about his words for a moment. The choice wasn't hard; I had nothing to lose and everything to gain. "Yes, we have a deal."

"Wonderful, I didn't think for a moment we wouldn't," he stated matter-of-factly.

"When do we start?" I asked.

"We already have. Even before we first met, I knew you and was working with you to bring about the present situation."

For some reason, I wasn't surprised by this. When we were first introduced, I had asked him if we'd met before, as he seemed familiar. 'We have,' he had replied while shaking my hand, 'but not face to face.' I wondered then what he meant, but before I could question him, he was whisked away to meet someone else.

"I have read about spirits and such, but what exactly are they?" I asked.

"As I said earlier, they are energy, but in a different form and existing on a different level of awareness than we do," Michael replied. "Everything which exists is energy in one form or another. Because we can't see it, does it mean it doesn't exist? Electricity is a classic example, no one can see it, but its energy can be felt, measured, and used. You need to see, taste, or smell something before you'll accept it exists, and there are many like you. But equally, many accept other forms of existence."

"I can't disagree with you, Michael. I am as you say."

"Then you need to acknowledge the other senses you possess besides the five used every day," he told me.

"What do I have to do?" I asked.

"Become aware of the inner you, the part which knows no limitations. We are all limitless beings, but we often limit and confine ourselves by arresting our growth. I remember when my thinking was tunnel-like, and I never allowed myself the luxury of going beyond the limitations I had placed on myself. I was bigoted, stubborn, and refused to budge on my opinions about religion and its importance in our lives. There was no room in my thinking for subjects which espoused a different view. I labelled all these extra subjects, spirits, telepathy, etc., as nonsense and those who spoke of them as crackpots. I suppose you could say I held a similar view to the one you have now."

"It does sound like it," I remarked. "What made you change your mind?"

"A similar incident to yours, but for me, it was more dramatic. I steadfastly refused to get the message, even though it was thrust at me on many occasions. In retrospect, I can look upon my awakening with a light heart, but when it happened, I wasn't as magnanimous. Like you, I was prodded awake, but not from a night's sleep. I was involved in an accident which led me to being hospitalised, and I was seriously ill. I slipped in and out of consciousness. I remember it vividly, even though it was many years ago.

I had had a fitful night, and it was nearing dawn. I was lucky to have a room with a view, and seeing the sunrise each day reminded me I was still living. I had drifted off to sleep as the sun was turning the night sky into day when I was jolted by a vivid flash of white light.

I thought I would be blinded. I heard a voice, and I still remember what it said. Later, when the doctor came to see me, he asked how I was, and I told him I was on my way back. 'You feel you are?' he asked. 'Yes,' was my reply, 'I'm back.' I was discharged within the week."

"Some awakening," I ventured. "What did you hear to make you take notice?"

"You'll have to wait another time for the answer, Peter. Let's walk."

At this rather ambiguous statement, I was prompted to ask, "What do you mean by doing the work you choose to do?"

"Before I came here, I was able to choose the life I wanted to live. We all get to choose each incarnation, and I chose this one. It's worked out well."

"How do you know?"

"I accept it as part of my reality. I once thought we had one lifetime and went to heaven or hell depending on how we lived. I changed my mind when presented with new information. To my way of thinking, we have many incarnations, some here and some in other places. To me it's a fact. I don't need to question or rationalise it because once I understood its principles, I found it easy to assimilate."

"I'm not unfamiliar with the concept, but I couldn't accept it as fact. Maybe it was because of my upbringing," I stated.

"What do you think now?" he asked.

"I'm starting to think maybe I'm wrong," I answered. "It doesn't seem possible we have multiple lives, but I also rejected the notion of heaven and hell. I don't have any idea of what happens when we pass."

"Sounds similar to my train of thought I had many years ago," Michael stated. "How glad I am I found The Knowing. I have nothing against any religion; I chose to follow a different path which led me to discover things I never knew existed. In the beginning, it wasn't easy because I had to discard most of what I had been taught, but as I progressed, it became easier."

"You don't think there is a heaven or hell?" I asked him.

"What I think, is immaterial. After all, many would disagree with me, but conversely, many agree. What's important is how you see it and your understanding of it. Incidentally, it also applies to all things, especially to The Knowing. It has no dogma or creed; it comes from within, and each has to discover it for themselves.

"Tell me more," I prompted.

"I can tell you about my experiences with The Knowing, Peter, not another's. One of the most important understandings, to me, was about taking responsibility for all my thoughts, words, and deeds. I know this is a basis for many religions, and it's not something I didn't know previously. The difference is taking full responsibility for myself, and in doing this I discovered the deeper meaning. I was taught right from wrong from an early age, but I also learned to blame others if things didn't go my way, and I became particularly good at getting others into trouble to save my neck. Learning the difference wasn't hard, but applying it was."

"Please continue," I asked.

"The Knowing, is at times, subtle and at other times obvious. Each of us has to decide for ourselves what it is and isn't. Say, for example, I was asked to do a deed without any reward. I could do it and complain inwardly I was being imposed on, or I could do it because I chose to. The difference is subtle, but a difference there is. The same applies to what I say and think. When I choose freely, it comes from the heart, and I'm happy to do it expecting nothing, not even acknowledgment, in return."

"I think I understand the difference," I said. "But how does knowing it help in life? After all, 'it's a do it to them before they do it to us' mentality which exists, or seems to exist, in society."

"I'm sure it's true for some, but The Knowing is about personal growth and finding the true self. Each of us is free to choose or exclude whatever we wish. I believe we inherently know right from wrong, and any behaviour we develop can be changed. Even a thief knows stealing is wrong but will still go ahead and do it and suffer the consequences if caught. What a waste of the opportunity life offers if it's squandered. However, I know enough about reincarnation to know not to judge and to be in acceptance of whatever is."

"How does one accept whatever happens, especially if violence is associated with it?" I asked.

"By being aware any situation could occur whether we like it or not. Personally, I am horrified at times about the level of man's inhumanity to his fellow creatures, but there's nothing I can do to stop it. All I can do is become a detached observer and ensure I don't commit such acts myself."

"You don't seem to subscribe to the theory of prayer and divine intervention, Michael."

"No, I don't now. To me, prayers are little more than wish lists, and divine intervention is wishful thinking. Humanity has to transform itself, individually and then collectively, before the violence will cease, and I don't envision it happening for some time. My point is we are responsible for everything we do, whether we are aware of it or not."

"Your statement seems a bit unfair," I exclaimed.

"Why is it?" Michael asked me.

"How can anyone be expected to know something which has never been shown to them?" I replied.

"A little thought of your own will provide the answer to your question, Peter."

He was right. I did get the answer, but I wasn't happy with it, but the more I thought about it, the more it made sense. We do have within us the answers to our questions, providing we are willing to listen and take notice. If it had been said to me six months ago, I would be listening to my inner-self, I would have told the person they were crazy, but now...

Melissa appeared from around the corner of the house and cheerfully greeted us. "You both look relaxed and pleased with yourselves," she said.

"We are," replied Michael, "or should I say I am, for I can't speak for Peter, although I think you'll find him a bit better than he was this morning. I'll leave him with you to look after while I do the dishes."

We sat together, basking in the sunshine, and in the quiet and stillness, I started to understand my inner voice and what it had to say.

CHAPTER 16

MICHAEL, THE HEALER

'Every human being is the author of his own health or disease.'
– Gautama Buddha

Michael is a true medicine man, blending intelligence, compassion, and a deep spiritual connection. His journey through The Knowing has given him profound insights into the human condition, making him a healer of the body, mind, and spirit. Unlike traditional healers who focus solely on medical knowledge or those who concentrate on spiritual rituals, Michael combines both into a holistic practice. Through his connection to all life, he channels healing energy to those who ask for his help.

He sees illness not as physical symptoms but as signs of deeper imbalances in thoughts, emotions, and energy. Michael aims to address these core issues, helping people restore their inner balance. Working with the body's subtle energies, he senses blockages and uses his hands and focused intention to clear them. His gentle touch radiates a calming warmth which penetrates deeply, rebalancing the body's energy connections and promoting natural healing.

Understanding how emotional and mental states affect health,

Michael listens closely to his patients' stories. He meets them where they are, offering insights to help them move beyond their pain. With his gift of The Knowing, he guides people toward inner peace, helping them connect with their soul and release deep-seated wounds which may block healing.

Michael believes true healing comes from reconnecting with one's inner self and the greater flow of life. He guides those in need through meditation, visualisation, and gentle affirmations to help them rediscover their inner light. His approach isn't tied to any specific doctrine; it's about fostering a personal connection to deeper truths.

Rooted in The Knowing, Michael sees healing not as fixing what's broken but as a journey back to wholeness. He believes illness and pain are messages highlighting areas needing care and transformation. He encourages them to view their struggles as opportunities for growth and self-discovery, walking alongside them as they find their own path to well-being.

A key part of Michael's philosophy is believing in the body's innate ability to heal itself. He teaches, while external help can be valuable, true healing comes from within. Empowering people to tap into their healing potential, he encourages them to listen to their bodies, trust their instincts, and cultivate positivity and self-love. His practice is holistic, considering all aspects of a person's life, and understanding physical health is intertwined with emotional, mental, and spiritual well-being.

Michael's practice is known for its serene and nurturing atmosphere. Whether in his healing space or visiting someone, he creates environments where people feel safe, seen, and heard. His calm presence provides comfort even before any healing begins. Believing the environment is crucial to healing, he carefully crafts a sanctuary with soft lighting, soothing sounds, and subtle scents, allowing individuals to relax and open up to the healing process.

He tailors each healing session to individual needs, beginning by understanding their physical and emotional concerns. Using his intuition, he senses what kind of healing is required, be it energy work, emotional release, or spiritual guidance. No two sessions are alike. Recognising healing is ongoing, he provides continued support, often following up after sessions to offer advice or to listen to a client's concerns. For Michael, healing isn't about the session; it's about helping people cultivate lasting change.

Michael's healing work profoundly impacts those who seek his help. Many experience relief from physical ailments and undergo deep personal transformations. They leave his sessions feeling better but also with a renewed sense of purpose and a deeper understanding of themselves.

One of the most significant effects of Michael's work is the empowerment it brings. By guiding individuals to tap into their healing potential, he helps them reclaim their power over their health and well-being. This often leads to lasting change as people adopt healthier choices and more positive lifestyles. His holistic approach ensures healing extends beyond the physical, fostering emotional balance, mental clarity, and spiritual connection, helping people live more fulfilling lives.

Michael's impact extends beyond those he heals directly. Through his teachings and example, he inspires others to embrace a more holistic and compassionate approach to health. His work ripples outward, creating a movement toward healing which honours the interconnectedness of body, mind, and spirit.

His identity as a healer is deeply intertwined with his journey through The Knowing. His practice isn't a profession but a mani-festation of his profound understanding of existence, compassion for others, and commitment to fostering holistic well-being. To fully grasp the depth of Michael the healer, it's essential to explore his life, methods, and the transformative impact he has on those he assists.

Michael's path to becoming a healer wasn't straightforward. Shaped by suffering, discovery, and transformation through The Knowing, his early encounters with illness and personal loss sparked his desire to understand the deeper causes of pain. Witnessing chronic illness in his family exposed him to the limitations of conventional medicine and ignited his interest in alternative healing.

At fifty, he experienced a profound shift, moving from structured religious practices to embracing The Knowing. This epiphany redefined his spiritual beliefs and reshaped his under-standing of healing, realising it requires nurturing the entire being, body, mind, and spirit. Guided by mentors, he developed his healing abilities through practices like Reiki, meditation, and energy work, crafting a unique methodology which is both intuitive and structured.

Michael's Healing Methods:

Michael's healing methods are diverse, addressing different aspects of well-being. He tailors his approach to each person, believing the body's energy centres, or chakras, play a crucial role in health. Assessing clients' chakras, he identifies blockages contributing to their issues through verbal communication, observation, and energy sensing.

To restore balance, he uses techniques like guided visualisation, sound healing with crystal bowls, and specific hand positions. Meditation and visualisation help clients access deeper conscious-sness, release emotional burdens, and foster inner peace. He creates tailored meditation scripts, guiding clients into relaxation and introspection.

Emotional well-being is central to his philosophy. Recognising unresolved emotions can manifest as physical ailments, he provides a safe space for clients to express their deepest feelings without judgment. Using techniques like Emotional Freedom Techniques (EFT) and guided emotional release, he helps them release pent-up emotions and foster resilience.

Drawing from The Knowing, Michael offers spiritual counselling to help clients connect with their higher selves. He encourages exploration of purpose and alignment with their true selves, providing life coaching to overcome barriers and build self-esteem.

His healing principles combine ancient wisdom with modern knowledge, aligned with The Knowing. He considers all dimensions of a person's life, believing true healing occurs when physical, emotional, and spiritual aspects are addressed. Advising on lifestyle, environment, nutrition, and stress management, he ensures the healing process is collaborative and empowering.

Michael is committed to ongoing growth, attending workshops and training to keep his practices current and effective. He remains flexible, modifying his approach based on clients' needs to ensure his practice is impactful.

Case Studies:

Sarah's Story: Sarah is a lady of forty-five years and had suffered from chronic migraines since her teenage years. Sarah found relief through Michael's energy balancing and guided meditation, which addressed blockages in her third chakra. She booked five sessions with Michael and her migraines lessened, virtually stopped all-together. She felt stronger and less tense and felt empowered to continue with treatments as her day-to-day life improved.

John's Journey: After being married for fifty years John was devastated by his spouse's sudden death. He was suffering from insomnia and depression when he first attended Michael's clinic. Michael supported him with deep listening and EFT, guiding him toward inner peace and meaning. John emerged from depression, channelling his grief into volunteer work and went on to lead a rewarding life.

Emily's Awakening: Feeling spiritually disconnected; Emily sought Michael's help. After talking and listening deeply to what Emily had to say Michael recommended guided meditation and chakra align-ment. She reconnected with her spiritual core, pursued her passions, and once again felt fulfilled and connected.

Challenges and Growth:

Michael faces challenges like dealing with others' deep emotional pain, which can be taxing. He sets boundaries and practices self-care to stay grounded. Encountering scepticism, he addresses it by explaining his methods and sharing success stories, integrating his practices with conventional treatments when appropriate. As an educator, he advocates for an integrative view of health through workshops and community outreach.

The Knowing and Healing:

Michael's method of healing is rooted in The Knowing, focusing on the interconnectedness of body, mind, and spirit. He believes illness often reflects disconnection and healing involves restoring harmony on every level. Viewing the body as a system of energy flows, he works to realign these flows, helping people tap into their inner healing reservoirs.

His sessions are unique and intuitive, creating a sacred space conducive to healing. The effects go beyond the physical, leading to profound changes in mindset and lifestyle. Many who work with Michael experience an awakening, realising their challenges are opportunities for growth. His healing fosters resilience, peace, and a deeper connection to the world. The positive changes in individuals ripple outward, inspiring others and contributing to a broader movement of healing and awakening.

Michael's life as a healer is one of service, driven by deep compassion and a desire to alleviate suffering. His journey and work inspire others to explore their potential as healers in their own interactions. In essence, Michael represents a profound blend of wisdom, compassion, and spiritual insight. His work is a living expression of The Knowing, bringing healing, transformation, and awakening to those who seek it. Through his gentle, intuitive practice, he helps people reconnect with themselves and the deeper currents of life, guiding them on a healing journey which touches every aspect of their being.

CHAPTER 17

PETER'S UNDERSTANDING OF THE KNOWING

'There are only two mistakes one can make along the road to truth; not going all the way and not starting.' — Gautama Buddha

I have learned profound lessons through my journey, particularly in my interactions with Michael and my exploration of The Knowing. These lessons have reshaped my understanding of life, healing, and identity.

One of the most significant lessons is the importance of confronting and accepting my past. Initially, I tried to bury painful memories of my lonely childhood, believing ignoring them would make them disappear. However, through conversations with Michael, I realised these suppressed memories continued to influence my life, manifesting as emotional wounds and unresolved fears. True healing comes not from forgetting the past, but from facing it with courage and acceptance. By acknowledging my childhood experiences and the pain they caused, I could finally begin to release their hold and move forward with a lighter heart.

I also learned trauma, while deeply impactful, does not have to define my life. Michael's wisdom about the nature of trauma, how it diminishes once faced and accepted, helped me see I could transcend my past rather than be perpetually trapped by it. The wounds of the past do not have to be permanent scars. Through introspection, acceptance, and self-compassion, it's possible to heal and transform trauma into a source of strength and wisdom.

Through The Knowing, I've gained a deeper under-standing of the interconnectedness of all aspects of life: body, mind, and spirit. I've begun to see how my physical health, emotional state, and spiritual well-being are intertwined, and how imbalance in one area can affect others. I've learned the importance of holistic well-being, recognising true healing and growth require attention to all dimen-sions of existence. This under-standing has led me to adopt a more balanced and mindful approach to life, valuing my emotional and spiritual health as much as my physical and intellectual pursuits.

I've come to appreciate the significance of my relationship with Melissa in a new light. While our connection has always been passio-nate and deeply engaging, I now see our bond is also crucial to my healing and growth. Melissa's presence has provided a safe space to explore my vulnerabilities and experience unconditional love and support. I've also learned relationships are about companionship; which can also be powerful catalysts for personal growth and healing. My relationship with Melissa has taught me about the importance of mutual support, understanding, and shared journeys in navigating life's challenges.

I've also learned life is a continuous journey of discovery and growth. The Knowing has taught me there is no final destination, no ultimate understanding to reach. Instead, life is about embracing the journey itself, with all its ups and downs, and allowing each experience to deepen one's understanding of existence. Life is not about reaching a state of perfect knowledge or happiness, but about continuously learning, growing, and evolving. This realisation has helped me let go of the need for certainty and control, allowing me to live more freely and fully in the present moment.

Through these lessons, I've evolved from a man burdened by my past and uncertain of my path to someone more self-aware, resilient, and connected to the deeper currents of life. My journey is ongoing, but with each step, I become more aligned with the essence of The Knowing, experiencing an ever-deepening connection to life's mysteries and trusting in the wisdom which emerges from within.

My journey of learning and transformation has been profound, touching multiple layers of my existence. As I delve deeper into the teachings of The Knowing and integrate the wisdom shared by Michael, I uncover new dimensions of under-standing which have reshaped my perception of the world and also my sense of self.

My initial approach to life was one of self-protection, shaped by my lonely and often painful childhood. I had built walls around myself, using my intellect and success as a writer to shield my inner world. Through my relationship with Melissa and conversations with Michael, I've learned true strength lies in embracing vulnerability. I discovered vulnerability is not a weakness, but a source of power. By allowing myself to be open and honest about my fears, insecurities, and past traumas, I've discovered a deeper connection with myself and others. This openness has led to greater emotional intimacy with Melissa and a more authentic way of living. I've also learned when I embrace vulnerability and stop hiding my true self I heal, and I also inspire others to do the same.

My journey of healing is deeply tied to my ability to accept myself and my past. For years, I struggled with feelings of inadequacy stemming from my childhood experiences and my shy, awkward nature. My initial attempts to suppress these memories led to more pain and inner turmoil. Through talks with Michael, I've learned acceptance is a critical step in the healing process. Instead of battling against my past or trying to erase it, I've begun to embrace it as an integral part of who I am. This acceptance doesn't mean I condone the pain or it no longer affects me; rather, it means I acknowledge it, allowing it to inform but not control my present life. This shift in perspective liberates me from the need to be perfect and helps me find peace with my imperfections and experiences which is truly the healing power of acceptance.

As a successful writer, I have always derived a sense of identity from my work. However, my creativity had become stifled, reflecting the emotional blocks I carried. The pressures of success and unres-olved issues from my past had drained me of the joy and spontaneity which once fuelled my writing. Through the process of healing and self-discovery, I've begun to reconnect with the joy which once inspired my creativity. I've realised creativity is not a professional pursuit, but a vital expression of my inner self. As I've healed emotionally, my writing has become more vibrant and authentic, reflecting my newfound freedom and depth of understanding. I've learned creativity thrives in an environment of emotional and spiritual well-being, and as I've nurtured these aspects of myself, my work has flourished.

My journey has also led me to explore the concepts of compassion and forgiveness, both for myself and for those who may have hurt me in the past. My childhood was marked by feelings of abandonment and neglect, leading to resentment and bitterness which lingered into my adult life. Through Michael's guidance, I've learnt holding onto anger and resentment perpetuated my suffering. I've begun to practice compassion, first towards myself, recognising I did the best I could with the circumstances I was given, and then towards others, including my parents. This act of forgiveness is not about condoning their actions, but about freeing myself from the emotional chains which bound me to the past. Compassion has allowed me to release the heavy burden of my anger, creating space for healing and peace.

A crucial aspect of The Knowing which I've internalised is the transient nature of all things: joy, sorrow, success, and failure. Life, I've learned, is a constant flow, and clinging too tightly to any one state or experience leads to suffering. I've begun to embrace the concept of impermanence, understanding life's ups and downs are natural and inevitable. This awareness brings me a sense of calm and resilience, allowing me to face challenges without being overwhelmed by them. I've learned to appreciate moments of joy without fearing their end and to endure pain with the knowledge it too will pass. This understanding has transformed my approach to life, making me more present, patient, and accepting of whatever comes my way.

My exploration of The Knowing has opened me up to a new dimension of spiritual awareness. Previously, my life was largely guided by intellect and reason, but as I've engaged more with Michael and delved into The Knowing, I've begun to tap into a deeper, more intuitive understanding of life. This spiritual awakening is not tied to any specific religious practices, but rather a broader sense of connection to the universe and the mysteries of existence. I've begun to trust my inner guidance more, feeling a sense of alignment with something greater than myself. This shift brings me peace and a profound sense of purpose, as I realise my life is part of a larger, interconnected whole. My spirituality has become a source of strength and inspiration, guiding me through both my creative work and my journey.

My relationship with Melissa has evolved as I've deepened my understanding of myself and my life. What began as a passionate and engrossing connection has become something even more meaningful: an authentic partnership based on mutual respect, understanding, and freedom. I've learned true love is not about possession or control, but about allowing each other to grow and evolve. My relationship with Melissa has taught me the value of space and freedom within a partnership, where both individuals can pursue their paths while supporting each other. This balance of closeness and independence enriches our bond, making it more resilient and fulfilling. Moreover, my relationship with Melissa has become a reflection of my inner growth, as we both navigate our lives together with a deep sense of love, respect, and mutual understanding.

Finally, I've come to see life as a continuous journey of learning, rather than a quest for a final, unchanging truth. The Knowing has taught me there is always more to discover, to experience, and to understand. This realisation has helped me let go of the pressure to have all the answers or to reach a certain level of achievement before I can be happy. Instead, I've embraced the process of learning itself, finding joy in the journey rather than fixating on the destination. This mindset brings me a sense of freedom and curiosity, allowing me to live more fully in the present moment and to approach each day as an opportunity for growth and discovery.

My journey has been one of profound transformation, marked by lessons about vulnerability, acceptance, creativity, compassion, impermanence, spirituality, relationships, and continuous learning. Each lesson has contributed to my growth as a person, helping me shed layers of pain and fear which once defined me, and I was able to step into a new phase of life with greater clarity, purpose, and inner peace. As I continue to navigate life with the wisdom of The Knowing, I become a more fulfilled and resilient individual, and also an inspiration to others on their journeys of self-discovery and healing.

CHAPTER 18

MELISSA'S EMBRACING OF THE KNOWING

'When you realise how perfect everything is you will tilt your head back and laugh at the sky.' — Gautama Buddha

The following is from a talk Melissa gave about The Knowing at a Ladies' luncheon. I include it because I feel it's important to bring balance to The Knowing, and to advise all, there are no restrictions as to sex, race, or even age as we can all benefit from getting to know our inner selves.

I remember the first time Peter told me about The Knowing. It felt like one of those moments where the world shifts, for a brief second, it's subtle and easy to miss. He was talking to Michael, engrossed in one of their long conversations filled with words I could barely catch. They were discussing life, purpose, and everything beyond the surface. Michael was calm, as though he had found some hidden treasure deep inside himself. Peter, on the other hand, was still searching, but I could feel it meant everything to him.

At the time, I didn't pay much attention. I love Peter and always give him space with his thoughts, but this 'Knowing' puzzled me. I've always been practical as life has its ups and downs, its joys and pains, and I've learned to accept them. I didn't see the need for a deep search for meaning. Life was, and I lived it. However, Peter seemed drawn to this idea, and I didn't want to hinder something which appeared to be tugging at his soul.

Michael first suggested I, too, might be on the path to discovering it. He didn't push; he never did. Michael has a gentle way of speaking, like a soft breeze which invites you to walk alongside it.

He said, 'Melissa, you already know what it is. It's not something to be taught or handed down. It's something which is already within you.'

At the time, I didn't believe him. I had never been one to dwell on spiritual matters. Sure, I have tried meditation and yoga, like most women my age, which was more for the physical benefits than anything else. Spirituality? Meaning? I had enough to deal with in the real world. Still… his words lingered.

For weeks after our conversation, I found myself pondering it, often in the oddest moments: while preparing dinner, watching the sunset from our balcony, or lying in bed with Peter after making love. What if Michael was right? What if there was something more to life, something deeper, which I had overlooked all these years?

I think the moment it all began to shift for me was during a quiet afternoon alone. Peter was away at a meeting, and I had the apartment to myself. There was nothing extraordinary about the day. I wasn't doing anything special. But something inside me told me to sit still. It was a strange feeling because I'm not one to sit idle for long. I'm always moving, always doing, always thinking about the next thing. But on this day, I stopped. I made a cup of tea, sat on the couch, and waited.

For a while, nothing happened. I felt silly, sitting there with my thoughts, waiting for some magical moment. But then, gradually, I noticed something. It wasn't an epiphany, not a voice from the heavens or a sudden flash of understanding. It was more like a soft, quiet knowing, like a whisper inside me. I didn't need to do anything. I didn't need to search for answers or meaning because everything I needed was already here. In me. Around me. I had been looking for something bigger, something grand when in reality, it was all in the simplest of things.

I think it's the difference between how I came to understand The Knowing and how Peter or Michael see it. For them, it's this deep, intellectual quest, especially for Peter. He's always analysing, always searching, constantly trying to put the pieces together. And Michael, well, he's been on this path for decades, peeling back the layers of life like some kind of spiritual onion. But for me, The Knowing wasn't about peeling away layers or analysing anything. It was about embracing what was already there, what had always been there, and maybe it's also because I'm a woman.

I think, as women, we tend to experience life more intuitively. We don't always need to search for answers in the way men do, because we live them, and we feel them. I've always felt there's a deeper rhythm to life, but I didn't see it before because I was caught up in the day-to-day of living. But once I stopped and listened, once I allowed myself to be, I realised I was already in harmony with the rhythm.

It's not to say life became perfect because I had all the answers. The Knowing doesn't work in this way. Also, it is not some magical solution to all of life's problems, but what it does, for me at least, is it makes those problems feel less overwhelming. It gives me a sense of peace, a sense of no matter what happens, everything is exactly as it's meant to be.

I remember one evening when Peter came home looking troubled. He had one of his bad days, the kind where his childhood memories crept back into his mind, filling him with doubt and insecurity. I could see it in his eyes the moment he walked in.

Normally, I would have rushed to comfort him, to say the right things, to try to fix whatever was hurting him. But, something inside me told me to wait. I didn't speak right away. I took his hand, led him to the couch, and sat beside him. We didn't talk for a long time. We sat there, in silence, holding hands. Slowly, Peter began to relax. He didn't need me to say anything. He didn't need me to fix him. All he required was for me to be there with him, to share in his pain without trying to change it.

Maybe, it's what The Knowing has taught me more than anything; life isn't about fixing things or finding answers. It's about being present, about accepting what is and knowing, in the grand scheme of things, everything is exactly as it should be.

Over time, Peter began to notice the change in me. He would often ask, 'Why are you as calm as you are? How do you always seem to know what to do?' I didn't have a clear answer for him because it wasn't something I could explain in words. It was more like a feeling, a deep, quiet assurance I was precisely where I was meant to be, doing exactly what I was meant to do.

One day, I shared this with him. I told him about the afternoon, about the stillness I had found within myself. I told him The Knowing wasn't something I had found through thinking or searching. It had come to me when I stopped looking for it. When I allowed myself to be. It's not something which can be explained or taught. It's something you feel, deep within your soul. For me, it wasn't about understanding life's mysteries or searching for some hidden meaning. It was about embracing the simplicity of life, the beauty in the everyday moments, and trusting everything, good and bad, was part of a larger, perfect whole.

Peter is still on his journey, and I love him for it, but his path is different from mine. The Knowing doesn't look the same for everyone. For some, it's a quest for understanding. For others, like me, it's about surrender. Surrendering to life, to love, to the moment, and in surrender, I've found a peace I never knew I was missing.

And here I am, a woman who once thought she had life all figured out, but I discovered there was much more beneath the surface. Not in the grand, dramatic sense Peter or Michael might describe it, but in the quiet moments: the warmth of the sun on my skin, the laughter shared with Peter, the stillness in the early hours of the morning. Not in the answers, but in the silence. In the presence. In the acceptance of life as it is. And, for me, this is more than enough.

When Melissa explains her beliefs about The Knowing to other women, she does it with warmth, empathy, and calmness, trusting each person can find their path to understanding. Here's how she might approach this conversation:

Melissa's Explanation of The Knowing to Other Women:
The Knowing isn't something I can hand over to you. It's not a concept you can memorise or a belief system you can adopt like a new diet or hobby. It's something much deeper and more personal. I believe every woman can come to her understanding of it in her own time. I'll share my experience, and perhaps something I say will resonate with you. If it doesn't, let it be okay too.

I didn't always have this sense of peace and comfort in being myself. Like many of us, I spent much of my life rushing from one thing to the next. There's immense pressure on women to have it all figured out, to balance everything, relationships, family, personal time and to do it all effortlessly, without showing any cracks.

For me, The Knowing was about letting go of the need to do it all. It wasn't a grand epiphany or spiritual awakening. It was subtle, like learning to trust the natural flow of things. As women, we often have a quiet strength within us, an intuition we don't always heed because we're too busy trying to keep everything together. The Knowing is about trusting your inner voice and recognising the wisdom we need is already within us.

This doesn't mean life rapidly becomes perfect. Challenges still arise and pull us in different directions. What changed for me was how I approached these challenges. I stopped trying to control every-thing and worrying about what was beyond my control. Instead, I began to accept life unfolds as it should, both the good and the bad.

The Knowing has taught me we don't need to have all the answers immediately or know how everything will turn out. I used to believe I had to plan everything perfectly, if I could arrange all the pieces correctly, life would make sense. Exhausting, isn't it? Our energy is wasted on worrying and overthinking, and most of those worries never materialise.

When I embraced The Knowing, I realised life is simpler than we often make it out to be. At its core, it's about presence, being fully here, in the moment, with yourself and your loved ones. It's about understanding whatever is happening now is part of your journey, even if it doesn't make sense at the moment. Most importantly, it's about trusting you already have everything you need inside you to navigate life.

For me, this has meant listening to my body more. As women, we have a deep connection to our bodies, but society often teaches us to ignore it, to push through pain, exhaustion, or doubt. The Knowing has helped me reconnect with my inner wisdom, the signals my body gives me, whether it's telling me to rest, let go, or nurture myself.

We often fall into the trap of thinking we need to seek answers outside ourselves. We look to gurus, self-help books, social media, and even well-meaning friends for advice on how to live better, be more fulfilled, and be more of everything. But The Knowing isn't out there, it's within you. It's in those quiet moments when you stop and breathe, when you allow yourself to be without the pressure to perform, fix, or achieve.

It's similar to how we care for others. As women, we're often caretakers. We know how to nurture, soothe, and make others feel safe and loved. But sometimes, we forget to give the same care to ourselves. The Knowing has reminded me I deserve the same gentleness, love, and care. It's permitted me to be softer with myself, to stop striving for perfection, and to trust I'm already enough, exactly as I am.

I want to emphasise The Knowing isn't a religious doctrine or a set of spiritual rules to follow. It's not about conforming to anyone else's path. Every woman's experience with it will be different because it's a deeply personal journey. For me, it's about feeling connected to myself and the world around me, without needing to control or define it.

I've found The Knowing often appears in the little things, the quiet moments when you're alone or with someone you love. It's in the way sunlight filters through trees in the afternoon, the sound of your breath during a deep inhale, the warmth of a hug, or how you feel after a good cry. It's in those moments of stillness, where there's nothing to do and nowhere to go, and you realise this moment is enough.

If there's one thing I hope you take away from this, it's this: You don't need to search for The Knowing outside yourself. You don't need to chase it or work for it. It's already within you, waiting for you to recognise it. When you do, you'll find life becomes less about solving problems and more about harmonising with what is. You'll start to trust yourself more, and trust will bring a peace you didn't know you were missing.

Lastly, don't rush. Don't feel like you need to figure it all out at once. Life unfolds exactly as it should, and The Knowing will come to you when you're ready. Be open, be kind to yourself, and trust everything you need is already here

For Melissa, The Knowing isn't about convincing or conv-erting others; it's about sharing her experience. She understands every woman is on a unique path and the wisdom of The Knowing will reveal itself in its own time and way.

CHAPTER 19

FINDING THE KNOWING

'No one saves us, but ourselves. No one can and no one may.
We ourselves must walk the path.' — Gautama Buddha

From the vantage of my many years and the countless roads I've travelled, I can tell you this: The Knowing is not something you find by looking outside of yourself. It's a matter of turning inward, of coming face to face with the truth within. It is not a teaching from any sage or scholar, not written in any book or carved in stone. It exists in the silent spaces of the mind, and in the quiet beat of the heart. To walk the path of The Knowing, is to peel back the layers of whom you think you are and come to understand what has always been.

In my journey, the realisation came gradually, like the slow bloom of a flower in spring. I had spent my younger years in study, searching for meaning in religious texts, sacred doctrines, and the words of great minds. Yet, it wasn't until I turned inward I began to glimpse the true nature of life, the essence of what is called The Knowing. Now, as I walk through life with this awareness, I under-stand the steps one must take, not in any dogmatic way, but as guiding lights for those seeking their understanding.

For me, the gateway to The Knowing was through silence and meditation. Early on, I'd sit for hours, wrestling with my thoughts, then gradually sinking into the quietude beneath them. I realised in this stillness, this space where the mind's noise settles like dust in an empty room, truth emerges. The Knowing is not something forced; it rises when you are still enough to hear it.

Mindfulness, too, was crucial. As I became more aware of the present moment, whether in prayer or walking through a forest, I found each moment carries a richness, a connection to the greater whole. This awareness, cultivated in meditation, seeped into my everyday life, allowing me to access The Knowing not in sacred spaces, but in the mundane practice of daily tasks.

There were days when I questioned the path I walked. Doubts, fears and old wounds would resurface, clouding my mind. But I learned self-reflection, truly sitting with those emotions, allowed me to delve deeper into myself. Journaling became a tool of great value, capturing fleeting thoughts and emotions, and uncovering various patterns in my mind.

I remember, during one of these reflective moments, recognising the deep void left by my lack of family life, and the aftermath of a marriage which didn't last long. Rather than suppress these feelings, I sat with them. Then I wrote about them and in the process, learned the emptiness I felt was an invitation, not to fill it with external things, but to come to terms with my inner completeness.

For years, I wandered in nature, and in those sacred landscapes, I found the earth itself reflected the truths I sought. Nature speaks without words, yet its lessons are profound. There were times I felt as though the wind carried whispers of ancient wisdom, or the stillness of a mountaintop mirrored the stillness within me. Nature reminds me everything is interconnected, the trees, the rivers, the sky, each is part of a larger, pulsing reality. In those moments of connection, I glimpsed The Knowing more succinctly, realising we are not separate from the world, but deeply embedded within it.

Despite the necessity of turning inward, my intellectual curiosity never faded. I continued to read widely, drawn to the words of mystics, philosophers, and thinkers. But rather than seeking answers in those texts, I used them as mirrors, reflecting my understanding. The truth is, no book can tell you what The Knowing is, but they can help you ask the right questions.

I found myself particularly inspired by the writings of those who walked their own unique paths to truth. The beauty of their stories was not in their answers, but in their courage to question, to venture beyond the known, searching for something deeper. If there is one lesson I have learned, it is this: trust the voice within.

Over time, I realised The Knowing speaks through intuition. It is not always loud or obvious, but it is persistent, a quiet nudge in the direction of truth. I learned to take notice of the gut feelings which arose, and to the dreams which visited me when I slept. And over time, I began to distinguish between the voice of fear and the voice of truth.

There was one night, not long after I'd begun this journey, when I awoke with a sense of profound clarity. The dream had been simple, a quiet landscape, a single tree bending in the wind, but the message was clear: trust the stillness, trust the movement.

While much of this journey is solitary, I found great value in the company of like-minded individuals. There were others, too, who sought The Knowing, some through meditation, others through prayer, some through simple contemplation of life's mysteries. These conversations were illuminating.

I remember one evening, sitting with a small group of seekers, each sharing their journey. As we spoke, something clicked within me: we each walked different paths, yet the essence of what we sought was the same. In our shared stories, I found reflections of my own. The Knowing is not a solitary discovery, but a shared truth, manifesting in many ways.

If I have learned anything from this journey, it is patience is required. The Knowing does not come all at once. There are moments of great clarity, and there are stretches of fog and confusion. But persistence, a quiet dedication to the path, is what brings you through. I often think of it like walking through a dense forest where at times, the way is clear, at others, you must navigate through the thick underbrush, but always, the path is there.

The most challenging part, I found, was not in glimpsing The Knowing, but in living it. It is one thing to have moments of insight, quite another to align your life with deeper truth. Over time, I began to see the insights gained in meditation, reflection, and conversation, were for the moment and I wasn't meant to stay in those moments. They were to be lived, to guide my decisions, relationships, and actions.

In the end, The Knowing is not something to be attained; it is something to be lived. It is not a destination, but a way of being. Each day, each moment offers a new opportunity to live from a place of profound awareness, of connection with the truth which lies within. As the journey continues, unfolding in new and unexpected ways, always leading deeper into the heart of existence.

The journey toward The Knowing has been the centrepiece of my later life, a path I didn't consciously choose, but rather one which chose me. It wasn't a moment of enlightenment which struck me, nor was it a revelation delivered by a master or a sacred text. No, it was a slow, gradual unveiling, as if layers of illusion were being peeled back, one by one. I came to understand The Knowing is not something external. It's not out there to be discovered, it is within, quietly waiting for us to turn inward, to stop looking with the eyes and start seeing with the soul.

But no matter how much I read or how deeply I studied, something always seemed to be missing. It wasn't until later in life, when I began to question the foundations of what I believed I understood, the essence of what I'd been seeking all along. This is The Knowing, not the answers themselves, but the space within which the answers arise.

Meditation became a cornerstone of my journey. When it was suggested to me, I resisted the practice. My mind was too busy, filled with thoughts racing from one idea to the next, cluttered with fears, desires, and memories. But as I persisted, I began to realise meditation wasn't about achieving anything. It wasn't about silencing the mind or reaching a specific state. It was about allowing; allowing everything to be as it is and sitting in stillness. As I sat longer, the noise in my mind began to quiet, not because I forced it to, but because I no longer fought against it.

Through meditation, I came to understand The Knowing is not intellectual; it is experiential. It is the quiet, profound understanding which comes when the mind is no longer frantically searching for meaning. I often found myself in states where time seemed to dissolve, and I was left being, no judgments, no thoughts, existing in awareness. It was in these moments I touched some-thing vast, something beyond myself yet intimately familiar. This is when I realised The Knowing isn't something you find; it's something you return to.

Mindfulness, as an extension of meditation, became a way of living. I learned to bring the same quiet attention to everyday active-ities. Washing dishes, walking, and eating, were no longer mundane tasks, but opportunities to remain present, and to engage fully with life. I found a deeper connection with myself, and the world around me. The Knowing isn't an abstract concept, it's the lived experience of being fully here, in the present, where life unfolds.

One of the most difficult aspects of this journey was confronting myself. There's a tendency to avoid the parts of ourselves we don't like, the parts which carry pain or shame. But The Knowing requires complete honesty, and a willingness to look inward, even when it's uncomfortable. I spent many nights in reflec-tion, questioning my beliefs, my desires, and my motivations. The journaling process was cathartic for me. It wasn't about recording thoughts, it was about unravelling them, exposing them to the light.

I would write about moments in my past which still haunted me, memories of missed connections, regrets, and the pain of feeling like an outsider in my life. As I wrote, I began to see patterns. These weren't random events; they were expressions of the same wound, the wound of separation, the feeling I was disconnected from something greater. Writing gave me the clarity to see this discon-nection was an illusion. In those quiet moments of self-reflection, I started to realise I had never been disconnected from life; I had been looking in the wrong places for connection.

Through journaling, I discovered The Knowing is not about finding peace; it's about integrating all parts of yourself, the good, the bad and the ugly. It's about accepting ourselves fully, with all our flaws and imperfections, and understanding we are part of the greater whole.

Nature, I found, has always been the greatest teacher. There is quiet wisdom in the cycles of the earth, the ebb, and flow of the tides, the changing of the seasons. In my younger years, I overlooked this. I was too caught up in the intellectual pursuit of truth. But as I grew older and began spending more time in nature, I realised the truths I had been seeking were all around me, reflected in the natural world.

I would spend hours walking through forests or sitting by rivers, not seeking anything, but being myself. There were moments when I felt as though the trees, the wind, and the water were speaking to me, not in words, but in a deeper language, a language of stillness and presence. In those moments, I realised nature embodies The Knowing. It exists, without striving or searching and in its quiet presence, it holds the entire universe.

The more time I spent in nature, the more I felt my sense of separation dissolve. I was no longer a man walking through the woods; I was part of the woods. The lines between me and the world around me blurred, and I understood, in a way I never had before, we are all connected, to each other, and to everything. The Knowing is this sense of interconnectedness, a realisation we are not isolated beings, but expressions of the same life force which flows through everything.

One of the most transformative aspects of this journey was learning to trust my intuition. For years, I had relied on external sources for guidance. But I began to realise true guidance comes from within. Our intuition is like a compass, always pointing us toward The Knowing, but we often ignore it, caught up in the noise of the mind.

I began paying attention to my gut feelings, the subtle nudges which seemed to come from nowhere. In the beginning, it was difficult to distinguish between the voice of fear and the voice of intuition, but with practice, I became more attuned. There were times when I would have a sudden insight or a feeling something was right or wrong, and I would follow it, even when it didn't make logical sense. More often than not, these intuitive leaps led me exactly where I needed to be.

Intuition, I discovered, is the voice of The Knowing. It doesn't come from the mind; it comes from a deeper place, a place beyond thought. Learning to trust the voice was one of the most liberating parts of my journey.

Although much of my journey was solitary, I found great value in the company of others who were also seeking. There is something powerful about shared experiences, about speaking with someone who understands the questions you are grappling with. I would often meet with small groups of people, some spiritual, some curious about life's more in-depth meaning, and we would talk for hours, sharing insights and challenges.

These conversations were not about finding answers. They were about exploring, about delving deeper into the mystery of life. Each person brought their perspective, their piece of the puzzle and in those dialogues, I frequently found the answers I sought arose naturally, not from anyone else's words, but from within myself.

Community, I realised, is about support; it's about reflection. In others, we see ourselves. In their stories, we find echoes of our own. And in those moments of connection, we realise The Knowing is not an individual pursuit, but a shared truth.

Perhaps the most difficult lesson I learned was the importance of patience. In our modern world, we are conditioned to seek quick results, and instant gratification. It is not something you can grasp or achieve. It is something which unfolds, slowly, over time, as you walk the path.

There were times when I felt frustrated, when I doubted whether I would ever truly understand. But as I persisted, I realised even in those moments of doubt, The Knowing was present. Every step on the journey, every challenge, every setback, was part of the unfolding. There is no endpoint to this journey, no final destination where you arrive and say, 'I have found it.' The journey itself is the goal, and it is through patience and persistence we come to realise this.

The greatest challenge, of course, is not in glimpsing The Knowing, but in living it. It is one thing to have moments of insight, moments when you feel connected to something greater. It is quite another to bring awareness into your everyday life. But this, I believe, is the ultimate goal; not to attain it, but to embody it. Living The Knowing means aligning your actions, your decisions, and your relationships with more in depth understanding. It means letting go of the need for control, for certainty, and allowing life to unfold as it will. It means trusting in the wisdom of the present moment and living from a place of openness and connection.

In the end, The Knowing is not something you find. It is something you become. It is the realisation you are not separate from life, but an integral part of it. And as you walk this path, you come to understand everything, every experience, every challenge, every joy; is an expression of a deeper truth.

The journey continues, always unfolding, always revealing new layers of understanding and as I walk this path, I know The Knowing is not some distant goal to be reached, it is within me.

CHAPTER 20

ACCESSING THE KNOWING

'The seeker who sets out upon the way shines bright over the world.
Like the moon, come out from behind the clouds! shine.' — Gautama Buddha

Accessing The Knowing is a deeply personal and transformative process. It's not about acquiring external knowledge or following a specific doctrine, but rather about tapping into inner wisdom which guides one's life. Michael, who has spent years on this journey, sees it as something which each individual can access in their own unique way.

The first step to accessing The Knowing is cultivating awareness an awareness of self, one's thoughts, emotions, and the world around self. Michael believes true awareness comes from mind-fullness and being fully present in each moment.

'Start by quieting the mind and observing your thoughts without judgement. Pay attention to your emotions, your reactions, and the way you interact with the world. The Knowing begins when you become fully aware of the present moment. In this state of heightened awareness, you start to see patterns, connections, and truths which were previously hidden. This is where the journey begins.'

Michael emphasises the importance of silence and stillness in accessing The Knowing. In a world filled with noise and distractions, finding moments of quiet allows one to connect with the deeper layers of their being.

'In silence, the mind quiets and the heart speaks. Create moments of stillness in your daily life, whether through meditation, spending time in nature, or sitting quietly. In these moments, you can tune into the subtle currents of wisdom which flow within you. The Knowing is often found in the spaces between thoughts, in the calm which comes when you're fully present and at peace. Allow yourself to be still and listen to what arises from within.'

Intuition is a key aspect of The Knowing. Michael believes everyone has an inner voice, a gut feeling or instinct, which guides them. Trusting this intuition is essential in accessing more in-depth wisdom.

Intuition is the language of The Knowing. It's your inner voice which guides you, even when logic or external advice says otherwise. To access The Knowing, you must learn to trust your intuition. It's a direct line to your more in-depth wisdom. When faced with decisions, instead of overthinking, tune into how you feel. What does your intuition tell you? The more you trust it, the clearer it becomes and the more connected you'll be to The Knowing.'

Michael understands The Knowing is not something to be found in isolation. It's deeply intertwined with life's experiences, the joys, the sorrows, the successes, and the failures. He advises embracing all aspects of life as opportunities for growth and learning.

Life itself is a teacher and every experience is a lesson in The Knowing. Embrace everything which comes your way, the good, and the not so good. Each moment has something to teach you, something which brings you closer to understanding the deeper truths of life. Reflect on your experiences, learn from them, and allow them to shape your understanding. The Knowing is not static; it evolves with you as you live your life fully and consciously.

A significant barrier to accessing The Knowing is the need to control outcomes and the fear of uncertainty. Michael advises letting go of this need for control and learning to trust the flow of life.

The Knowing cannot be forced or controlled. It comes when you let go of the need to know everything or to control every outcome. Trust your life is unfolding as it should, even when things don't go according to plan. When you surrender to the flow of life, you open yourself up to The Knowing. This doesn't mean being passive; it means being actively engaged in life while also trusting in the process. Let go and allow The Knowing to guide you.

Michael emphasises The Knowing is more about feeling than think-ing. It's about connecting with the heart and allowing it to guide your actions and decisions.

The heart is the seat of The Knowing. While the mind analyses and rationalises, the heart understands and feels. To access The Knowing, you must connect with your heart; your true emotions, your compassion, and your love. Let your heart guide you in your interactions with others, in your decisions, and in your understanding of life. When you lead with the heart, The Knowing flows naturally, guiding you with wisdom and grace.

For Michael, accessing The Knowing involves aligning one's thoughts, emotions, actions, and intentions with their true self. This inner alignment creates a harmonious state where The Knowing can emerge.

Inner alignment is key to accessing The Knowing. When your thoughts, emotions, actions, and intentions are in harmony, you create a clear channel for more in-depth wisdom to flow. Reflect on your life, are you living in alignment with your true self, or are there areas where you're out of balance? The more aligned you are, the more easily The Knowing will come to you. It's about being true to yourself and living in a way which resonates with your deepest values and beliefs.

Michael teaches The Knowing is not about having all the answers, but about embracing the mystery of life. He encourages others to be comfortable with not knowing and to find peace in the uncertainty.

The Knowing is not about certainty; it's about embracing the mystery. Life is full of unknowns and where its beauty lies. Be comfortable with not knowing everything. In fact, the more you accept the mystery, the more open you become to it. It's a paradox, the less you seek definitive answers, the more understanding you gain. Trust in the journey and in the wisdom, which reveals itself along the way.

He reminds Melissa and others, accessing The Knowing is a continuous practice, not a one-time event. It requires patience, dedication, and a willingness to grow and evolve.

The Knowing is not a destination; it's a lifelong journey, something you access through continuous practice, daily awareness, reflection and inner work. Be patient with yourself; growth takes time. Some days you'll feel deeply connected to The Knowing, and other days it might seem out of reach. This is natural. What matters is your commitment to the journey. Keep practicing, keep exploring and over time, it will become a natural part of your life.

Accessing is a deeply personal and spiritual journey, one which involves cultivating awareness, embracing silence, trusting intuition, and letting go of control. It requires connecting with the heart, seeking inner alignment, and being comfortable with life's mysteries. Michael's guidance shows The Knowing is both a goal and a process, a continuous practice which evolves as one lives a life of authenticity, openness and trust in the inner wisdom which lies within.

Awareness is the first and most essential step on the path to The Knowing. It involves more than mindfulness; it is about cultivating a deep, non-judgmental presence in every moment. This awareness is the gateway to understanding the subtle layers of existence which are often overlooked in the hustle and bustle of daily life. Awareness requires an individual to engage with life above a superficial level. It also requires you to tune into the underlying currents of energy and intention. This means being acutely aware of one's thoughts, emotions, and reactions as they arise. It also involves recognising the interconnectedness of all things, seeing beyond the immediate and obvious, and sensing the subtler forces at play in each situation. To cultivate this awareness, practices such as mindfulness, meditation, deep breathing, and reflective journaling are invaluable. These practices help quiet the mind and open the heart, creating space for the more in-depth insights of The Knowing to emerge. It's about slowing down, tuning in, and becoming fully present, allowing every moment to be a potential doorway to more profound wisdom.

Silence and stillness are not the absence of noise and movement; they are the language through which The Knowing speaks. In a world which constantly demands our attention, embracing silence and stillness is a revolutionary act which allows us to access the depths of our inner wisdom. In stillness, the noise of the external world fades and the internal landscape becomes clearer. This is where the mind's incessant chatter quiets down, making room for the subtle whispers of intuition and inner guidance. It's in these moments of stillness the truths of The Knowing can be most readily perceived.

Michael might suggest incorporating moments of stillness into daily life, not in formal meditation, but in the quiet pauses throughout the day. Whether it's a few moments of deep breathing before starting a task, or a quiet walk in nature without distractions, these moments of stillness allow The Knowing to surface. They are opportunities to listen deeply, and to tune into the inner wisdom which is always present, but often drowned out by the noise of everyday life.

Intuition is often described as a gut feeling or a hunch, but in the context of The Knowing, it is much more. It's the inner compass which guides one's path, a direct connection to the deeper truths which lie beneath the surface of conscious thought. Trusting intuition means learning to listen to your inner voice and allowing it to guide decisions and actions, even when it defies logic or conventional wisdom. It requires a willingness to follow the path which feels right on a deeper level, even if it's not the most straightforward. To develop a stronger connection to intuition, one must practice tuning into it regularly. This could involve reflecting on past decisions where intuition played a role, paying attention to how it feels when intuition speaks, and learning to differentiate it from fear or wishful thinking. The more one trusts and acts on their intuition, the stronger and clearer it becomes, serving as a reliable guide on the journey of The Knowing.

Life itself is the curriculum through which The Knowing is accessed. Every experience, whether joyful or painful, contributes to the understanding and wisdom which form it. Michael would likely emphasise nothing in life is wasted or without purpose. Every experience, even those which seem negative or challenging, offers a lesson which brings one closer to it. This perspective transforms the way one views life's challenges, they are no longer obstacles to be avoided, but opportunities for growth and more in-depth understanding. Embracing life's experiences means approaching each moment with an open heart and a willingness to learn. It involves reflecting on experiences, asking what lessons they hold, and integrating those lessons into one's understanding of the world. Over time, this process of reflection and integration deepens one's connection to The Knowing, creating a rich tapestry of wisdom drawn from the full spectrum of life's experiences.

The need to control outcomes, and resist uncertainty is one of the greatest barriers to accessing The Knowing. Letting go of this need for control is essential to allow the flow of life to guide one toward a more in-depth understanding. Letting go does not mean passivity or inaction; rather, it means releasing the tight grip on how things should be and opening up to how they are. It is about trusting life which has its own wisdom and by surrendering to its flow, one aligns with the deeper currents of The Knowing. Michael guides myself and others to practice this surrender in small ways, by letting go of rigid plans, being open to unexpected opportunities, and trusting; even setbacks are part of a larger, wiser plan. This practice of surrender allows one to move from a state of resistance to a state of flow, where it can emerge naturally and effortlessly.

The Knowing is not an intellectual understanding; it is a deeply emotional and embodied experience. Connecting with the heart is essential to fully access it, as it is through the heart one feels the truths the mind cannot fully grasp. Michael would emphasise the importance of emotional intelligence in accessing it. This involves being with one's emotions, understanding what they are signalling, and allowing the heart to guide decisions and actions. The heart has wisdom of its own, often leading to deeper, more compassionate choices which align with The Knowing. Practices which connect with the heart, such as loving-kindness meditation, gratitude journaling, and heart-centred breathing, can help one tune into this emotional core. By leading with the heart, one becomes more attuned to the truths of The Knowing, which are often felt more than they are thought.

Inner alignment is the process of bringing all aspects of oneself, thoughts, emotions, actions, and intentions, into harmony. This alignment creates a state of coherence where The Knowing can flow more freely. Michael would likely stress true inner alignment requires ongoing reflection and self-awareness. It involves regularly checking in with oneself to ensure one's actions are in line with their deeper values and intentions. When there is a misalignment, such as acting out of fear rather than love, it creates a dissonance which can block access to it. Aligning with it means living authentically, where what one thinks, feels, says, and does are all in harmony. This coherence creates a state of inner peace and clarity, allowing new found knowledge to guide one's life with ease and grace.

The Knowing is not about having all the answers; it is about embracing the mystery of life. In this acceptance of the unknown, one finds the deeper truths which cannot be fully articulated or understood through conventional means. Michael might explain the paradox of it as the more one accepts not knowing, the more one knows. It is in the surrender to the mystery, in the acceptance of life's uncertainties, more in-depth insights emerge. This requires humility and a willingness to be comfortable with ambiguity, trusting the answers will reveal themselves in time. By embracing the mystery, one becomes more open to the unexpected and the unknown, which are often the sources of the most profound wisdom. The Knowing, in this sense, is not a fixed state of knowledge, but an ongoing, dynamic relationship with the mystery of existence.

This requires patience, as there will be times when The Knowing feels distant or unclear, but with continued practice, whether through meditation, reflection, or living with intention, it becomes a natural part of one's being. This continuous practice involves a commitment to self-awareness, growth, and the ongoing exploration of life's mysteries. Over time, knowing becomes not an occasional insight, but a steady, guiding presence in one's life, leading to greater wisdom, peace, and fulfilment.

When The Knowing transforms into Your Knowing, it signifies the insights and understanding you've gathered have settled into your being. This wisdom is no longer something you seek externally or attempt to grasp; it becomes an integral part of who you are. Your Knowing is deeply personal, tailored by your experiences, reflections, and the unique path you've walked. In this phase, the truths you once explored in abstract terms become living realities in your daily life. You no longer merely contemplate the mysteries of existence; you embody them. The lessons learned along the way, about love, loss, joy, and sorrow are no longer external concepts, but truths which guide your every decision and interaction.

As Your Knowing takes root, a whole new dimension of existence opens up. This dimension is characterised by a profound sense of connection, clarity, and peace. You begin to perceive life not as a series of events, but as an intricate, interconnected web of meaning. Every moment, every interaction becomes infused with a deeper significance. In this new dimension, you experience a heightened awareness of the subtleties of life. You see beyond the surface of things, recognising the underlying patterns and rhythms which govern existence. This is where intuition sharpens, where synchronicities become commonplace, and where life's mysteries feel intriguing, and also deeply familiar.

Your Knowing is not a static state, but one of continuous growth and expansion. As you live with it, you find your understanding deepens and evolves. The more you engage with life from this place of inner wisdom, the more you uncover new layers of meaning and insight. This phase of Your Knowing is marked by an ease and flow which wasn't present before. Decisions are made with confidence, not from a place of uncertainty, but from a deep-seated trust in your inner guidance. Challenges are met with resilience, as you now have the tools and understanding, to navigate life's complexities with grace.

In this stage, Your Knowing becomes a guiding light; for yourself, and for others as well. You find your presence, words, and actions naturally inspire and uplift those around you. You don't need to preach or teach; living from this place of inner wisdom radiates a quiet power which others are drawn to. You become a beacon of understanding in a world often clouded by confusion and fear. Your Knowing allows you to see readily, to discern truth from illusion, and to act with compassion and integrity. This new dimension of life is one where you are fully aligned with your highest self, living in harmony with the greater whole.

Even as Your Knowing becomes established, the journey does not end. The new dimension which opens up is vast and full of potential for further exploration. There is always more to discover, more layers to peel back, and more depth to experience. The path of Your Knowing is one of infinite possibility, where each step leads to greater wisdom, connection, and fulfilment. In the end, Your Knowing is a culmination of years of seeking, it is the flowering of your true self. It is the realisation the wisdom you sought was always within you, waiting to be uncovered and lived, and as you continue on this journey, you find life itself becomes the ultimate teacher, revealing ever-deeper truths and guiding you toward an ever-expanding understanding of existence.

As The Knowing gradually transforms into Your Knowing, a profound and deeply personal shift occurs. This transition signifies more than a shift in understanding; it marks the culmination of years of spiritual exploration, self-reflection, and life experience. The Knowing, once an external concept or goal, has now become internalised, woven into the fabric of your being.

This is the point where wisdom is no longer something you seek, but something you embody, a natural, intuitive guide which influences every aspect of your life.

CHAPTER 21

A Personal Journey to The Knowing

No one saves us, but ourselves. No one can and no one may.
We ourselves must walk the path.' — Gautama Buddha

The journey to accessing The Knowing is as unique as the individual undertaking it. Michael said there is no one-size-fits-all approach, and no rigid set of rules or practices to follow. Instead, the path to it is deeply personal, shaped by one's experiences, challenges, and inner reflections. It's a process of peeling back the layers of societal conditioning, self-doubt, and fear to uncover the truth which has always resided within all of us. For some, this journey might involve meditation, self-inquiry, or deep introspection. For others, it could be sparked by life-altering experiences or quiet moments of clarity in nature. What remains constant is the transformative nature of this journey. As one delves deeper into their consciousness, they begin to uncover a profound sense of understanding, a connection to something greater than themselves.

Accessing The Knowing requires trust in one's intuition and inner guidance. This inner wisdom, often overlooked or ignored in the hustle and bustle of everyday life, is the key to unlocking The Knowing. It's not about seeking answers from external sources or relying on the teachings of others, but rather about tuning into the quiet, yet powerful, voice within. This inner wisdom speaks in subtle ways, through gut feelings, dreams, or moments of deep resonance with certain ideas or experiences. Michael regularly advises those on this path to cultivate stillness and mindfulness, allowing themselves to become attuned to these inner signals. Over time, as one learns to trust and follow their intuition, The Knowing begins to unfold naturally, offering insights and guidance which are deeply aligned with their true self.

One of the most profound aspects of The Knowing is it manifests differently for each person. There is no universal blueprint or final destination. What we all come to realise is it is less about arriving at a definitive understanding and more about embracing the ongoing process of discovery. For some, it might be experienced as a deep sense of peace and contentment, a knowing everything is as it should be. For others, it could be a heightened awareness of life's interconnectedness, or a profound sense of purpose and direction. The Knowing might reveal itself in creative expression, in acts of service, or in simple moments of presence. Michael sees this diversity in experiences as a testament to the individuality of each person's journey. The Knowing, while universal in its potential, is expressed in ways which are unique to each person's path, personality, and life circumstances.

Another key understanding Michael imparts is accessing The Knowing is not a linear process. There are no clear milestones and the path is rarely straightforward. It's a journey which involves moments of clarity and understanding, often interspersed with periods of doubt, confusion, and even setbacks. Michael encourages those on this path to be patient and compassionate with themselves. The Knowing doesn't always reveal itself in grand epiphanies; sometimes, it's found in the small, quiet realisations which slowly shift one's perspective. It's a journey which requires faith in the process, even when the destination is unclear.

Despite the unique nature of each person's experience, Michael firmly believes The Knowing is accessible to everyone. It's not reserved for a select few or those who follow a particular spiritual path. It is an intrinsic part of being human, available to anyone willing to embark on the journey within. Michael's teachings emphasise it is not something to be attained, but rather something to be remembered and reconnected with. It's a return to the natural state of wisdom and understanding which resides within every individual. Accessing The Knowing is about stripping away the layers of ego, fear, and doubt which obscure this inner wisdom, allowing it to shine through.

Once accessed, it becomes a guiding force in one's life. It helps to shape relationships and provides a sense of direction which is deeply personal yet universally connected. For Michael, living with it means moving through life with a sense of ease and trust, knowing you are aligned with your true purpose. There is a sense of freedom which comes with having The Knowing. It frees one from the need to conform to societal expectations or to seek validation from the outside. The Knowing is a profound understanding your path is yours to follow and every tool you need to forge it, is already in your possession. In this sense, it becomes both a destination and a journey, a state of being which keeps evolving with you. For Michael, sharing this insight with others is not to provide a specific path, but to inspire those he speaks with, to find their own. It's available to whosoever will seek after it, and its healing power is for everyone who will take the inward journey.

When you start this personal journey towards The Knowing, it is often deeply introspective and transformative, marked by moments of clarity and self-discovery. It begins with a yearning for something more, a desire to understand one's place in the world, to find meaning beyond the superficial or external influences. This journey is unique to each individual, unfolding at its pace and guided by inner curiosity, intuition, and a willingness to explore beyond the familiar.

The early stages may involve questioning long-held beliefs, patterns, and expectations imposed by society, family, or oneself. It requires embracing uncertainty and letting go of the need for external validation or approval. As the journey progresses, there is typically a shift in focus from the outside world to an internal landscape. One begins to listen more intently to inner guidance, trusting emotions, instincts, and quiet insights which may have been ignored or undervalued in the past.

During this time, individuals may encounter challenges, doubts, and fears. These obstacles, however, serve as opportunities for growth, pushing them to dig deeper and uncover hidden truths about themselves. It starts to emerge as a deep, intuitive under-standing life is interconnected and one's path is inherently personal and meaningful, regardless of external circumstances.

As one moves closer to The Knowing, a profound sense of peace, trust, and freedom begins to take root. There's an alignment with one's true self and decisions become more authentic, driven by a sense of purpose rather than obligation. Relationships shift as well, becoming more genuine and reflective of this inner clarity. It is not about having all the answers, but about embracing the journey itself, realising everything one needs to navigate life is already within.

The journey toward The Knowing is a deeply personal and often transformative process which requires a willingness to step beyond the boundaries of the familiar and venture into the unknown. This path is less about following a set road map and more about peeling back the layers of conditioning, expectations, and preconceived notions which have accumulated over time. As one embarks on this journey, several key phases and experiences typically mark the transition from living in uncertainty to living with a deep sense of inner clarity and trust.

The journey typically begins with a sense of dissatisfaction or restlessness. Life as it has been lived no longer feels fulfilling or authentic. This can manifest as a feeling something is missing or an internal nudge life is meant to hold a more profound meaning. This phase frequently feels like an awakening of sorts, where one becomes aware there is more to life than the roles, labels, or identities they've previously accepted. The Knowing, though still undefined, beckons from within, urging the individual to question the path they are on.

As the individual begins to question their old patterns, they are often confronted with doubt, fear, and discomfort. This is the phase where many question whether they should continue along their current path or break free into uncharted territory. This uncertainty can feel disorienting, as it challenges the foundations on which their life has been built. There may be moments of second-guessing, feelings of vulnerability, or even a desire to turn back to the safety of what is known.

This period of doubt is crucial because it forces the individual to sit with their discomfort and learn to trust in the unfolding of the process. Rather than seeking immediate answers or resolutions, they are guided to become comfortable with not knowing, to trust clarity will come in time. It's during this stage an individual often encounters what can be described as the 'dark night of the soul,' a period of deep introspection, where they feel lost, disconnected, or uncertain about their direction. Yet, it is through this darkness the seeds of The Knowing begin to take root.

One of the most pivotal stages of the journey is the act of surrender. Here, the individual realises the need for control, external validation, or fixed outcomes is hindering their progress. To access The Knowing, one must relinquish the desire to fit into society's mould, to impress others, or to meet expectations which do not align with their true self. This surrender is not about giving up; rather, it is about allowing life to unfold without forcing it into rigid frameworks.

In this space of surrender, the individual begins to listen more closely to their intuition, the quiet voice within which guides them toward authenticity. They start to recognise the subtle signs, synchronicities, and insights which life offers when they are open and receptive. The journey becomes less about seeking external solutions and more about tuning into the inner voice which has been there all along, waiting to be heard.

As the individual continues to trust the process, they start to access it in profound ways. The Knowing is an inner compass, a deep, intuitive wisdom which transcends logic and analysis. It speaks in a language which is personal to each individual, offering guidance which is both unique and universally connected.

During this phase, the individual experiences moments of clarity and insight where decisions, actions, and relationships begin to align with their true purpose. There is a newfound confidence, not in the ego-driven sense, but in the deep trust they are precisely where they need to be. The Knowing offers reassurance they are on the right path, even when the path seems unconventional or misunderstood by others.

As one continues to cultivate The Knowing, life begins to flow with greater ease and grace. Living in awareness is about moving through the world with a sense of trust and alignment. Challenges still arise, but the individual no longer views them as obstacles. Instead, they are considered growth opportunities, as part of the greater journey of self-realisation. In this phase, the individual also experiences a sense of liberation. They are no longer bound by the need to conform to societal norms or seek approval from others. There is an understanding their path is uniquely their own and the external world's opinions hold less weight. The Knowing instils a deep sense of freedom, allowing the individual to live authentically, unapologetically, and with purpose.

At this point in the journey, there is often a natural desire to share the wisdom of The Knowing with others. For Michael and many who reach this stage, it is not about dictating a specific way of life but encouraging others to embark on their journey of self-discovery. Everyone has access to this inner guidance if they are willing to seek it and trust in the process, and be guided by Your Knowing.

Instead of offering a set path, those who live with The Knowing often become guides, helping others tap into their inner wisdom. They encourage others to listen to their intuition, trust their journey, and embrace the uncertainty which comes with growth. Your Knowing becomes a gift which is shared, not through instruction, but through the embodiment of living authentically and inspiring others to do the same.

The journey toward Your Knowing is personal, ever-changing, and profoundly transformative. It is an invitation to step into the unknown, trust in the wisdom which lies within, and live a life which is aligned with one's true self. It is always available, patiently waiting for you who are ready to embrace the journey within.

For Michael, his own religious background had initially made him believe there was a specific path to enlightenment or truth, but the deeper he ventured into his journey, the more he realised this belief had been a constraint. The Knowing was not about following someone else's map; it was about uncovering the truth which had always been within. This process of discovery was unique, as it would be for anyone else who sought it.

The Knowing is a way to strip away the layers of societal conditioning, self-doubt, and fear which has built up over time, obscuring the inner wisdom which resides within all of us. For some, this might involve practices like meditation, self-inquiry, or long periods of introspection. For others, it could come through life-altering experiences, or even quiet moments in nature which bring unexpected clarity. The common thread was the transformative nature of the journey itself.

What Michael realised most profoundly was accessing The Knowing required trusting in one's intuition. It wasn't about seeking answers from books or teachers, but about tuning into the quiet voice within, the one which speaks through feelings, dreams, and moments of deep resonance with certain ideas or experiences. He frequently advised people to cultivate stillness and to become attuned to these inner signals because the more you trust and follow your intuition, the more The Knowing begins to unfold naturally. There is no universal blueprint, no final destination. For some, it might be a deep sense of peace and contentment, a certainty everything is as it should be. For others, it might manifest as an awareness of the inter-connectedness of life, or a renewed sense of purpose and direction. The Knowing could emerge through creative expression, acts of service, or simple moments of presence in the everyday. Michael found this diversity to be a testament to the individuality of each person's journey. There's no milestones and no clear progression from one point to another. It's a path filled with moments of clarity, often punctuated by periods of doubt, confusion, or even setbacks. Michael encourages all to be patient with themselves and to embrace the journey with compassion because it doesn't always arrive in grand epiphanies. Occasionally, it's in the small, quiet realisations which slowly shift one's perspective, one step at a time.

Despite the challenges, Michael was adamant The Knowing is accessible to everyone. It's not reserved for a select few, or for those who follow a particular spiritual path. The process is about peeling back the layers of ego, fear, and doubt, to reveal the inner wisdom which has always been there.

Once accessed, The Knowing becomes a guiding force. It shapes decisions, relationships, and the way one moves through life. For Michael, living with The Knowing meant living with a sense of ease and trust, knowing he was aligned with his true purpose. It freed him from the need for external validation and from the pressure to conform to societal expectations. He saw it as a reminder each person's path is their own and everything, they need to navigate is already within them. It evolves as we do, growing and expanding alongside us. For him, sharing this insight was not about providing others with a specific path, but about inspiring them to find their own. The Knowing, he believed, was available to anyone willing to seek it and its healing power was for everyone who dared to take the inward journey.

CHAPTER 22

THE KNOWING TO YOUR KNOWING

'In the end, only three things matter: how much you loved, how gently you lived and how gracefully you let go of things not meant for you.' — *Gautama Buddha*

After years of searching through books, consulting mentors, and life itself, something begins to shift within you. Slowly, then with greater clarity, The Knowing transforms into Your Knowing. Initially, you might not even notice it. You're still immersed in learning, seeking guidance, and trying to understand life's complexities. But one day, you wake up and realise you no longer look outward for answers. Instead, they have started to come from within.

This shift doesn't occur with a flash of brilliance or any fanfare. It is subtler. It happens in moments when you notice your decisions aren't made with the same hesitation or doubt. Moments when you find yourself responding to life not from a place of fear, but from a place of grounded confidence. It's a quiet yet profound evolution: you are no longer someone who knows; you are someone who understands.

Your Knowing isn't about accumulating knowledge; it's about

embodying knowledge as well. It's the difference between someone who can recite facts and someone who has lived them. In this space, you're not piecing together fragments of wisdom from external sources. Instead, you weave the wisdom you've gathered into the fabric of your daily life.

As this transformation unfolds, you feel a sense of ease. You stop chasing perfection or needing all the answers. You begin to realise life isn't to be figured out; it's to be lived. The messiness, unpredictability, highs, and lows are all part of it. Instead of trying to control every aspect, you navigate it with deep self-trust.

In this space, Your Knowing takes root. You see how your responses to challenges change. Where there was once anxiety, there's now calm. Where there was uncertainty, there's now a quiet conviction. It's not about knowing what will happen next; it's you trusting yourself to handle whatever comes.

This self-trust is liberating. It frees you from the constant need for approval, validation, or external guidance. You no longer need others to define what's right for you because you've cultivated a deep, inner compass guiding your decisions. This doesn't mean you stop listening to others or seeking advice when needed, but outside voices are now considered rather than relied upon. They are part of the process, not the decisive factor.

As Your Knowing deepens, you become more authentic. Layers of pretence and masks worn to fit in or meet expectations fall away. You stop living for approval, and start living in alignment with who you truly are. This authenticity isn't about being perfect; it's about being real, showing up as yourself without apology or hiding parts of who you are.

This authenticity is magnetic. People sense it, even if they can't articulate it. They feel your presence, confidence, and calmness, and they're drawn to it. You become a source of stability for others, not because you have all the answers, but because you're connected to your truth. You've stopped trying to impress or convince; instead, you've become a living example of walking through life grounded in Your Knowing.

Getting to this place wasn't easy. It took years of trial and error, heartache and healing, searching and stumbling. It took countless moments of doubt and questioning, it was messy and unpredictable, full of setbacks and breakthroughs. This is what makes Your Knowing powerful because it wasn't handed to you; it was earned, shaped by your unique experiences, struggles, and resilience.

Looking back, you might recognise difficult moments forged your inner strength. When you felt lost or broken, those moments deepened your wisdom. They forced you to dig deeper to find resources within yourself you didn't know existed. Now, with hindsight, every challenge was a stepping stone toward Your Knowing.

What's even more profound is Your Knowing isn't a final destination; it's a process, a constant unfolding. When you think you have understood something, life presents a new layer, a new challenge, inviting you to deepen your understanding further. It's dynamic, always evolving and growing. There's never a moment of finality. And it's a beautiful thing because it means there's always more to learn, experience, and integrate.

Moreover, the more you trust Your Knowing, the more resilient you become. Life will still present challenges, but you'll navigate them differently. Instead of being thrown off course, you'll adapt with greater ease. You'll bend without breaking because you understand these challenges aren't meant to defeat you; they're part of the process. They are opportunities to deepen Your Knowing and test the wisdom you've cultivated.

In difficult moments, you'll return to your center more quickly. You won't remain lost in chaos because you've built an inner foundation of strength. You'll face pain, confusion, and uncertainty, yet you know this too shall pass. When it does, you'll be stronger, wiser, and more connected to your inner truth.

Consider the ripple effect of living from Your Knowing. When you show up authentically, living from a place of deep self-trust, you inspire others. Without realising it, you become a beacon for those around you. Your calm, confidence, and clarity are contagious. People are drawn to your energy and the way you move through life with grace and resilience. You don't need to teach or preach; your presence becomes a lesson in living in alignment with your deepest truth.

Remember, Your Knowing doesn't mean you've figured everything out. You'll still have doubts and moments of uncertainty. The difference is you've learned to trust yourself, and in these moments, you don't panic or crumble. You sit with uncertainty, knowing clarity will come, as it always has. When it does, you act from a place of inner alignment, not fear or desperation.

In daily life, Your Knowing manifests in subtle yet profound ways. It's in how you navigate difficult conversations with grace and empathy. It's in decision-making, big or small, without overthinking, trusting the right path will reveal itself. It's how you approach work, relationships, and creativity with purpose and ease. You stop forcing outcomes, allowing life to unfold, trusting whatever happens, you can handle it.

In these moments, you realise Your Knowing is not something you practice, it is who you are. It's woven into your being, showing up in every aspect of life, from the mundane to the extraordinary. It's not something you consciously think about anymore. It's there, guiding you, quietly yet powerfully, in everything you do.

Ultimately, Your Knowing is a gift, to yourself, and to the world around you. It's a gift which continually evolves, grows, and deepens. It is a reminder life's greatest wisdom comes not from outside sources, but from within. The more you trust it, the more fully you'll live, with peace, purpose, and authenticity.

Your Knowing represents a profound integration of spiritual depth with practical wisdom, marked by continuous growth, authentic expression, and a compassionate perspective toward life. It is both a personal journey and a collective contribution, as the wisdom gained is not kept in isolation, but shared and demonstrated through meaningful actions.

CHAPTER 23

MICHAEL'S JOURNEY TO THE KNOWING

IN HIS OWN WORDS

'Quiet the mind and the soul will speak.' — *Gautama Buddha*

The morning was different, though I couldn't pinpoint why. I had woken up countless times in the same bed, under the same ceiling, with the same routine ahead of me, but this day, something shifted. I sensed a pull, a deep restlessness gnawing at my thoughts before I could even understand it. It wasn't a fleeting feeling; it was more like an itch in the deepest part of me, a whisper telling me I was meant for something else, something attainable and within my reach.

I couldn't ignore it. As the day began, I moved through my familiar tasks, brushing my teeth, making coffee, staring at the news, but everything felt irrelevant and hollow. My mind wasn't in it; it was elsewhere, chasing something I didn't yet have a name for, but I could feel it, a distant echo of something important; like a calling, or perhaps an awakening. The Knowing, they called it, and now, for the first time in my life, it was as if it was calling me.

The Knowing was one of those things people never spoke about directly. It was always in the background, mentioned in passing, as though it was too elusive to be fully explained. Friends had spoken of it as if it were a myth, something whispered about in quiet moments, but no one could ever define what it truly meant.

'You'll know when it's time,' they'd say with a smile which was equal parts mystery and gloominess. I had never pressed them for answers.

I packed a small bag with the bare essentials, not knowing how long I'd be gone or where I was headed. I knew I needed to leave. The weight of my old life felt too heavy, too constricting, as though it was holding me back from something I couldn't yet see. I closed the door behind me, feeling a strange sense of finality, though I wasn't certain if I'd be back or what I'd return to.

There was no map to follow, no set path to The Knowing. I knew it from the beginning. Every story I had heard was different. Some people found it in the depths of their darkest moments; others claimed it came in dreams. I didn't know where I would find mine, but I knew the journey wasn't about searching for something external. It was about finding what had been inside me all along.

Within hours, I left the city behind, its noise fading into the background as I ventured further into the unknown. The buildings, the streets, and the people all blurred together as if they belonged to another life. The road ahead was long and winding, stretching out before me like an open invitation. I walked without real direction, trusting the pull which had started from deep within me.

By the second day, I found myself deep in the wilderness. The air smelled different out here, cleaner, more ancient. It was as though the trees, the earth, and the sky were all part of something bigger, something I had always missed in the chaos of everyday life. Out here, the world moved at its own pace, untouched by the rushing hands of the clock. Time seemed to slow down, practically stop, it was a surreal moment.

The wilderness had a way of stripping everything down to its essence. There were no distractions, no voices, no obligations. There was me, the sound of my footsteps crunching through the forest floor, the wind brushing against the trees, and in the silence, I began to hear things I hadn't heard before, not with my ears, but with something deeper, more primal. The voice inside me grew louder, clearer. It wasn't speaking in words; it was more of a feeling, an understanding I had always known but had somehow forgotten.

Each night, I set up camp under the stars, staring up at the vastness of the sky above me. The stars seemed brighter out here, more real. Their light less like distant fire and more like a connection to something ancient, something beyond the comprehension of my day-to-day life. Each night, as I lay there, I felt myself falling deeper into the journey, both physically and spiritually. I had been walking for days, but it seemed I hadn't even scratched the surface of what lay ahead.

The deeper I ventured, the more the outside world faded into insignificance. My old concerns, my old goals, they seemed laughably small now. I had spent much of my life chasing success, recognition, and control. But out here, none of it mattered. The trees didn't care who I was. The wind didn't ask me about my accomplishments. Out here, I was another seeking soul, wandering through a vast, unknowable universe.

By the fifth day, I found myself in a clearing. The forest had opened up, revealing a wide expanse of open sky, the sun hanging low and casting a golden light across the landscape. I had seen sunsets before, but this one was different. There's a stillness in the air, a kind of quiet which pressed against my skin, and then it happened, without fanfare, without drama. The Knowing arrived.

I can't say exactly what it was or how it affected me. It wasn't like a lightning strike or a sudden epiphany. It was more like a subtle shift, as if something inside me had quietly clicked into place. I sat down in the middle of the clearing, feeling the cool grass beneath me, and for the first time in my life, I was truly at peace. It was as though the universe had whispered its deepest secrets to me, not in words, but in a profound, wordless understanding.

I realised then The Knowing wasn't something to chase; it had been with me all along, waiting for me to slow down and listen. It wasn't about acquiring new wisdom but recognising the quiet truth within me. As I sat there, time seemed irrelevant. The stars appeared and by the time I stood up, the sky a vast ocean of light above me. I now understood the journey had never been about reaching a destination. The Knowing wasn't something you could find on a map or measure with steps. It was about understanding the real journey was the one unfolding within me.

I didn't need to go any further or look for answers because I had found what I was seeking, not out there, but within myself. The Knowing wasn't a moment, place, or achievement; it was a state of being. As I stood there under the vastness of the sky, I finally understood. The journey I had embarked on was not about finding something external or reaching a particular destination. I realised The Knowing a mysterious revelation, a place, or a piece of wisdom to be sought and captured. Instead, it was an inner transformation, an in-depth awareness which had always been within me, waiting for me to slow down, listen, and understand.

I grasped the answers I had been searching for were not in the world around me but in the silence and stillness of my being. The Knowing was the realisation life's greatest truths don't come from chasing achievements, external validations, or knowledge. Instead, they come from recognising the quiet wisdom which already exists within all of us. Ultimately, I understood the journey itself was the purpose and true clarity comes from embracing who we are, not what we accomplish. It was a shift in perspective, a profound under-standing everything I needed was already inside me and peace, acceptance, and self-awareness were the essence of The Knowing.

When the moment of revelation arrived, I sensed an overwhelming peace wash over me, like a weight I had been carrying for a long time had finally lifted. It wasn't sudden or jarring; there was no dramatic moment of clarity, but rather a quiet, gentle unfolding of truth. I had been searching for something, for answers, for meaning, as if they existed somewhere outside of me, waiting to be discovered. But now, sitting there, it all seemed quite clear.

I remained calm, serene, as if the turbulence of my thoughts had stilled, leaving a deep sense of knowing. It wasn't an intellectual understanding; there were no words, no formulas, no clear-cut realisations. It was something far deeper, something I had realised all along but had never truly grasped. There was a strange mix of relief and joy within me. Relief because the endless searching, the striving for something elusive, had come to an end. And joy, not the loud, exuberant kind, but a quiet, fulfilling happiness which came from knowing I didn't have to look any further. The answers were never out there; they were always inside me, in the stillness I had been too busy to notice.

For the first time in what seemed like forever, I wasn't caught up in questions, doubts, or the need to achieve something. I was connected, to myself and to everything around me. The trees, the sky, the wind, they were all alive, and I realised they had always been part of the same truth I was now living.

I felt gratitude, too. Not for the destination, because I now understood there was none, but for the journey itself. Every step I had taken, every doubt, every struggle, it had all led me here, to this simple, profound understanding. And for this, I felt a deep, abiding appreciation. In the clearing, under the vastness of the sky, I was no longer searching, no longer striving. I was aware, and in my awareness, I was whole.

As I sat there in the clearing, under the open sky, I felt the weight of my old beliefs pressing in from the edges of my mind. My faith had been a cornerstone of my life for as long as I could remember, an anchor in times of uncertainty, a guiding light when the world felt chaotic. I had always turned to my religious convictions for answers, for structure, for comfort. And yet, in the quiet of the moment, something was different.

I had expected The Knowing to align with my faith, to perhaps deepen my understanding of the divine in the ways I had always been taught. But as the realisation unfolded within me, I found myself questioning everything. It wasn't as if I had lost my belief in something greater, far from it, but the way I understood it, the way I had framed it in my mind, it was too small, too rigid. My faith had always been built around ideas, rules, and doctrines which tried to explain the unknowable, to put it into neat, understandable boxes.

It was as if I had glimpsed something far beyond those boxes. The Knowing wasn't something which could be contained in words, symbols, or rituals. It was bigger than any one belief system, vaster than the confines of my religious teachings had ever allowed. It wasn't about dogma, right and wrong, or a clear set of answers. It was a simple, profound awareness of interconnectedness, of being part of something infinite which defied explanation.

A strange mix of emotions were swirling in my mind. There was a sense of loss, like mourning, as if the version of my faith I had held on to tightly was slipping away. But at the same time, there was relief. I no longer needed the pressure to understand everything, to fit the mysteries of existence into the framework I had been given. I didn't need to have all the answers anymore.

I realised this peace came from accepting the unknown, from letting go of the need for control and certainty. It was about trusting in the flow of life, in the idea everything was connected and I didn't need to understand how or why. For the moment, it didn't matter what came next, or where my path would lead. I didn't need to know the answers to the questions which had haunted me for a long time. I didn't need to label the divine or define the purpose of my existence. The peace I felt came from knowing it was all okay, I was part of something vast and infinite, and this alone was enough.

It wasn't a peace which could be explained to others, or what made it powerful. It wasn't about convincing myself or anyone else of a particular truth. Furthermore, it was beyond words, beyond reasoning. It was a deep, abiding calm I carried within me, untouched by the circumstances of the world or the questions of the mind.

It wasn't something I could explain, but it didn't need explaining. It was there, filling me from the inside, grounding me in the present moment, and making everything else, every worry, every doubt, every unanswered question, seem small and insignificant in the face of this quiet, boundless peace. It was then, I realised, I had found the greatest freedom of all.

CHAPTER 24

MICHAEL, PETER, AND MELISSA SHARE EXPERIENCES

'Happiness does not depend on what you have or who you are.
It solely relies on what you think' – Gautama Buddha

In the stillness of Michael's Garden, the air hung heavy with the sweet scent of blooming Jasmine and the gentle rustling of leaves. Michael, Peter, and Melissa sat together in a circle on the cool stone benches, the garden's serene beauty wrapping around them like an embrace. Nature, with its winding paths, soft fountains, and towering pine trees, seemed to stand watch over their conversation. The sun, casting its golden farewell light, dipped low, bathing everything in a warm, contemplative glow.

Michael, ever the steady presence, spoke first. His voice, calm yet layered with meaning, broke the silence.

"This garden... it's seen much of my journey toward My Knowing," he stated, eyes sweeping the familiar trees as though greeting old friends. "It wasn't always easy. In fact, the road was filled with challenges and doubt. But it led me here, to understand The Knowing reveals itself from within, not something found out there."

Peter, seated across from him, nodded slowly, his gaze thoughtful.

"I used to believe it was something external, something I had to hunt for or achieve like a goal. But now, after everything, I've come to realise it's been inside me all along. The trick is quieting the noise of the world long enough to hear it." He paused, looking at the small fountain nearby, where water trickled softly over smooth stones. "For a long time, I doubted it. Doubted myself. But now, I'm learning to trust my inner voice, even when I can't see the full picture."

Melissa, her legs folded beneath her, listened quietly, her eyes soft with reflection.

"For me," she began, her voice gentle but resolute, "My Knowing wasn't about understanding myself. It was about stripping away all the layers, layers of expectation, both from others and from myself. I spent too much time living for people's approval. It's taken a long time, but now, I'm starting to live for me, to trust who I am is enough." She smiled, wistfully. "The Knowing, for me, is about embracing vulnerability and understanding I don't need to prove anything to anyone."

Michael's eyes crinkled in a quiet smile.

"It's remarkable how our paths have been quite different, yet they've all led us to this same place. It's like we've been walking separate roads which all converged here, in this moment."

Peter leaned forward, elbows resting on his knees.

"What I've found fascinating is The Knowing isn't about certainty. It's about learning to trust the process, even when everything feels uncertain. I've realised I don't need all the answers, sometimes, it's enough to trust where I'm headed."

Melissa, playing with the edge of her scarf, nodded in agreement.

"Exactly. I used to think I needed control over everything in my life. But now I see there's more freedom in letting go, in allowing things to unfold as they will. It's in surrendering to the flow, and it's there I've found my strength."

The breeze whispered through the trees as if nature itself was participating in their conversation. Silence settled between them, a peaceful, reflective silence where their words echoed in the air.

Michael spoke again, his voice was soft but full of conviction.

"The Knowing doesn't end with us. It's a journey which continues to evolve as we do. We can share it, not by telling others how to find it, but by living in alignment with it ourselves, and by showing the way."

Peter smiled; his expression thoughtful. "Maybe this is why we're here together, in this moment. We've each found our way, but now we can support each other and be a source of inspiration for those still searching."

Melissa's eyes shone with quiet understanding.

"Yes. The Knowing isn't about reaching a destination. It's about embracing the journey, with all its uncertainties, trusting we're exactly where we need to be, even if the path is winding."

The sun dipped lower, casting long, soft shadows across the garden. The three sat in peaceful harmony, more connected than ever, to each other and to the quiet truth of The Knowing which bound them.

Michael's smile deepened. "It's wonderful to see how far both of you have come on your paths. Tell me, what does The Knowing mean to each of you now?"

Peter, his gaze distant as he reflected, spoke first.

"For me, My Knowing was about finding peace, peace from my past, my insecurities, from everything which used to weigh me down. I thought if I could find it, everything would be perfect. But now, I realise peace isn't something external. It's something I carry with me, no matter what's happening around me. The world can be chaos, but My Knowing keeps me grounded."

Melissa smiled; her face soft with understanding. "For me, it started as a way to connect more deeply with others, especially with both of you. I thought The Knowing would help me understand people better, to align with them more. But it's become much more personal. It's about connecting with myself. The more I know myself, the more authentic my connections with others have become. It's like by knowing myself, I can truly be present with everyone else."

Michael nodded, his smile widening as they spoke.

"Yes, The Knowing often starts as one thing and transforms as we grow. Therein lies the beauty of it, ever-evolving, as we do."

Peter leaned back; his expression thoughtful. "I've also learned it's not about adding more, but about letting go, letting go of the noise, the expectations, all the things which aren't necessary. It's about stripping away and finding what's always been there underneath."

Melissa tilted her head, her eyes thoughtful. "It feels like learning to listen to a language I've always known but somehow forgot. Now, I try to listen more, to myself, to the world, and to the spaces between words. There's much wisdom in the silence."

The three sat quietly for a moment, the garden around them a reflection of the stillness in their hearts. Michael looked at them, his voice filled with gratitude.

"The Knowing is personal, yes, but it's also something we can share through presence, through holding space for each other's journeys, allowing them to unfold in their own time."

Peter nodded, his eyes softening. "It's not about fixing or solving. It's about being present, for ourselves, for each other. The Knowing helps me remember."

Melissa's smile warmed, reflecting the beauty of the moment. "And sitting here, sharing this understanding, it reminds me of how beautiful the journey is. We may walk different paths, but The Knowing connects us in ways words can't express."

The air felt lighter, the garden itself offering a quiet affirmation. Together, they sat in peaceful reflection, aware their paths would continue to evolve but being aware, through The Knowing, they were forever connected.

Michael's voice broke the silence again, filled with curiosity. "What's been the most challenging part of this journey for you both?"

Peter, with a steady but contemplative tone, responded first.

"Letting go of my need to control everything, was the hardest. I had to trust in the process, in what you taught us about surrendering."

Melissa, eyes soft yet filled with depth, added, "For me, it was facing the truths within myself. Some were painful. Accepting my vulnerabilities, not hiding from them, was challenging. But it's also been liberating. It's strange how the things we resist the most often set us free."

Michael nodded; his eyes full of understanding. "The chall-enges we face on this path are often the greatest growth oppor-tunities. It's not about what's comfortable, but about embracing discomfort, knowing it has something to teach us."

Peter, placing his hand over his heart, reflected, "It's been a journey of turning inward. I always thought the answers were out there, but they've been in here, all along."

Melissa smiled warmly at Peter. "Sharing this journey with you, Peter has brought us closer. It's made our bond stronger. I've learned as much from you as I have from The Knowing itself."

Michael's eyes sparkled with pride.

"The Knowing doesn't isolate us; it connects us. You two are living proof of this. The way you've grown, both together and individually, is a testament to the power of this journey. The Knowing is personal, but it's also collective. We're all connected."

Peter, his voice a mix of curiosity and reverence, asked, "What about you, Michael? How has your understanding of The Knowing evolved?"

Michael smiled softly; his gaze thoughtful.

"Every person I meet, every story I hear, enriches my understanding. The Knowing is boundless, always growing, always flowing. What I knew ten years ago is different from what I know now, and it will continue to evolve. The Knowing adapts as we do, offering new layers as we're ready for them."

Melissa, filled with gratitude, looked at Michael. "Thank you, Michael, for guiding us with such patience. This journey has been transformative."

Michael's response was simple yet heartfelt. "Thank you both for trusting the process. The Knowing is in all of us; but we need to listen. It's always there, waiting."

And as the three sat in the garden, their conversation lingering in the air like a gentle breeze, they knew they were part of something far bigger than themselves.

Connected by their journeys, bound by their shared experience of The Knowing, they understood this was the beginning.

CHAPTER 25

THE IMPACT OF THE KNOWING ON PETER AND MELISSA

'If you want to fly, give up everything which weighs you down.'
– Gautama Buddha

The Knowing isn't a lofty idea or a distant, abstract philosophy, no, it's something far deeper, more immediate. It's a way of being, a state of flowing effortlessly with life's unpredictable rhythms. Imagine living in a world where you can embrace uncertainty, not with fear, but with quiet confidence. The Knowing invites you to step into the present moment without constantly grasping for control, without needing to explain or justify everything. It's a profound shift, introduced by Michael, a man whose presence embodies this concept. For Michael, it isn't something to ponder; it's a lived experience, a way of navigating life's chaos with unshakable calm, resilience, and grace.

At its core, The Knowing is about realising one simple but transformative truth: we are not separate from the world around us. We are intricately connected, woven into a vast web of experiences, relationships, emotions, and forces far beyond our comprehension. Michael lives by example. His unwavering calm, the way he remains steady no matter what life throws his way, is a testament to his Knowing. His love for humanity, his quiet strength, and his ability to face challenges without flinching, all reflect a deeper understanding of life's inherent complexities.

For Michael, The Knowing isn't some abstract theory to be dissected and debated. It's a lived, tangible experience. Each day, he approaches life with a palpable grace, an awareness life, no matter how messy, unpredictable, or painful, can still be fully embraced. He doesn't seek to control life; he embraces it. And through this acceptance, he finds peace. It's this peace which gives him the ability to face any challenge, no matter how daunting, and without fear.

Peter's Journey into The Knowing:

I began my journey with a different mindset. Logic, control, and analysis have always defined my approach to life. For me, every problem has a solution, every outcome could be controlled if I worked hard enough, thought long enough, planned meticulously enough. Yet, despite my best efforts, fulfillment remained out of reach, like a shadow I could never quite catch. My relentless pursuit of answers brought more stress, more questions, and a deep sense of disconnection, from others, from myself, and from life itself.

When I first met Michael, I was both intrigued and perplexed. There's something about Michael's calm, his effortless peace, which stirred something in me, something I didn't even know was missing. Initially I was sceptical, but as I watched Michael's unruffled demeanour I slowly began to wonder if there might be something to this thing called The Knowing. But I am a man of logic. I want to understand, to dissect, to categorise. And The Knowing defies all of this. It cannot be understood in the traditional sense; it has to be experienced.

Gradually, as I opened myself up to this new way of living, subtle but powerful changes start to take root. I began to notice my need to control every situation started to fade. Life, once a series of problems to be solved, begins to feel like a series of moments to be experienced. I pause before reacting, breathing through moments of tension, and I start trusting I can handle whatever life throws my way. The Knowing brings me calmness, clarity, and most importantly, the realisation life doesn't need to be wrestled into submission to be enjoyed.

This shift transformed my relationships as well. Where I once felt the need to guide, fix, or control, I now listen more deeply, to Melissa, to my friends, and myself. My connection with Melissa, in particular, deepened. I no longer feel the need to protect or guide her constantly, I have learned to be with her and accept her as she is. In my professional life, my writing began to reflect this inner transformation. My work, once driven by the need to construct meaning, now flows naturally from the truths I have discovered within myself.

But perhaps the most profound change is the newfound confidence The Knowing gives me. It's not the kind of confidence which comes from knowing all the answers, but the quiet assurance which comes from trusting life's flow. Challenges no longer seem like battles to be won but opportunities to grow. My self-doubt, my anxiety over the future, and my obsessive need for certainty began to dissolve as I embraced life's uncertainty with calm acceptance.

Melissa's Evolution Through The Knowing:
Melissa, intuitive and emotionally aware by nature, finds The Knowing resonates deeply with her. Always someone who nurtured others, Melissa sometimes found herself overwhelmed, carrying the weight of other people's emotions. But The Knowing has taught her a valuable lesson: she doesn't have to carry the world on her shoulders.

Because of it, Melissa learns she can support others without absorbing their pain. She can be compassionate without losing herself in the process. This shift brings her a sense of freedom and resilience. She no longer feels the need to manage every detail or to ensure everyone around her is happy. Instead, she trusts life is unfolding as it should, as each person's journey is their own to walk. This new understanding allows her to focus on her growth and happiness, free from the weight of guilt and responsibility which once burdened her.

In her relationship with me, The Knowing created a deeper harmony. Melissa meets me where I am, without trying to change me, without trying to fix me. Our bond strengthened as we both learnt to be fully present with each other, creating a space for growth and healing. Melissa becomes more attuned to her emotions and the emotions of those around her, navigating her relationships with greater empathy and understanding.

With The Knowing, Melissa faces life's challenges not with fear, but with an openness to the lessons they bring. Life's obstacles no longer feel like burdens, but like opportunities for deeper self-understanding. In The Knowing, she draws strength from within, a quiet confidence which comes from being fully aligned with the present moment.

The Lasting Influence of The Knowing:

Michael's embodiment of The Knowing acted as a catalyst for Melissa and me, guiding us on our separate journeys of self-discovery. His wisdom, patience, and love for humanity created a space for exploration and growth without pressure or force. Through his quiet example, we began to understand life is not about control, it's about presence. It's about trusting life's flow, even when the current pulls us in unexpected directions.

The changes we experienced weren't dramatic or sudden, they unfolded gradually. As The Knowing weaved its way into the fabric of our everyday lives, we noticed the subtle shifts were trans-formative. As we embraced The Knowing, our relationship grew more harmonious, the challenges less daunting, and our inner worlds more peaceful. We learned life's greatest wisdom doesn't come from understanding everything, it comes from being open to everything.

The Reader's Invitation to The Knowing:

As a reader, you too are invited to reflect on your own life. What would it be like to live with this kind of presence and acceptance? To let go of the need to control outcomes or understand every twist in your path? Imagine facing each day with the quiet confidence, no matter what happens, you have the resilience to meet it.

The Knowing offers you a life of greater peace, clarity, and connection. It teaches peace doesn't come from avoiding life's difficulties, but from embracing them with an open heart. By practicing The Knowing, the things you once feared, uncertainty, change, and challenge, may become your greatest sources of growth and fulfillment.

In embracing the concepts, you will discover the peace which you have been searching for, has always been within you, patiently waiting to be remembered.

CHAPTER 26

LEONARD AND MICHAEL

'Believe nothing, no matter where you read it, or who said it, no matter if I have said it, unless it agrees with your own reason and your own common sense.' — Gautama Buddha

Leonard stands tall, at a solid six feet. An imposing figure which commands the room with every step. His presence is not about his height, though. It's the meticulous grooming, the silver-grey hair swept back with precision, and the eyes, those deep-set brown eyes, sharp, probing, always calculating. He's the kind of man whose appearance mirrors his life: disciplined, structured, and efficient. His tailored suits? They aren't for show. They reflect the detail and order he's infused into every corner of his existence, from his booming career to his ironclad belief system.

Leonard's strengths are clear. He's a businessman to his core. Also, a strategist, a negotiator who can spot an opportunity from a mile away and close a deal before anyone else even realises what's happening. He navigates complex situations like a sailor in familiar waters, calm, steady, with an unwavering hand. His Christian faith is his anchor, the moral compass which keeps him steady in both life and work. Integrity, discipline, loyalty, these aren't mere words to him, they're principles etched into his being, and people respect him for it.

But, there's always a '*but*,' isn't there? His convictions, as noble as they may be, can sometimes trap him, and his unwavering certainty can harden into rigidity. Leonard, the master of negotiation, and the pragmatic thinker, can become locked in his beliefs, unwilling to bend or even entertain an idea which doesn't fit neatly into his worldview. New ideas? Alternative approaches? They seem flimsy, uncertain, and even reckless to a man who thrives on structure. And, when something like The Knowing comes along, something intangible, fluid, it grates against everything he stands for. He resists and dismisses it as fantasy, a crutch for those who can't handle reality.

Yet, here he is. Sitting across from Michael, the man who introduced him to The Knowing. Leonard had been sceptical then, he's still sceptical now, but something about Michael's words lingered on his conscience. Something which wouldn't let him walk away.

Michael leans back in his chair, eyes calm but piercing. He doesn't beat around the bush.

"Leonard, when we first met, you made it clear you thought my lecture was fantasy. You called The Knowing wishful thinking, for the weak-minded."

Leonard doesn't blink. "Yes, I did say it. And believe me, I thought a lot worse which I didn't say out loud."

"And yet," Michael's voice is steady, "you're here."

Leonard shifts slightly, the discomfort of being challenged evident, but his composure remained intact.

"Yes, I am. I've been thinking about what you said. It's... it's the opposite of everything I've built my life on; Structure, certainty, and belief, but there's something about it... I couldn't shake it from my mind." Michael's nod is imperceptible, as if he expected this all along.

"It's natural to resist, Leonard. Especially when your core beliefs have served you as long as they have. But something brought you here today. You wouldn't be here if there wasn't something deeper pushing you to explore this."

Leonard, always one for directness, cuts to the heart of the matter. "I still can't fully buy into this idea of The Knowing. It feels...

reckless. Uncertain. I've built my life, my business, and my faith, on solid and proven principles. You're talking about something without a framework, without structure. Which goes against everything I know."

Michael leans forward, eyes locking onto Leonard's, the intensity of the moment rising.

"This is what makes it difficult, Leonard. You've built your life on certainty, on structures which have served you well. The Knowing doesn't ask you to abandon any of it. It invites you to look beyond it. To see there's something more, something intuitive, fluid. It's not about rejecting what you know; it's about deepening your understanding."

Leonard, arms crossed now, his posture guarded. "But how can something without a clear structure provide any real guidance? In business, if you don't have a plan or a strategy, you fail. You can't leave things up to chance."

Michael's voice remains steady, unflinching.

"Here's where you're misunderstanding. The Knowing isn't about leaving things to chance. And it's not without structure, the structure isn't external, it's internal. It's about trusting yourself, your intuition, your connection to life, and the divine flow through it. Sometimes, no matter how essential your plans and strategies are, they can't capture the full spectrum of what's possible."

Leonard leans back, his gaze still locked on Michael, his mind racing.

"You're saying I should abandon everything I have relied on. Everything which has given me success and certainty, to follow... what? A vague feeling? It sounds dangerous. It sounds like a way to lose focus, to get lost in your mind."

Michael shakes his head; his voice is soft but resolute.

"No, Leonard, not at all. You don't abandon anything. The strength, discipline, and principles you've cultivated, remain. The Knowing complements them. It allows you to see where rigidity might blind you to other possibilities. It's not about losing yourself. It's about opening yourself to what you already know, deep down, but maybe haven't yet acknowledged because of the structure you rely on."

Leonard exhales, his arms uncrossing as he considers Michael's words. "This could enhance what I already know? Not tear it down?"

Michael smiles slightly, nodding. "Exactly. Think of it this way: in business, you rely on numbers, data, and analysis. But sometimes, you go on instinct, don't you? A gut feeling which tells you to make a certain move, to trust a certain person, even when the data doesn't quite add up? The Knowing is like instinct. It's the part of you which understands things before your mind can rationalise it and it also goes much deeper."

Michael leans back, his eyes softening as he speaks, his voice a whisper.

"And maybe, Leonard, the greatest faith is the one which allows you to embrace the unknown."

Leonard sits in silence, absorbing the weight of truth. For the first time, the rigid lines of his certainty begin to blur. The Knowing, elusive as it may be, seems less like chaos and more like... possibility.

"I've had those moments in business, where my gut told me something before, I could explain it. But this is different, isn't it? This is about faith... about something bigger."

"Yes, it is. The Knowing invites you to recognise this same instinct. This same inner guidance, applies to business and to life itself, to your faith, to your understanding of the world and your place in it. It's about listening to the deeper voice, Your Knowing, which is often drowned out by the noise of everyday life and external expectations."

"I've always been taught to trust in the Church, to follow its teachings unquestionably. This... this feels like questioning every-thing."

"I understand how these ideas could feel unsettling. But The Knowing doesn't ask you to reject your faith. It often deepens faith by encouraging you to see it as a living, breathing relationship with the divine, rather than something static. It's about moving from belief to experience, from the mind to the heart. It's about trusting the answers you seek are not found in doctrine but it's within you, in the quiet places of your soul."

Leonard sat quietly for a moment, staring at the floor.

"It's hard to let go of control, Michael. I've built my life around being in control, of having things mapped out."

"And you've done well because of control, Leonard. But perhaps now, you're being invited to let go, a little bit, not to lose control, but to allow yourself to see what else might be waiting for you when you do. Your Knowing is not about chaos; it's about trusting the flow of life, knowing you don't need to control every moment to find meaning or truth."

Leonard looked up, a hint of vulnerability in his eyes. "What if I don't like what I find when I let go?"

"Then you will have learned something valuable. But more often than not, Leonard, when we allow ourselves to truly let go, we discover what lies beneath the surface is far more beautiful, far more connected, than we ever imagined. The Knowing is about trusting the divine is with you, in you, guiding you, whether you are in control or not."

"I'm not sure, I'm ready to dive in, Michael. But... I'll think about what you've said."

Michael gently replied, "Leonard, thinking is the first step. And when you're ready, whether it's today, tomorrow, or years from now, The Knowing will be there, waiting for you."

"We'll see. I'm not one to rush into things, but maybe... maybe there's more to this than I thought." He nodded.

"I believe there is. And whenever you're ready, the journey will begin at the right time. I understand your commitment to Christian teachings. They provide structure and a foundation for many, but The Knowing is not about replacing belief systems. It's about an inner recognition, a personal understanding of existence which transcends doctrine."

"But Michael, you're talking about something without any foundation. Christian teachings are grounded in centuries of study, scripture, and tradition. The Knowing, as you call it, seems like a vague concept, how can it compare to the solid ground of faith?"

"Faith is personal, Leonard, as is The Knowing. It's not about dismantling Christianity or any religion. It's about understanding the life force which binds us, the connection to all things. Christianity provides answers, yes, but The Knowing encourages us to ask more in-depth questions, to explore beyond what is written."

"Questions? What more do we need to ask when the Bible gives us the answers? The teachings of the Church are clear. We have a guide to salvation, a clear path. Your Knowing is nothing more than speculative philosophy."

"Speculative, perhaps, from where you stand. But consider this: The Church teaches faith in the unseen; in things we cannot fully comprehend. The Knowing invites us to explore those same mysteries, not as rigid dogma, but as lived experiences. It's not bound by texts or traditions, it's discovered within."

"The Church isn't about restricting discovery; it's about finding the truth! There's a difference between personal feelings and objective reality. Christianity provides answers and guidance. What you're suggesting leaves people adrift, chasing illusions."

"On the contrary, Leonard. The Knowing doesn't leave any-one adrift; it guides them to understand the truths, within themselves. The Church speaks of a personal relationship with God, yes? The Knowing is another way of seeking a relationship, without the boundaries of institutional frameworks. It's not about illusion; it's about embracing the unknown as part of the journey."

Leonard replies firmly, "You can't replace tradition and Scripture with this abstract idea of 'personal truth,' Michael. It's dangerous to think this way. The Church is the one true path to understanding God and salvation. Without it, where is the certainty?"

"Certainty, Leonard, is often an illusion itself. Life is filled with uncertainty, but within it, we find growth. The Knowing isn't a rejection of truth, it's an acceptance truth may be more expansive than any one belief system. You may find your answers through the Church, but others may find them through different means. Neither is invalid." Replied Michael calmly.

"We'll have to agree to disagree, then. I need the grounding Christianity offers. What you're talking about seems too loose, too uncertain for me."

Michael, smiling gently, "Leonard, the beauty of life is we each walk our path. My hope is, in time, we learn to respect all paths as valid, even if we don't fully understand them. You're right, Christianity has given many people a firm foundation, and a sense of guidance. It answers questions about life, morality, and the afterlife.

But The Knowing isn't an answer in the same sense. It's not about providing a set of rules or an ultimate destination. It's about the journey itself, the constant unfolding of life as we experience it."

"But it's here where we fundamentally disagree. Faith is supposed to give you certainty. We are not meant to wander, searching for some undefined truth. The Church offers the clearest path, through scripture, through the teachings of Christ. It's not what you feel at the moment or what you experience. It's about what is."

"I respect what you say, Leonard. The Church, through its structure and teachings, offers a kind of certainty which many need. But isn't it also true, even within Christianity, there are mysteries which defy explanation? The Trinity, for example, or the concept of grace? These are not concrete facts; they require faith and an openness to the unknown. The Knowing is an invitation to sit with those mysteries rather than forcing them into a rigid understanding."

"Those are mysteries, yes, but they're divinely revealed mysteries. We may not fully comprehend them, but they have been given to us by God. They aren't open-ended ideas for us to interpret however we wish. There's the danger of what you're proposing. You're talking about letting people define truth for themselves as if each person's truth is equal."

Michael calmly and with conviction replies.

"I understand your fear, Leonard. It seems chaotic to think everyone can have their truth. But what I'm saying is truth is not relative. Rather, truth is multifaceted, and each person is equipped to discover their relationship to it. The Knowing acknowledges the divine or whatever name you want to give it, and it speaks to each of us in a way we can understand. For some, their path is Christianity, for others, it may be through nature, through silence, through the simple act of being. None of these paths invalidates the others."

"But it's here where I struggle, Michael. The Church has already given us the right way to know God. Through scripture, the sacraments, and the teachings of the saints; it's all there. What need do we have of this Knowing? You're advocating for people to stray from the true path which can lead to moral chaos."

"I'm not asking people to abandon their faith, Leonard. I'm suggesting faith can be more expansive than we allow. The saints themselves, many of them mystics, often stepped outside the boundaries of the institutional Church in their search for God. St. John of the Cross spoke of the 'dark night of the soul,' where even the most devout believers experience doubts and a lack of clarity. The Knowing encourages us to sit with doubt and uncertainty. It doesn't reject tradition but allows it to breathe, to grow alongside our personal experiences."

"And yet, those mystics always returned to the Church! They didn't abandon its teachings; they deepened their understanding within the framework God provided. This is what you're missing, Michael. All these personal explorations you talk about, they're dangerous without the Church's guidance. You can't rely on personal feelings or experiences. Truth is not subjective."

"But Leonard, even within the Church, people experience God differently. One person's experience of faith is not the same as another's. It doesn't mean one is more valid than the other. Look at the diversity of saints, some were scholars, others simple people of deep prayer. Their paths to God were unique. The Knowing says we must honour those differences in how we approach the divine, even if the destination is the same. It's not about subjectivity, it's about respecting the divine reveals itself in myriad ways."

"There's one way to the divine, Michael, and it's through Jesus Christ, the Son of God. 'I am the way, the truth, and the life. No one comes to the Father except through me.' It's not open to interpretation." Leonard replied firmly but with growing frustration.

"And I don't dispute it, Leonard. For you, and many others, it's the absolute truth. But consider this: what if The Knowing is another way of understanding Christ's word? What if, in discovering The Knowing, people are ultimately drawn back to the truth you hold dearly? It doesn't threaten faith, it deepens it by encouraging exploration, by allowing people to question and seek answers, as Christ himself asked his disciples to 'seek, and you shall find'."

Leonard, after a pause, calmer but still resolute, "I understand what you're saying, but it's still too uncertain for me. I can't follow a path which doesn't offer the certainty of salvation. The Church gives me certainty, Christ gives me certainty. I can't rely on something as vague as The Knowing."

Michael smiled gently, "I understand, Leonard. Faith, like The Knowing, is deeply personal. For some, certainty is essential. My hope is, in time, we can accept certainty for one may be different for another, and both paths lead to the same source of truth. We are all seekers in this life, and the ways we find meaning may differ, but the divine remains at the heart of it all."

Leonard sighs, nodding slowly, "I suppose we'll have to agree to disagree, Michael. But I appreciate the conversation."

As do I, Leonard. Overall, it's these conversations which help us grow, whether we change our minds or not, the exchange of ideas is part of the journey." Michael answered. "Let me explain The Knowing in more detail. It's not some abstract or fanciful idea. It's quite practical, though its origins are rooted in something beyond the ordinary. The Knowing is about awareness, a kind of deep inner awareness which transcends the everyday noise of life. It's about being in touch with the essence of existence, not as an intellectual exercise, but as something you feel and live every day."

"I hear what you're saying, but it still sounds vague to me. What exactly is this essence of existence you're talking about?" Asked Leonard.

"It's hard to put into words because it's not a concept which fits neatly into language. Imagine for a moment, you've been looking at the world through a fogged-up window. You can see shapes and outlines, but the clarity isn't there. The Knowing is like wiping a window clean. Everything comes into sharp focus, but not in a way you could have expected. It's not because new information is revealed, but rather the same world takes on a depth, a meaning, which wasn't apparent before."

"But it sounds to me, subjective. How can you trust something which is based on a feeling or personal experience? It could be misleading."

"Yes, it is subjective in a sense, but it doesn't make it unreliable. It's about a shift in perception, not a belief in an external doctrine. Think about the times when you've felt the presence of God in a deeply personal way, beyond the words of scripture or the rituals of the Church. In those moments, didn't you feel something greater, something more intimate? Your Knowing is an ongoing state of a similar kind of awareness. It's the recognition life itself is sacred and this sacredness can be felt, seen, and known in every moment if you are present enough to it."

"I've had those moments, yes, but the Church helps me understand them. Without structure, those feelings could be misinterpreted."

"I understand why structure feels necessary. We crave cert-ainty, especially when dealing with something as profound as the divine. But The Knowing doesn't dismiss the structure; it allows us to see beyond it, to see the essence which gave rise to it. It's like a river. The Church provides the banks to guide the flow, but The Knowing allows you to feel the current itself, to understand the water, the force, and the source which feeds it."

"But how do you know when you've found The Knowing? What does it feel like?"

"It's less about finding and more about realising it's always been there. In moments of profound clarity, when the chatter of your mind quiets down, and you are present, whether in the beauty of nature, in the silence of contemplation, or the love shared between people; there's a sense of connection. You know you are part of something much larger than yourself, but also this larger thing is not separate from you. It's knowing you are deeply interconnected with everything and everyone and life itself is imbued with meaning."

"But life doesn't always feel connected or meaningful. Occasionally, it's chaotic and full of suffering. How does The Knowing account for this?"

"There's the paradox, Leonard. The Knowing doesn't deny suffering or chaos. It acknowledges them as part of the whole, but it doesn't let them define the entire experience. Think of it this way: a storm doesn't invalidate the existence of the sun, periods of suffering don't negate the deeper reality of connection and meaning. The Knowing helps you see, even in the darkest moments, there is still something sacred at work. It doesn't eliminate pain, but it gives you the perspective to see beyond it."

"What you are suggesting is The Knowing offers a way to understand suffering." Leonard remarked.

"Yes, exactly. It's not a solution to suffering, but a shift in how you relate to it. Instead of resisting or fearing it, you begin to see it as part of the unfolding of life. You realise everything, even the painful moments, has its place in the grand tapestry of existence. The Knowing gives you the capacity to accept life as it is, without needing it to conform to your expectations or desires."

"And what about God in all of this? Where does God fit into The Knowing?"

"God is central to The Knowing, though not always in the way people expect. In The Knowing, God isn't a distant figure or a concept to be worshipped from afar. God is the essence of life, the spark within every moment, every breath, every interaction. It's the divine presence which permeates all things. In The Knowing, you come to realise God is not separate from you, but is woven into the fabric of your being. You are an expression of divine presence, as is everything around you."

"If I understand you correctly you are saying, we are all connected to God?"

"Yes, it's what I believe Leonard. The Knowing reveals separation is an illusion. We are all connected; to God, to each other, to all creation. It's not about abandoning your faith, but about deepening it by recognising the divine in every moment of life. The Knowing doesn't ask you to leave behind the Church or its teachings; it asks you to see those teachings as part of a larger, living reality, one which is constantly unfolding, constantly speaking to you if you are open to it."

After a long pause, Leonard replies, "I'm not sure I can fully accept what you say, Michael. But I can understand it comes from a place of sincerity. Maybe there's more to explore here than I originally thought."

"The path to The Knowing isn't something to be rushed, Leonard, it's a gradual unfolding, and it meets each of us when we are ready. The fact you're even considering it is the beginning of the journey." Michael smilingly replied.

CHAPTER 27

THE KNOWING AND CHRISTIANITY

'Three things cannot be long hidden: the sun, the moon, and the truth.' — *Gautama Buddha*

The Knowing, as experienced by Michael, and Christianity, particularly as taught by the Catholic Church, share a focus on understanding life and the divine. However, they differ significantly in their approach to spirituality, truth, and the nature of the relationship between humanity and God. Below is a comparison of The Knowing with Catholic teachings, highlighting their similarities and differences.

The Nature of God and Divinity

Catholic Church:
In Catholicism, God is viewed as a personal, omnipotent, and omniscient being who is separate from His creation. God is the Creator of the universe, the source of all life, and His will governs all things. Catholics believe in the Holy Trinity: God the Father, God the Son (Jesus Christ), and God the Holy Spirit. The relationship between humans and God is based on faith, prayer, and adherence

to His commandments. God reveals Himself through Scripture, tradition, and the Church's teachings, and salvation is achieved through grace, faith, and works.

The Knowing:

The Knowing, as understood by Michael, does not center on a personal, omnipotent God. Instead, it emphasises a more abstract understanding of the divine, one which is intertwined with life itself. The Knowing suggests divinity exists in all things, in nature, in human interactions, and in the flow of life. It is more of a spiritual connection to the universe and its mysteries rather than a relationship with a personal deity. There is no concept of a singular, authoritative God in The Knowing, and instead, divinity is seen as something to be experienced within oneself and the world around them.

Revelation and Sources of Truth

Catholic Church:

In Catholicism, truth is revealed through the Bible (Scripture) and Church tradition. The Church, guided by the Holy Spirit, is considered the authority on interpreting God's will and teachings. Catholics believe in divine revelation, where God actively communicates with humanity through prophets, saints, and most notably through the incarnation of Jesus Christ. The sacraments, particularly the Eucharist, are central to this belief system, acting as a direct encounter with God's grace.

The Knowing:

The Knowing does not rely on any external scripture, revelation, or formal tradition. It is a deeply personal understanding of life's mysteries which arises from within the individual. For Michael, The Knowing was not taught or imparted by any religious authority but discovered through his own experiences and reflections. It is an internal process of awareness rather than an external revelation from a divine source. Unlike Catholicism, where truth is found in religious doctrine, The Knowing emphasises personal insight and a fluid, experiential connection with the universe.

189

The Role of Jesus Christ

Catholic Church:
Central to Catholic teaching is the belief in Jesus Christ as the Son of God, the Saviour of humanity. Catholics believe through His death and resurrection, Jesus redeemed mankind from sin and opened the path to eternal salvation. The Church teaches a personal relationship with Jesus is essential for salvation and through the sacraments, especially baptism, confession, and the Eucharist, Catholics partake in Christ's grace and salvation.

The Knowing:
The Knowing does not place importance on the figure of Jesus Christ in the same way Catholicism does. While Michael may recognise Jesus as a historical or even spiritual figure, The Knowing does not rely on the idea of a Saviour or the need for redemption through another being. Instead, The Knowing focuses on personal under-standing and connection to the greater flow of life. There is no concept of original sin or salvation in The Knowing, and as such, the role of Jesus as a divine redeemer is not part of its framework. Spiritual enlightenment is seen as something to be attained indiv-idually, not through a messianic figure.

Salvation and the Afterlife

Catholic Church:
Catholicism teaches salvation is achieved through grace, faith in Jesus Christ, and good works. Salvation is the deliverance from sin and its consequences, allowing believers to enter eternal life with God in heaven. Catholics also believe in the existence of purgatory, a state of purification for souls who die in God's grace but still require cleansing from venial sins before entering heaven. Hell is considered the ultimate separation from God for those who reject Him.

The Knowing:
The Knowing does not address salvation or the afterlife in the same way as Catholicism. There is no formal concept of sin or redemption,

nor is there an emphasis on the afterlife as a reward or punishment for one's earthly actions. Michael's understanding of The Knowing is more focused on living in the present moment and embracing life as it unfolds, without concern for what comes after death. The Knowing suggests a sense of peace and acceptance of the mysteries of existence, including the uncertainty of death, rather than the pursuit of eternal life in heaven or fear of hell.

Moral Guidance and Sin

Catholic Church:
Catholicism provides a clear moral framework based on the Ten Commandments, the teachings of Jesus, and Church doctrine. Sin is a central concept in Catholicism, representing a violation of God's law. Catholics are taught to avoid sin, seek repentance through confession, and strive to live virtuous lives in adherence to the teachings of the Church. Moral conduct is essential for one's relationship with God and for achieving salvation.

The Knowing:
The Knowing does not prescribe a specific moral code. Instead, it encourages individuals to live in harmony with the world around them and to be present in each moment. The moral framework in The Knowing is more fluid and arises naturally from an understanding of interconnectedness and compassion for others. Rather than focusing on sin and moral absolutes, The Knowing emphasises living with awareness, presence, and authenticity. Michael's approach to ethics in The Knowing is personal and intuitive, not dictated by an external authority or set of rules.

The Role of the Church

Catholic Church:
The Catholic Church plays a central role in the spiritual life of its followers. It is seen as the mediator between God and humanity, providing guidance, sacraments, and moral teaching. Catholics are encouraged to attend Mass regularly, participate in the sacraments,

and follow the Church's teachings. The Church also serves as a community of believers, offering support, fellowship, and a sense of belonging.

The Knowing:

The Knowing is an individual experience which doesn't require an organised community or institutional framework. Michael did not need a church, priest, or congregation to experience The Knowing. His journey was deeply personal, and while he encountered wisdom from various cultures and teachers, The Knowing did not depend on any formal religious structure. It is a solitary journey of discovery, where one finds their path without relying on a religious institution for guidance or validation.

Spiritual Practice and Rituals

Catholic Church:

Catholicism is rich in rituals and practices, including the celebration of the Mass, the sacraments (such as baptism, communion, and confession), prayer, fasting, and devotion to saints. These rituals are seen as a means of receiving God's grace and maintaining a close relationship with Him. The liturgical calendar, with its various feasts and holy days, also plays an important role in the life of Catholics.

The Knowing:

The Knowing does not have formal rituals or religious practices. It is less about structured actions and more about living with mindfulness and presence. For Michael, The Knowing might involve moments of quiet reflection, meditation, or connection with nature, but these practices are informal and spontaneous. There are no prescribed rituals or ceremonies in The Knowing, and spiritual practice is based on personal intuition and experience rather than external require-ments.

Summary

While both The Knowing and Catholicism seek to provide a deeper understanding of life and existence, they do it in fundamentallydifferent ways. Catholicism offers a structured, theistic worldview centred on God's relationship with humanity, the need for salvation through Jesus Christ, and adherence to moral laws and sacraments. The Knowing, by contrast, is a more fluid, individual experience which focuses on personal awareness, interconnectedness, and embracing the mysteries of life without the need for formal doctrine, institutions, or external authority.

In essence, Catholicism provides a well-defined path to salvation through faith, worship, and the sacraments, while The Knowing emphasises a personal, experiential understanding of life and is centred on presence, acceptance, and living in harmony with the world without concern for salvation or divine intervention.

CHAPTER 28

THE KNOWING AND BUDDHISM

'If you light a lamp for somebody, it will also brighten your path.' – Gautama Buddha

The Knowing, as Michael experienced it, shares similarities with certain aspects of Buddhism, but it also diverges in notable ways. Both The Knowing and Buddhism focus on an inner understanding of life and existence, emphasising a departure from rigid structures or dogmatic beliefs. However, their approaches and underlying philosophies provide different perspectives on the nature of reality and enlightenment.

The Nature of Truth

Buddhism:

In Buddhism, truth is deeply connected to the Four Noble Truths and the realisation of the nature of suffering (Dukkha), its causes, and the cessation of suffering through the Eightfold Path. Central to Buddhist philosophy is the idea all of life is impermanent (Annica), and clinging to desires and attachments results in suffering. The ultimate goal is to attain Nirvana, a state of liberation and the extinguishing of desire and ignorance, which ends the cycle of rebirth (Samsara).

The Knowing:

The Knowing, on the other hand, is not a formalised or codified truth like the Four Noble Truths. It is less about structured realisation and more about a deep, personal understanding of life's mysteries. For Michael, The Knowing was about embracing life as it is, without needing to define or categorise it into systems of belief. It's an open-ended awareness, a state of being which allows for the recognition of life's interconnectedness and the beauty of the unknown, without the need for complete comprehension. Unlike Buddhism, which provides a pathway to liberation, The Knowing is about accepting the journey itself without striving for an end goal.

The Role of Suffering and Attachment

Buddhism:

A key element of Buddhist teaching is the understanding suffering arises from attachment to transient things. The Buddhist path advocates for the reduction of attachment, leading to detachment as a way of finding inner peace. This process of letting go of desires and ego is considered crucial for achieving enlightenment.

The Knowing:

In The Knowing, Michael also encountered the idea of letting go, but in a more fluid and less prescriptive way. The Knowing involves an acceptance of both the good and the difficult aspects of life, without the desire to escape or transcend them. It doesn't directly address suffering as Buddhism does; rather, it's about living fully in the present moment and being at peace with uncertainty. The focus is more on experiencing life in all its forms rather than systematically reducing suffering through renunciation of attachment.

The Approach to Enlightenment

Buddhism:

Buddhism offers a structured path toward enlightenment, often referred to as the Middle Way. This path involves moral discipline, mental cultivation (such as meditation), and wisdom. Meditation plays a central role in attaining enlightenment, as it helps practitioners develop insight into the nature of reality, leading to Nirvana, where ignorance, craving, and suffering cease.

The Knowing:
The Knowing does not have a structured path or formal practices. For Michael, enlightenment was not about following a set of guidelines but rather about understanding through lived experience and personal insight. The Knowing is about being open to the unfolding of life and the mysteries it presents, without the need to achieve a specific spiritual milestone. It is more about living in a state of mindfulness and presence without the pressure of attaining a higher state of consciousness or escaping suffering altogether.

The Concept of the Self

Buddhism:
Buddhism teaches the concept of anatta, or 'no-self.' According to this belief, the idea of a permanent, unchanging self is an illusion. Understanding the illusory nature of the self is essential for overcoming attachment and achieving enlightenment. Buddhists aim to transcend the ego, recognising the self is a collection of ever-changing physical and mental components (the five aggregates) and not a fixed entity.

The Knowing:
In The Knowing, the self is neither affirmed nor denied in a strict sense. Michael's experience of The Knowing is deeply personal, but it does not focus on dismantling the ego or transcending the self in the same way Buddhism does. Instead, The Knowing involves a harmonious balance of understanding one's place in the universe while still living within the self. The self is seen as part of a greater interconnected reality, but there is no explicit need to dissolve the

ego or transcend the idea of selfhood. It's more about an alignment with life rather than a rejection of personal identity.

Spiritual Practices

Buddhism:
Buddhism emphasises meditation, mindfulness, and ethical living as core spiritual practices. Monks and laypeople alike are encouraged to engage in regular meditation to cultivate insight and compassion. The teachings of the Buddha provide a clear framework for understanding right conduct, mindfulness, and concentration.

The Knowing:
The Knowing, as Michael discovered, does not prescribe specific practices such as meditation or ethical codes. Instead, it is more about living with awareness, presence, and an openness to life's experiences. There is a spiritual practice in The Knowing, but it is informal and arises from the individual's relationship with life. It may involve periods of quiet reflection, moments of deep connection with nature, or being fully present in everyday actions. The emphasis is on experiential learning rather than formalised practice.

The Afterlife and Rebirth

Buddhism:
In Buddhism, the cycle of death and rebirth (Samsara) is central to understanding the human condition. Through karma, beings are reborn into different existences based on their actions in previous lives. The goal is to break free from Samsara and attain Nirvana, ending the cycle of rebirth and suffering.

The Knowing:
The Knowing does not directly address concepts like reincarnation or an afterlife. Michael's understanding of life's mysteries is more focused on the present moment and the experience of being alive. It is less concerned with what happens after death and more about finding peace and meaning in the here and now. The Knowing

embraces uncertainty, including the uncertainty of what comes after life, without trying to define or control it.

Summary

While Buddhism offers a structured approach to understanding suffering, the nature of self, and the path to enlightenment. The Knowing is more fluid and less defined, allowing for a highly personal exploration of existence. Buddhism, founded on the teachings of Siddhartha Gautama, presents a systematic framework which guides practitioners through the complexities of human suffering, known as Dukkha and outlines practical steps to overcome it. Central to this path is the understanding of impermanence (Annica), the non-self (Anatta), and the interdependent nature of all things. Buddhism seeks to provide clarity on the causes of suffering and offers tools such as the Four Noble Truths and the Eightfold Path, which guide adherents toward ethical living, meditation, and insight into the nature of reality.

In contrast, The Knowing lacks a formalised doctrine or rigid steps. It emphasises a more fluid, personal journey of spiritual awareness, one which is centred on the acceptance of life as it unfolds. Rather than offering a specific framework for addressing human suffering, The Knowing invites individuals to embrace life's mysteries without seeking definitive answers or solutions. It focuses on living in harmony with the present moment, accepting both the joys and challenges of life without attempting to transcend them or reach a state of enlightenment.

Both Buddhism and The Knowing emphasise inner under-standing and self-awareness, but they diverge in their approaches. Buddhism presents a clear goal: to transcend suffering and break free from the cycle of rebirth (Samsara) through practices which lead to the cessation of craving and attachment. It encourages practitioners to follow a disciplined path, utilising meditation to cultivate mindfulness, concentration, and ultimately, (Nirvana), a state of liberation from the cycle of birth, death, and rebirth. Through ethical living, meditation, and insight, Buddhism aims to transform one's relationship with suffering, leading to a profound inner peace which is not subject to the changing conditions of the external world.

The Knowing, on the other hand, does not emphasise the transcendence of suffering or an ultimate liberation from the cycle of life. Instead, it finds peace in the acceptance of life's uncertainties, imperfections, and transitory nature. There is no clear objective of liberation or release from the human condition; rather, The Knowing encourages individuals to embrace the present moment fully, without striving for an end goal. It suggests life's difficulties and pleasures are part of a greater, interconnected whole and true understanding comes from accepting this interconnectedness without the need to escape it. The journey is not about reaching a higher state of consciousness but about recognising and appreciating life's inherent beauty.

In essence, Buddhism offers a formalised path to enlight-enment, complete with ethical guidelines, meditative practices, and philosophical teachings aimed at transforming the mind and liberating the individual from the cycles of suffering and rebirth.

The Knowing, by contrast, is an individual's embrace of life's unfolding mysteries without striving for an end goal. It allows for a more open-ended exploration of life, where meaning is found in being present, aware, and accepting of life's unpredictability.

Where Buddhism seeks to free the individual from suffering, The Knowing invites a deeper engagement with it, encouraging a mindset of acceptance rather than transcendence.

CHAPTER 29

THE KNOWING AND HINDUISM

'The tongue like a sharp knife… Kills without drawing blood.' – Gautama Buddha

The Knowing is a spiritual concept which reflects a deep understanding of the ways of life, its meaning, and the pursuit of inner truth, as experienced by individuals like Michael. It is not religious by nature, but rather a personal journey of discovery which guides seekers toward insight and peace. It lacks a formal structure or set of rituals, making it highly individualised. Hinduism, on the other hand, is one of the world's oldest organised religions, encompassing a wide array of beliefs, practices, rituals, and philosophies which have evolved over thousands of years. It offers a structured approach to spiritual life, deeply rooted in tradition and community.

Core Principles and Understanding:

The core principle of The Knowing is the idea of uncovering a personal truth which brings about a profound understanding of oneself and one's place in the world. It emphasises the fluid, nondogmatic nature of spiritual exploration, where meaning is shaped by the individual seeker. Hinduism, conversely, has core principles such as Dharma (righteous duty), Karma (cause and effect), and Moksha (liberation from the cycle of rebirth). It offers multiple paths toward spiritual realisation, including paths of devotion (Bhakti), knowledge (Jnana), and righteous action (Karma Yoga).

While The Knowing does not insist on any particular dogma or a universal set of beliefs, Hinduism accommodates a wide diversity of thought, including atheistic, polytheistic, and monotheistic perspectives. In Hinduism, seekers can explore different gods, texts, and practices, but they are often guided by a teacher or guru, as well as centuries of sacred literature, such as the Vedas, Upanishads, and Bhagavad Gita.

The Individual Experience:

In The Knowing, the individual's journey is the essence of the experience. There is no central authority or scripture; rather, it is about looking inward, examining one's life, and coming to an authentic understanding of existence. Michael embodies this journey, offering insights to others but never imposing his ideas, allowing the seeker to interpret and experience The Knowing for themselves.

In contrast, Hinduism provides a framework which supports both communal practices and individual exploration. It often encourages devotion to a chosen deity (e.g., Shiva, Vishnu, or Devi) and engagement in community rituals and festivals. However, Hinduism also recognises the importance of personal experience and self-realisation, particularly through practices such as meditation, yoga, and philosophical inquiry. The concept of Atman (the inner self or soul) in Hinduism bears a similarity to the internal journey of The Knowing, where the ultimate goal is to realise one's true nature.

Hinduism also emphasises the interconnectedness of all beings, which is encapsulated in the concept of Brahman, the ultimate reality or cosmic spirit. This idea encourages individuals to see beyond their ego and realise their unity with the broader universe. In The Knowing, the emphasis is more on the individual's subjective experience and personal understanding rather than a cosmic unification, but both paths ultimately guide the seeker toward a deeper awareness of themselves and their relationship to the world.

Rituals and Spiritual Practices:
Unlike Hinduism, The Knowing does not involve any formalised rituals, temples, or sacred ceremonies. It is a direct and personal path without prescribed rites of passage or specific prayers. It invites individuals to cultivate awareness and understanding through introspection and dialogue, as seen with Michael's willingness to share but not to enforce his knowledge.

Hinduism, by contrast, is rich in rituals and sacred practices, including daily prayers, Pujas (worship ceremonies), Yajnas (sacrificial rituals), and festivals like Diwali and Holi. These rituals help practitioners connect with the divine and foster a sense of belonging within the community. Though it offers these practices, Hinduism also encourages meditation and self-inquiry, aligning with the introspective aspect of The Knowing.

Rituals in Hinduism are often seen as tools to help individuals internalise spiritual concepts and connect with the divine. For example, yoga is a physical practice but also a means of disciplining the mind and body to achieve spiritual growth. The Knowing lacks these external forms of practice but focuses intensely on inner exploration and personal insight, with each individual shaping their spiritual journey according to their own experiences and reflections.

Freedom and Structure:
The Knowing represents ultimate freedom in spiritual exploration, devoid of institutionalised teachings or external authority. This makes it accessible and adaptable, but also deeply personal and reliant on the individual's willingness to seek. There is no definitive scripture, no binding rules, and no specific spiritual leaders. This can be empowering for those who wish to forge their own path without external constraints but may also be challenging for individuals who seek a clear roadmap or community support.

Hinduism, while flexible and diverse, provides a structured path for those who seek spiritual growth. It offers well-defined teachings, sacred texts, and a framework which can guide individuals through the complexities of life, which can be reassuring for those who appreciate tradition and community support. The teachings of gurus and spiritual guides provide an anchor for seekers, offering wisdom which has been passed down through generations.

Hinduism also incorporates different yoga's or paths, Karma Yoga (the path of selfless action), Bhakti Yoga (the path of devotion), Raja Yoga (the path of meditation), and Jnana Yoga (the path of knowledge), each catering to different personality types and spiritual needs. This structured approach can help individuals find a path which resonates with them, offering practical ways to engage with the divine and progress spiritually. In The Knowing, the path is entirely self-directed, with the individual deciding how to proceed, which can lead to an authentic but sometimes solitary journey.

Community and Individuality

One of the key distinctions between The Knowing and Hinduism lies in the role of community. The Knowing is inherently an individualistic journey. It is about personal insight and the subjective experience of truth, often explored alone or through informal dialogue with others like Michael. There is no congregation, temple, or organised community which one must be part of to practice The Knowing.

Hinduism, however, places significant emphasis on community and the role of family and society in one's spiritual life. Festivals like Navaratri, Ganesh Chaturthi, and Raksha Bandhan are religious events but also social gatherings which reinforce familial bonds and community ties. Temples serve as centres for spiritual and social activities, creating a sense of belonging and shared cultural identity. This community aspect can provide support, encouragement, and a sense of continuity, which can be invaluable in a seeker's spiritual journey.

Complexity of Spiritual Insights

When it comes to spiritual insights, The Knowing embraces complexity and ambiguity. There are no absolute answers. This aspect of The Knowing makes it deeply enigmatic and introspective,

203

every individual's experience is unique, leading to a complex interplay of thoughts, realisations, and emotions. The nature of The Knowing encourages seekers to question their assumptions and embrace the unknown, which can result in significant internal transformation.

Hinduism also has a profound depth in its spiritual teachings. The sacred texts, such as the Upanishads, delve into metaphysical questions about the nature of reality, consciousness, and the self. The philosophical diversity within Hinduism, from Advaita Vedanta (non-dualism) to Dvaita (dualism), creates an intricate web of ideas which invite seekers to explore different viewpoints. This contributes to a burstiness in the Hindu tradition, where complex philosophical discourses coexist alongside simple, heartfelt expressions of devotion.

In both The Knowing and Hinduism, there is an element of mystery and depth which draws individuals toward spiritual exploration. However, The Knowing leans more heavily on personal interpretation and direct experience, while Hinduism offers a blend of personal and communal understanding, enriched by centuries of philosophical inquiry and shared traditions.

Summary

Both The Knowing and Hinduism offer paths to spiritual fulfillment, but they differ significantly in approach. The Knowing is a deeply personal, non-religious journey which places the individual's under-standing at the centre, free from ritual and structure. Hinduism pro-vides a rich, multifaceted tradition which encompasses both personal spirituality and communal worship, offering a vast array of teachings and practices to help seekers navigate their spiritual journey.

Ultimately, the choice between The Knowing and Hinduism (or the blending of aspects from both) depends on the seeker's nature and needs, whether they are drawn to personal, unstructured insight or to the deep heritage and ritualistic richness of a traditional religion. While The Knowing provides complete freedom in how one approaches spiritual understanding, Hinduism offers a supportive framework steeped in history, community, and diverse spiritual practices.

Both paths lead toward self-realisation and a deeper understanding of life, each in its own unique way.

Chapter 30

A Lecture Given by Michael

'Better than a thousand hollow words is one word which brings peace.' — *Gautama Buddha*

Good evening, and thank you for joining me today. I stand before you not as a teacher, nor as someone with all the answers, but as a messenger of The Knowing. I do not aim to instruct but to share, to offer an idea, a way of viewing life which may resonate with some of you. You may find what I say mirrors something you've always known, but never articulated. Or, perhaps it will challenge you in ways which make you uncomfortable. Either way, I intend to plant seeds, not build walls.

In The Knowing, we do not seek to master life, nor do we aim to control it. Instead, we aim to understand and harmonise with it. This is the first principle: Life is to be lived, not dominated. Too often, we spend our time and energy trying to bend life to our will. We want certainty, stability, and control, but life, in its essence, is fluid, ever-changing, and full of surprises. To attempt to control life is to resist its nature. It is like trying to stop the wind with your hands. You may feel powerful for a moment, but ultimately, the wind will pass through your fingers.

As we delve deeper into The Knowing, we encounter the second principle: connection is the essence of existence. In a world which often feels fractured, understanding our interconnectedness is vital. Every thought, action, and emotion we hold contributes to the collective tapestry of humanity. When we embrace this truth, we dissolve the barriers which separate us. We begin to see others not as adversaries but as fellow travellers on this journey of life. By fostering genuine connections, we find solidarity, companionship, and the shared wisdom which emerges from our diverse experiences.

The third principle guides us to liberate our understanding of self: The journey is as significant as the destination. In a society which intensely focuses on outcomes, we often forget the beauty of the journey itself. The Knowing teaches us every moment, every experience, whether pleasant or challenging, carries value. It reminds us to appreciate the simple acts of existence: the laughter of a friend, the turning of seasons, the quiet reflection in solitude. Each moment is a stepping stone, a crucial part of our unique narrative.

Now, some of you might wonder, how do we cultivate The Knowing? The answer lies in mindfulness, in being present. Life is riddled with distractions, pulling our attention in countless directions. We spend much of our time in our heads, analysing and worrying, and we often miss the richness of the world around us. The practice of mindfulness urges us to slow down, breathe deeply, and connect with the here and now.

Start by inviting moments of silence into your day. Allow space for contemplation and allow your thoughts to settle. Journaling can also help, as it provides an avenue to articulate feelings and insights which align with The Knowing. Allow your pen to flow without censorship.

Engagement with nature is another profound way to foster this understanding. Nature reflects the principles of The Knowing, a vibrant demonstration of connection, fluidity, and acceptance. When we immerse ourselves in its beauty, we re-awaken to the simplicity and profundity of existence.

Finally, surround yourself with a community which encourages growth and exploration. Share your thoughts and experiences with those who resonate with the concepts you are beginning to understand. However, remain open, challenge each other's ideas, and welcome discomfort as a sign of growth.

Remember, my intention today is not to prescribe a way of being but to plant a seed, a seed which may one day blossom into clarity, understanding, or a renewed sense of connection. We are all on this journey together. As we each awaken to The Knowing, we contribute to a collective understanding which can enrich our lives and the world as a whole.

The Knowing, at its core, is a deep, intuitive understanding of life, one which transcends words, doctrines, and creeds. It is not a religious concept, although it may touch upon spiritual dimensions. Nor is it a philosophy, although it encourages profound reflection. The Knowing is both personal and universal. It is the quiet, persistent voice within you which calls for truth, meaning, and connection, connection to the self, to others, and the vastness of existence.

I wish to add I have also found something fundamental: life cannot be fully understood through logic alone. Our modern world, with all its scientific advancements and technological wonders, often insists valid knowledge is those which can be measured, quantified, and repeated. But life itself defies such limitations. Life is chaotic, unpredictable, mysterious, and, at times, maddening. And yet, at its core, it is also incredibly simple. Life is, it exists, as we do. The great challenge is in accepting this existence for what it is, without always seeking to impose our desires or expectations upon it.

Instead, we must learn to move with the wind. To embrace uncertainty, to accept change, and to flow with life rather than fight against it. This is not a passive resignation, nor is it fatalism. It is a recognition about life, in all its chaos, which also has rhythm, flow, and harmony. To live well is to listen to this rhythm, to sense the flow, and to align ourselves with it.

Now, some of you may be wondering: How do we find this rhythm? How do we align ourselves with life? The answer is deceptively simple: we must listen. The Knowing is not about acquiring more knowledge or seeking new information. It is about listening deeply, to ourselves, to others, and the world around us.

I invite you to ponder the teachings of The Knowing when navigating the complexities of life. Embrace the idea which states understanding transcends logical reasoning. Be a witness to the beauty of connection; relish the journey; and cultivate presence in each passing moment.

The modern world is overflowing with information. At any given moment, we are inundated with news, opinions, advice, and instructions, from social media, news outlets, friends, family, and self-help gurus. Everyone seems to have an answer, a solution, or an opinion about how we should live our lives, what we should believe, and what we should strive for. We live in an age where information is more accessible than ever before, and while this is a powerful tool, it can also be overwhelming.

When we are constantly surrounded by this noise, by the voices of others, and by the external pressures of society, it can become difficult to differentiate between what is truly important to us. Over time, many of us become conditioned to seek validation, guidance, and approval from outside sources. We start to rely on others to tell us who we are, what we want, and how we should feel.

This relentless bombardment of external input can drown out the one voice which truly matters: 'our own'. The inner voice, which is deeply personal, intuitive, and authentic, often gets lost in the chaos of external influences. It's easy to confuse the noise for truth, mistaking the loudest voices for the right ones. But the reality is the wisdom we seek is not found outside of us, it has been within us all along.

Listening to our voice requires us to turn inward, to create space for introspection, and to trust ourselves. It involves developing the ability to tune out the distractions, to recognise when we are being swayed by others' opinions or expectations, and to ask ourselves: 'What do I feel? What do I think?' This process is not always easy because it can go against the grain of what we've been taught. From a young age, we are often conditioned to look outside ourselves for answers, whether it's from authority figures, institutions, or societal norms. But to truly understand ourselves and live authentically, we must learn to trust our inner guidance.

Our voice, our intuition, our inner knowing, has a quiet strength. It doesn't shout or demand attention like the external world often does. Instead, it whispers. It speaks in moments of stillness, in those quiet spaces where we can reflect and tune in to what we truly feel and believe. This voice is the one which knows what brings us joy, what causes us pain, what we need to heal, and what our deepest desires are. It knows the path we need to take, even when the external world tries to convince us otherwise.

When we forget to listen to our voice, we risk losing ourselves in the process. We start living lives which may not truly reflect our deepest values, desires, or dreams. We may find ourselves chasing goals which aren't our own, or adhering to beliefs which don't resonate with us on a soul level. We can feel disconnected from ourselves, even as we are inundated with information and advice which tells us how we should live.

The key is to reconnect with the inner voice. This doesn't mean rejecting all external advice or ignoring the opinions of others. There is value in learning from others, and sometimes outside perspectives can offer us valuable insights. But we must learn to filter this input through the lens of our inner wisdom. We must make space to ask ourselves: 'Does this resonate with me? Is this true for me?' It is this process of discernment which allows us to live authentically, guided by our inner knowing, rather than being swept along by the tides of external influences.

In a world which is constantly pulling us in different directions, listening to our voice becomes an act of empowerment. It allows us to reclaim our autonomy, to honour our unique path, and to live with a sense of integrity and purpose. When we listen to our voice, we can make decisions which are aligned with whom we truly are, rather than whom the world expects us to be. It is by turning inward and honouring this voice we can find the clarity and peace many of us are searching for in the external world.

Each of us carries within us a deep well of wisdom. This wisdom is not something which can be taught. It is not something which can be found in books or lectures, though they may help point us in the right direction. Rather, it is an intuitive understanding, a quiet knowing which resides within us all. The challenge is learning to access it.

In my life, I spent many years searching for answers outside myself

I studied religion, philosophy, science, and spirituality, hoping to find the one truth which would explain everything. But no matter how much I learned, I always felt something was missing. It wasn't until I turned inward, until I began to truly listen to my inner voice, I began to understand The Knowing.

To listen to this inner voice requires stillness. It requires us to quiet the noise of the external world and tune in to the subtle signals within. This is why practices like meditation, contemplation, or even spending time in nature can be powerful experiences. They help us create the space to hear ourselves and to connect with our inner wisdom.

But it's important to note The Knowing is not about with-drawing from the world. It's not about isolating ourselves in pursuit of some private enlightenment. In fact, The Knowing teaches us the opposite: true understanding comes through connection.

We are not meant to walk this path alone. Life is inherently relational. We exist in connection to others, to the natural world, and to the universe itself. These connections are not incidental; they are essential to our being. Every interaction, every relationship, no matter how fleeting, is an opportunity to learn, to grow, and to deepen our understanding of ourselves and the world around us.

But relationships, like life itself, are not always easy. They can be messy, challenging, and even painful. Yet, it is through these challenges we often come to know ourselves more deeply. Relationships act as mirrors, reflecting to us aspects of ourselves we may not always see. They show us our strengths, our weaknesses, our fears, and our desires.

In The Knowing, we do not shy away from these reflections. Instead, we embrace them. We recognise every relationship, whether it is with a friend, a family member, a romantic partner, or even a stranger, is a teacher. It offers us the opportunity to see ourselves more openly, to understand our place in the world, and to grow in compassion and empathy.

Compassion is a key aspect of The Knowing. True under-standing is not possible without compassion, for ourselves and others. Life is difficult. We all carry burdens, face challenges, and experience pain. The Knowing teaches us we are all in this together. No one is exempt from the difficulties of life, and no one is beyond the reach of compassion.

Compassion, however, begins with ourselves. This is the fourth principle of The Knowing: 'Self-compassion is the foundation of understanding.' Many of us are our own harshest critics. We judge ourselves for our mistakes, our shortcomings, and our perceived failures. But, by doing this, we create a barrier to understanding. We cannot see openly when we are clouded by self-judgement.

To practice The Knowing, we must first learn to be kind to ourselves. This doesn't mean excusing harmful behaviour or avoiding responsibility. It means recognising we are human, we are imperfect, and this is okay. Self-compassion allows us to see ourselves more lucidly, to accept our flaws, and to grow from experiences.

When we extend this compassion to ourselves, it naturally flows out to others. We become more patient, more understanding, and more empathetic. We understand others are doing the best they can with the knowledge and resources they have. This understanding is the basis for true connection.

Finally, the fifth principle of The Knowing is this: Life is a mystery to be embraced, not a puzzle to be solved. Too often, we approach life as if it were a problem to be resolved or a riddle to be unravelled. We want clear answers, definitive solutions, and absolute truths. But life doesn't work this way, because it's full of contra-dictions, uncertainties, and mysteries.

We embrace this mystery with The Knowing. We understand it is okay everything can't be explained. The beauty of life lies in its mystery, in its unpredictability, in the questions which remain unan-swered. To live in The Knowing is to be at peace with not knowing, to find joy in the journey rather than fixating on the destination.

The Knowing is not about acquiring more knowledge or mast-ering life. It is about deepening our understanding of ourselves, our relationships, and the world around us. It is about embracing life in all its complexity and mystery, with compassion, humility, and an open heart. We can't rush or force self-discovery; it's something which unfolds naturally for each of us, in our time and in our way. In today's world, where we're constantly connected, information comes at us from every direction. Whether it's news, podcasts, blogs, videos, social media, or even the conversations we have, we're bombarded with advice, opinions, and ideas. It feels like there's guidance for everything, from how to build our careers, improve relationships, or boost our self-esteem. And while having access to all this knowledge, in many ways, it can also be overwhelming.

The sheer ease of accessing information online has given us the freedom to explore any topic we're curious about. With a few clicks, we can dive into subjects, stay informed, and broaden our perspectives. But occasionally, all of this can blur the lines, making it challenging to figure out what truly resonates with us. When we're faced with an endless stream of opinions and instructions on how to live our lives, it's easy to lose track of our voice. The noise can make us feel unsure or disconnected from our beliefs and values.

When we are constantly surrounded by other people's expectations and opinions, it can be difficult to hear the quiet voice within, the one which reflects who we are, what we deeply believe, and what feels right for us. This inner voice is like a compass, guiding us toward choices which align with our true selves. But if we rely too much on external validation or let other viewpoints dominate our thinking, we risk losing touch with our inner guidance. Over time, our voice can grow quieter, overshadowed by the demands and criticisms of the world around us. We might even forget how to listen to it, and by doing this, lose sight of what's right for us.

It's natural to seek approval from others, especially when we're growing up. We look to authority figures, friends, or societal norms to help shape our decisions. Society tends to teach us validation from the outside world defines our success and happiness. But when we constantly seek approval, we risk drifting away from our instincts and intuition, which can lead to feelings of uncertainty or dissatisfaction. The nagging sense of something being off often comes from not honouring our inner truth.

It's important to remember the information and advice we get from others isn't inherently bad. Many external insights can be valuable and bring wisdom into our lives. The real challenge lies in how we process and prioritise this information. When we are hit with as many perspectives and viewpoints, it becomes harder to stay grounded in our beliefs. Over time, we might find it tough to distinguish between what truly reflects who we are and what's been imposed upon us.

Think about how the media influences our views on success, beauty, and happiness. We often compare ourselves to the curated lives we see online, which can make us doubt our decisions or feel like we're falling short. The more we are exposed to external standards, the more we might start chasing goals which don't resonate with who we are. It's easy to get caught up in pursuing things which don't truly align with our core values, because we've lost touch with our inner voice guiding us.

To navigate this complex world, we need to reconnect with our inner compass, the voice inside us which understands what we truly need. Finding our voice involves making space for reflection. It means stepping away from the noise and spending time with our thoughts, emotions, and desires. This journey isn't about shutting out external perspectives entirely. It's about finding a balance between external input and our internal knowing. Trusting our instincts and making choices which feel right for us is crucial. We need to own our path, instead of letting others chart it for us.

Listening to our inner voice can be tough, especially when it goes against what others expect or when it challenges societal norms. But real empowerment comes from having the courage to follow our path, even if it means making choices others may not understand. Trusting ourselves and staying true to our beliefs, despite outside influences, is an essential step toward self-acceptance. It's a step which allows us to live authentically and to be in harmony with our personal values.

Our inner voice is like a quiet, steady companion. It doesn't shout or demand attention like the external world often does. Instead, it whispers to us when we slow down and take the time to listen. It nudges us when something feels off, and it gently guides us when we need to shift direction. This voice holds the key to understanding our most significant moments, our deepest desires, and what truly lights us up. But to hear it, we need to practice the art of listening.

One way to do this is by finding peace amidst the chaos of life. Mindfulness practices like meditation or journaling can help us connect with our inner thoughts and emotions. Taking moments to step away from the hustle, whether by spending time in nature or sitting quietly with ourselves, allows us the space to hear our voice. These practices allow us to tune into our beliefs and values, helping us make decisions which reflect who we are at our core.

When we ignore our inner guidance, we risk living a life which doesn't align with our deepest aspirations. We might end up chasing after things which don't bring true fulfilment or adopting beliefs which don't resonate with our authentic selves. This disconnect from our inner voice can leave us feeling lost, unsatisfied, or even empty.

But the answer isn't to cut ourselves off from the world. Instead, we need to learn how to filter external advice through the lens of our inner wisdom. It's about asking ourselves whether the advice we receive aligns with our values and whether it feels true to who we are. This process helps us integrate outside perspectives in a way which feels authentic, instead of blindly following external expectations.

In a world full of distractions, turning inward to hear our voice is a choice we make for ourselves. It's a choice which allows us to take control of our lives, live authentically, and make decisions which truly align with who we are. When we tune into our inner wisdom, we free ourselves from the pressures of societal norms and external influences. We become the architects of our lives, guided by the quiet voice within us.

Ultimately, the clarity and peace we seek aren't found in the world around us, they reside within us. In those moments of stillness, when we listen to our inner voice, we find the direction and wisdom we need to live a life which reflects our true values, dreams, and purpose.

Thank You.

This lecture offers a glimpse into Michael's philosophy of The Knowing to Your Knowing – A Journey of Self Discovery, focusing on personal wisdom, life's inherent mysteries, compassion, and embracing the unpredictable flow of life.

AUTHOR'S NOTE

I first started writing The Knowing to Your Knowing back in 1994 and over the next 3 years wrote the first 5 chapters. Then living got in the way, and other projects and activities took precedent. But, about 12 months ago the urge to finish what I started came to a head and I was compelled to stop procrastinating and 'get it out there', which I have now done.

I originally planned it as a 3-book series and I'm now working on the second. It will be from Michael's point of view and a more in-depth view of The Knowing to Your Knowing, and how it can be used for personal use.

It took many years of searching before I discovered everything, we ever need is within us and writing reinforced my opinion there is a better way. All we need to do is listen to the quiet voice within. We never lose if we are willing to try something new, so begin today and transform your life.

At 77 years of age, I am embarking on a new chapter in my life as a debut author with The Knowing to Your Knowing, marking a culmination of years of reflection and writing. Though this is my first full-length book, my words have already made an impact through articles published in various magazines. Writing has been a natural extension of my well-read nature, and my literary interests span an eclectic range of titles, driven by a love for exploration rather than a preference for any particular genre.

I am happily married and have been with my partner for 33 years, having tied the knot 14 years ago. Family plays a significant role in our life. I am a proud parent of two adult children, and a loving grandparent to 11 grandchildren and 2 great-grandchildren.

In retirement, I have found a passionate outlet in woodturning, a craft I practice, both at home, and at a club alongside fellow enthusiasts. The precision and artistry of woodturning reflect my creative spirit and my appreciation for craftsmanship. This hobby has not only enriched my leisure time but also connected me to a community of like-minded individuals.

I'm a seasoned traveller, having experienced the world firsthand, visiting countries like the USA, England, Scotland, France, Germany, Russia, China, Japan, New Zealand, and more. Each journey has contributed to a rich tapestry of life experiences, shaping my worldview and inspiring my writing. My goal is to author as many books as possible, making the most of the time I have, and leaving a legacy of stories for future generations to cherish.

The Knowing to Your Knowing is something new. Don't be afraid to try it as the only thing to fear is fear itself.

Thank you for reading this story...

Happy Knowing.

The next book in the series

Michael's Journey to The Knowing

– A Journey of Self Discovery –

Step into the transformative journey of Michael's Journey to The Knowing, a profound tale of self-discovery, spiritual awakening, and the search for meaning beyond the ordinary.

Michael is a man of wisdom, shaped by a life steeped in religious study and philosophical exploration. But as he reaches a turning point in his life, he realizes there is more to existence than the confines of traditional beliefs. Determined to uncover life's deeper truths, he embarks on a journey that transcends the physical and ventures into the spiritual.

Through encounters with wise mentors, soul-stirring revelations, and moments of profound introspection, Michael discovers 'The Knowing,' an inner awareness that illuminates the mysteries of life and the universe. Along the way, he grapples with timeless questions: What is the purpose of life? How do we find inner peace? And what does it mean to truly understand ourselves?

This captivating book invites readers to walk alongside Michael as he unravels the layers of his soul and ventures into the boundless realm of understanding. Rich with inspiration and profound insights, Michael's Journey to The Knowing is a spiritual and philosophical guide wrapped in the engaging narrative of one man's quest for enlightenment.

If you've ever yearned for clarity, connection, or a deeper sense of purpose, this book will resonate with your heart and stir your spirit. Discover Michael's Journey to The Knowing, 'A Journey of Self Discovery' that may lead you closer to your own truth.

Available through Amazon Books

Here is the link:

https://www.amazon.com.au/dp/1763857204

www.ingramcontent.com/pod-product-compliance
Lightning Source LLC
Chambersburg PA
CBHW071250250626
47163CB00002B/406